HAPPINESS

A Novel

Sherrie Flick

UNIVERSITY OF NEBRASKA PRESS

LINCOLN AND LONDON

Library of Congress
Cataloging-in-Publication Data

Flick, Sherrie.
Reconsidering happiness : a novel
/ Sherrie Flick.
p. cm. — (Flyover fiction series)
ISBN 978-0-8032-2521-3 (pbk. : alk.
paper)
I. Title.
PS3606.L533R43 2009
813'.6 — dc22
2009004265

Set in Fournier by Kim Essman.
Designed by Nathan Putens.

For Rick and Nancy, my driving companions

ACKNOWLEDGMENTS

For the spectacular gifts of time and space, I would like to thank the Ucross Foundation, Atlantic Center for the Arts, Virginia Center for the Creative Arts (and the Heinz Endowments for a fellowship there), Pennsylvania Council on the Arts, the Flick Family Farm, and BD&E.

Endless gratitude as well to: Café Brioche, Ceres Bakery, and Sally's.

"Saving a Great Vision: Poet John Neihardt," by David L. Bristow, *Nebraska Life* July/August 2000, and *The Nature of Home*, by Lisa Knopp, were insightful, as was Nancy S. Gillis, executive director of the John G. Neihardt Center.

The idea of Vivette moving to Des Moines and early—albeit very different—incarnations of Robert and Susan began in the short story "Slow Fire Pistol," published in *Puerto del Sol*, 2003.

Many individuals contributed important advice, insight, and support along the way. This book would not exist without them: Brian Butko, Guy Capecelatro, Jim Crace, John Dalton, Noel Eicher, Charlyn Ellis, John Fleenor, Don and Shirley Flick, Scott Houston, Casey Huff, Cheryl Krisko, Nancy Krygowski, Elise Levine, Bob Marion, Anthony McCann, Jolene McIlwain, John McNally, Tim O'Brien, Steve Pesci, Ladette Randolph, Pam Raiford, Hilda Raz, James Simon, Pam St. John, Marly Swick, and John Talbird.

Last but not least: no one helped out more than my dear husband, Rick Schweikert.

RECONSIDERING HAPPINESS

1

Vivette, On the Road

Vivette knew nothing about Des Moines except for the lovely ease of the letters — the way its name sounded out like a yoga chant, exotic and foreign. *Des Moines*, with those silent s's beckoning with a sexy finger, a promise. It whispered to her as she lay in her tousled New Hampshire bedsheets. The wooden shutters on her windows escorting cross-stitched moonlight across the dusty floor. The tugboats, with their deep-throated howls, stretched at their moors, the buoys offering cowbell clangs. *Des Moines. Des Moines.* Her friends thought she was crazy.

Just like that, she was driving through Bucyrus, Ohio, the land turned from rocky, hilly East to something flat as a pancake. Silos sprouted along the pastures. Water towers loomed. Cornstalk stumps mishmashed in the fields like crooked razor stubble. Vivette sped on by.

Then at the Mayflower Bar and Grill in Plymouth, Indiana, Vivette did not, as she hoped, find a grill. Instead, thumbtacked to a post, there was a thin paper square that read: "Tunafish Sandwich $1.75." As she sat at the bar writing a postcard, surrounded by knotty pine walls and bustling small-town conversation, construction workers cashed paychecks with one of the two cute blondes behind the bar, the cash register already loaded down with $20 bills in anticipation of the rush. Under Vivette's forearms, a wooden bar stretched with thousands of names carved into it.

VIVETTE ON THE ROAD, Vivette scratched into the wood, tracing over the letters with her ballpoint pen.

Two plastic models of the *Mayflower* sailed along the top of a beer case packed shoulder to shoulder with bottles of Budweiser along with replicas of the *Niña*, *Pinta*, and *Santa Maria*. The rough and rugged man beside Vivette talked to no one in particular about the option of doing community service versus time. As the noise in the bar increased, she thought about doing time, what it meant to a person who'd pulled up her roots. Postcards sent and received. Mile markers passed. She mulled it over, content to be invisible. She drank her beer and ate her sandwich. White bread. Tunafish.

After the Mayflower, she was back on the road, past tidy houses with uptight porches. Vivette eased by chubby citizens wearing practical clothing who stood looking lost in their rectangular yards.

She made for the Mississippi River, like so many before her. Even in the haze of her endless driving, it was clear the river saved the country from its own monotony. Her car hovered above the roadway, and Vivette was flying in the midst of her own momentum. The flat, easy horizon. A red pick-up in a cornfield. A tractor trailer at rest on a rise. Ribbons of dirt roads to the left and right led to gullies and ravines and farmsteads with stacks of firewood on little islands in an endless sea of cornstalks. Her world was confined by a solid white line to the right and a dotted one to the left. The longer she drove the more the idea of never stopping, the ease of stepping on the gas, made sense.

Vivette had weaseled the Buick from her grandfather a few months before on a visit to her hometown, Wilkes Barre, Pennsylvania. She reminded him that it hadn't been driven in years. Rumor had it they'd taken his license away the last time he tried to make it downtown for bingo.

Vivette said, "Sit down and think about it, Grandpa. C'mon Joe-Joe, don't you want that car to go out in style instead of rusting in the garage with Sammy running it for fifteen minutes once a month?" Vivette settled her freckled face in close. She could smell Joe-Joe's old-man coffee breath. "You know I'm your favorite. All those other grandkids are spoiled and stupid. I won't tell anyone you let me have it. Hell, they won't even know the car's gone. I promise. I'll tell Uncle Sammy I paid a thousand for it. He'll think I got ripped off and be happy."

Joe-Joe fiddled with his pipe, knocking it against the thick sole of his work boot, scraping at its crusty bowl, packing it with Captain Black tobacco. Vivette stood on the cracked linoleum that stretched out around him—scuffed and neglected once-pretty flowers with green vines. After minutes passed and Vivette was sure he'd forgotten about her altogether, Joe-Joe smiled, let her know she wasn't his favorite, but said he'd give her the car anyway because she had spunk like her mother. Then there was a lengthy, numbing discussion concerning road safety, tire pressure, oil changing, and car washing. Finally he shuffled to the kitchen to fill a zip-lock bag with important items for the glove compartment: flashlight, Kleenex, Vaseline, tire gauge, breath mints.

With shaking hands he patted the bag closed and handed it to her along with the keys. The blue plastic keychain declared, "I'm Your Man—Sammy's Auto," in bold silver cursive. To seal the deal he tolerated a kiss on the cheek. The $20 she tried to poke into his shirt pocket only made him mad. He said, "If I'm giving you the car, I'm giving it to you—none of this halfway crap. I want it hanging over you. I want postcards to show the boys over at the VFW." Vivette brushed some scattered toast crumbs out of the way, tucked the twenty under a pretty blue sugar bowl when Joe-Joe wasn't looking.

Soon she was nestled into the Buick's big bucket seat. The car smelled of pine-scented air freshener and Irish Spring soap. The gearshift on the neck of the steering wheel was thick and solid. It was a sturdy car she wouldn't have to think twice about. She headed back to Portsmouth, ready to leave those five years behind, her friends. Robert.

Back in New Hampshire, she cruised down Main Street, eased to a stop and bought a postcard at the tobacco shop. A tacky collage — seagull/tugboat/drawbridge. She wrote:

To Grandpa Joe-Joe. I'm back to pack up my life. Haven't wrecked the car yet. Will keep you posted. Vivette

She knew better than to sign, "Love."

But that was 1,558 miles ago. Now Vivette made her way to Interstate 80's constant traffic and eased the old green Buick into a stark, cemented rest area. She wanted to make sure it was okay to visit for a week at Margaret and Peter's farmhouse. Before walking fifty steps to the map of Iowa and placing herself with a tiny finger within its veiny web, Vivette applied lipstick, messed with her hair, took some deep breaths. Fifty steps more to a shiny black-and-blue pay phone.

A stout, whiskery man in jeans and suspenders, his plaid flannel shirt straining its snaps, shuffled up to study a vending machine's options. He fed in a dollar bill, pushed a button, and a candy bar tumbled into view, his change dropping like rain into the tray. When he slipped a perfect white invitation from a pack of Camels and eased it into his mouth, Vivette reminded herself that she'd quit smoking. The low hum of rushing trucks mixed with the slow, chirping, long-distance ring of the telephone on the other end of the line.

Vivette clutched the hard black plastic of the phone, nodded through directions to the farmhouse, thanking Margaret, and then hung up the receiver with a broad click. She knew a complicated string of wires connected this pay phone to one particular phone on a coffee table in an apartment in New Hampshire. She would not, she told herself, make another call. One hundred steps back to her car, the impact of each splayed and sandaled foot rippling up to her jaw. She was safe, the engine a kitten, the Buick ready for anything she sent its way. Turn around or keep going. It was that easy: drive west, change a life; drive east, revise — drive, drive, drive. She put the car into gear, yielded to all that was oncoming.

Vivette drove right past the exit: DES MOINES. A cop-out, she knew. She didn't even pull off to take a peek. Both hands plastered to the wheel, she stayed on Interstate 80, navigating that black thread through Council Bluffs. Past fields of corn, truck stops, squeaky-clean subdivisions, and onward into Nebraska. The horizon a playing card, not a cloud in sight. For now, Des Moines could linger back there without her. Vivette wanted to see Margaret, whom she'd met in New Hampshire, but who had soon moved away to San Francisco. There were postcards, a letter or two to the Penhallow Bakery gang, many stories from shared friends — so many Vivette felt like she knew Margaret pretty well, the way she knew movie stars from reading magazines. Vivette was twenty-three years old, twenty-three hours from home, ready to start over on the Great Plains. She wanted some pointers.

As she neared her destination, off 80 again and onto a sketch of rural routes, there were no gas stations selling coffee or tall cups of fountain root beer, no restaurants or grocery stores, just brown fields stretched to the horizon. Tractors crawled like bright green beetles. Farmhouses perched like little miracles beside trees strung with clothesline. All this deep brown up against the bright blue sky broken by gray road. Vivette forged on. She pressed rewind, then forward, until REM's "Don't Go Back to Rockville" started up again. She turned it up, belted along off key. The double-yellow lines plowed across smaller dusty lanes with signs like exclamation points declaring rural routes. Daisies and phlox swayed at the side of the road, little notes of spring.

Finally, a farmhouse, familiar from a photograph taped above the sink at Penhallow Bakery, hovered on the thin horizon —

a cautious proclamation of humanity. Vivette signaled left onto South 283rd Street wondering what it was 283rd to, baffled at the meticulous grid that made up this new world. A dove balanced on an electric wire. The Buick pitched its way up Margaret and Peter's rutted drive. Sheep plodded to the edge of their fence line, little hooves stamping the ground, heads bobbing.

2

Vivette, Nebraska

It's morning. With a glass of water and a cigarette, Vivette stands on the porch, waiting. The sheep huddle near the far edge of the field. She pulls a wrinkled postcard from her bag, scoots onto a purple Adirondack chair after tugging it along the porch's floorboards for the best view. Using the chair's wide arm as a table, she wipes at the blank postcard with her pinky finger, brushing loose ashes to the wind.

Dear Grandpa Joe-Joe. I have started smoking again. Today it's Nebraska and the sheep already don't like me so much. Yours, Vivette

She pulls at the long string of postcard stamps snaking from her bag; puts one in place. The card is of a smiling farmer on a tractor pulling an enormous ear of corn down a country lane. Big, red, cursive letters spell out: "Iowa: The Corn State."

Tossing her butt into the yard, Vivette shivers into the kitchen, quiet and hungry. The screen door is a tiny clap at her back. All around her are ingredients: flour, sugar, butter, pecans, molasses, cornmeal, oats, honey, but she can't bring herself to make anything. Even coffee. She sighs. Fingers tapping lightly. She notices the kitchen is a sort of reenactment of Penhallow Bakery, which Margaret left behind long ago but Vivette just walked out of five days earlier: Hobart mixer, Cuisinart, ingredients within arm's reach, well-labeled. Knives on a magnetic strip, pots and pans hanging in a jumble from a steel rack, a big ceramic pot filled with wooden spoons, scrapers, spatulas, and pastry brushes. Spices in a huge rack. Cookbooks lining the far wall along with a row of wooden pegs that hold an apron, a coat. Vivette notes that Margaret not only owns sheep, but also a coat with a feed-store logo on its front pocket and practical shoes.

Vivette feels anxious, but she's not sure why. Beyond the hum of the refrigerator, the silence presses in, as does the weight of the expanse beyond the windows, the rise and fall of the wind. She's road weary and just plain exhausted from the life she left behind. A life she spent years putting together but only a few weeks taking apart. The going-away party at the bakery was tiresome too, because everyone thought Vivette was just getting this leaving thing out of her system, that driving out here was on an itinerary that included a gigantic U-turn. They gave her a compass for her dashboard and snacks for the road, but everyone wondered aloud what could possess her to leave such a beautiful place.

Vivette wants another cigarette, but instead she lifts the jacket from its hook. It's heavier than it appears. The thick green material, with a ribbing of glossy red fabric in its interior, glides over Vivette's arms. Big and comfortable, the cuffs of the sleeves dangle just past her fingertips. She pokes her thin feet into the worn brown clogs resting against the wall, a size too big.

Vivette paces the kitchen in Margaret's coat and shoes, making the farmhouse her house, those sheep her sheep—this kitchen hers. She stands at the window, admiring her land, musing over the possibilities, the renovations: a Jacuzzi, a screened-in porch, some apple trees, horses, goats, maybe even a donkey, large outdoor sculpture.

Yesterday's image of Margaret greeting her from the farmhouse steps—blanched, calm, and acclimated—Margaret rooted and bound to the earth with a big sky beyond her bright blue eyes

7

that stapled everything, including Vivette, into place. Margaret unfolded herself from the porch steps to give Vivette a hug. Vivette pressed harder, longer in the embrace, trying to find the Margaret she thought she knew instead of this pleasant paper sack, this drained aqueduct. She felt bad thinking it, but what did she expect? Later that peaceful reserve kept them seated around the dining room table drinking tea and then wine until Vivette pleaded exhaustion and fled to her room.

The sun peeks over the edge of the field, and the horizon is suddenly ridiculously beautiful, like a patriotic savings-and-loan calendar. Vivette presses her hands against the thin piece of counter lining the sink, tips the clogs forward onto their stiff toes. "This land is your land," she thinks, "this land is my land." She softly sings the few lyrics she remembers from elementary school. "This land was made for you and me." The silence takes over again when she stops singing, embarrassed by the sound of her voice. But by the time Margaret walks in, Vivette has taken up "America the Beautiful" and is following what seems like a pattern in the sheep's slow, pointless choreography.

"Cold?" Margaret asks. The word slices through the kitchen.

Vivette jumps, distracted from her reverie, and turns to face Margaret, her hands stashed behind her back like she's hiding a secret. "Yes. Yes, I was a little. I hope you don't mind." She knows she should slip the coat off and return it to the proper peg, but she can't. The clogs are big and sweaty on her feet.

"You were up early then. No problem. Let me know if you need to borrow a coat while you're here. I'm sure we have something. But you brought a coat with you, right? You're going to need a coat," Margaret says. She fiddles nervously with the bag of coffee, the grinder.

Vivette's wide-eyed night in the guest room clicks into memory, her body still vibrating from the car's accelerator. When she finally slept, trucks pushed her off the road; big green exit signs had no numbers. "I slept fine last night," Vivette says. "Great guest room. Except for all the silence. At first it was so loud. You know what I mean? But then, wham, I was out cold. Sorry, I just couldn't bring myself to make coffee. I'm feeling a bit immobilized." She knows she's talking too fast and too loud.

Margaret says softly, "Oh, it's okay. No problem. I'll get it going. You're a guest. You don't have to make coffee for me." She flips the switch on the coffeemaker, pops open a canister of oats.

Margaret frowns as she starts the oatmeal, pouring milk into a pan, dusting in the oats. Vivette stares intently at her back. Finally, Margaret says, "When I first moved out here? The bugs were so loud I couldn't imagine how anyone could get to sleep. They sounded like hundreds of car alarms. They haven't started up yet, or you'd know what I mean."

Vivette notices an orange dishtowel hanging from the oven door, presses her fingers into the grooves woven into the thick fabric. "Was it what you expected, though? Nebraska?" she asks. Vivette pulls herself up onto the kitchen counter, swinging her feet, the loose clogs tapping a cupboard on each backswing.

Margaret looks at the cupboard doors, the clogs, smiles. "It was nothing like I expected. Then, well, eventually I started looking at things differently."

Margaret knocks a wooden spoon along the edge of the oatmeal pan. "Like right now, it's tick season. When I see a tick on my arm, I just pick it off. It isn't like 'Oh, there's a tick! Gross! Get it!' It's just spring in Nebraska. There's a tick. Pick it off the dog, my arm, Peter."

Vivette runs her thin fingers through her long hair, expecting to find a little blood-filled thing sucking the life out of her. She wraps her skinny arms around herself, and then rubs her hands over her eyebrows, the short bridge of her nose, over her smooth, freckled cheeks, the soft hairs at the back of her neck.

The sheep aren't innocent after all. They're tick-filled time bombs lurking in the tall grass. Vivette pushes her arms up inside the sleeves of the coat. "No one told me anything about ticks," she says.

Margaret laughs, "Don't worry. Just give yourself a good once-over every few hours and you'll be fine." She pours the oatmeal into bowls, asks Vivette if she wants to sit outside at the picnic table. Vivette hesitates, but after changing into jeans and a sweatshirt, follows.

"At first I hated it here," Margaret says. The soft, constant breeze ruffles her practical haircut, parting it this way and that, leaving a few perplexed strands standing at attention. "Everything seemed so predictable and slow. I was constantly taking off, driving six hours to Minneapolis, sometimes ten hours to Chicago, but then, I don't know." Margaret looks up the lane, a tiny furrow forming between her pale eyes.

"What happened?" Vivette squints, turning her hair into a knot that unravels as soon as she lets it go. She looks in the same direction as Margaret. There's a rutted brown lane with two big, black mailboxes punctuating the end.

Margaret picks at a fingernail. "I don't know. I started seeing beauty in the smallest things." She smiles. "I know that sounds corny, but that's how it happened."

Vivette imagines the dusty back roads taunting Margaret as she looks for a cowboy bar to hide in — the window down, bright red lipstick, cat's-eye sunglasses, long, wild hair whipping in the wind, her arm soaking in the sunshine as she searches for something that could make this place work for her. "Happiness," Vivette says.

Margaret nods, "Maybe it was there all along, and in that moment I let it bubble to the surface? A curve in the road, blue sky, green fields, sunflowers beside a barn. I stopped, you know, felt this blip of joy—felt how simple and beautiful and easy the world could be. It was comforting."

"That's what I'm looking for, I guess," Vivette says. "Some kind of a sign. Something that says, 'Good choice, keep going.'" She pulls her feet up onto the bench, wondering if that's true.

"If only it was that easy, right?" Margaret stretches her legs out straight from the table, points her toes inside the brown clogs, and yawns. "Anyway. That's when I decided to focus on where I was instead of driving off to where I wasn't all the time. I gave in." She looks at Vivette a second too long, "But I realized I'd spent so many years leaving places, that leaving in itself had become a kind of monotony. I was bored."

"You're a legend at Penhallow, you know."

Margaret laughs, holding her cup near her chin with both hands. She swishes the coffee as she looks down, then back up at Vivette. "At first, I just said I was happy, then eventually I was. But I'm happy, you know? Here. And then I met Peter."

Vivette smiles, "So, you met Peter later, after the happiness?" A cow moos off in the distance, then another. It's quiet again—except for the wind. A tractor starts up, another cow. She imagines a giant game of musical chairs out there in the fields.

Sparky, a Labrador-collie mutt nuzzles Margaret's hand. "Yeah, you know, depending on a guy to bring you happiness just leads to all kinds of baffling agony." She forages a tick from Sparky's forehead. He wags his tail, scratches his ear. Margaret holds it carefully between two fingers and says, "Peter can squeeze them hard enough to kill them, but I have to flush them down the toilet." She walks with the tick into the house. Vivette hears the faint flush and marvels at the futility. Weren't there thousands of ticks in the grasses all around them? How could plucking one and sending it to a spiraling death make any difference?

Margaret holds a bright red ceramic carafe when she comes back, pours more coffee.

Vivette brings her hand up to her eyes, squints. "So, the ticks go away, right?"

"Oh, tick season leads into other things. The heat, the well running dry. Last fall hordes of spotted bugs took up residence on the kitchen ceiling, and then there's the grasshoppers. But that's not now—now this wind is gorgeous, isn't it? The blue sky? It's nice this time of year. Doesn't the sky remind you of New Hampshire? Sometimes it feels like the ocean is waiting just around the corner."

Vivette tips her head back so the wind nudges her hair. "Except without the tourists," she says. Then quietly she tries out, "It is lovely here." She thinks about happiness all on its own, no strings attached. She imagines it as a postcard with big, block letters: HAPPINESS.

Margaret leans toward Vivette, both hands on the table. "I'm glad you decided to visit," she says. "Hardly anyone travels out this way, you know. You'd think I lived on the moon. But that's okay. It's nice to catch up with people when I can. It's good to know the old world still goes on. But enough of this I'm-so-content talk. Give me the town gossip. All of it."

Vivette gives it to her, methodically going through a checklist of mutual acquaintances. Who makes a lot of money, who's changed, had babies, gotten married, divorced, split up—dead pets, new pets. Good news and bad.

She leaves out her own life entirely.

That night as Vivette dozes off in the cozy guest room, handmade quilts over her and black-and-white photographs of Margaret and Peter on the walls, she feels a twitch on her belly. Panic has her heart pounding before she can think, her hand electric as she traps the squirming bug. With the tick secured between her thumb and finger, she scurries down the hallway, throws it into the toilet, and flushes.

Back in the guest room, she pulls a postcard from the thick stack in her knapsack, fumbles for a pen, rubbing her eyes. *Grandpa*, she writes, *not everything is fun and games*.

She sleeps then in fits and starts the rest of the night, phantom ticks scurrying, her heart pounding in expectation while all around her the house sleeps soundly, silent and immaculate on the Great Plains.

3
Margaret, San Francisco

When she lived in San Francisco, after New Hampshire and before Nebraska, once a week Margaret rode the N Judah streetcar out to Ocean Beach. She strolled down the long, sandy shore toward the Musée Mechanique. The old Sutro Baths had been there once, burned down so many times now that they'd put an ugly, but sturdy, cement structure in its place. The oversized black-and-white photos on the walls of the visitor center showed a giant pool with trapezes and slides and men and women having a good old turn-of-the-century West Coast time in their wool bathing suits with striped leggings and big bows. Down beneath the visitor center, in the subterranean space that housed the museum itself, Margaret dropped quarters into the Cail-O-Scope peep shows called "The Belly Dancer's Day Off" and "The Artist's Model." Photos of robust, barely clad women from the early 1900s flipped unevenly, one after another, lit by a dim bulb. The whir of the motor and the sound of the metal plates flipping from one image to the next created a tiny background percussion. Her face pressed against the brass viewing piece, Margaret imagined the idle conversation while the photographer fixed his lens, arranged the silk scarf to barely cover a breast, asked the model to leave her shoes on, to grab the pillow, hold the hair brush just so.

Transported back to a time before the corner of Haight and Ashbury had a Ben and Jerry's and GAP, back to a time when San Francisco was newer and ready to be formed by those Americans who had persevered across an impossibly long expanse, Margaret felt a pure, sick nostalgia. To soften this inexplicable jealousy, she took clothed and coy pictures in the instant photo booth around the corner, letting her coins drop into the thin slot inside the box, resting her head against the short synthetic curtain behind her. In black and white, she traveled back in time. In these strips of photos, four stacked squares, she was an ancient movie star: head tilted, creamy white skin, mouth in an O of surprise, a pucker of dismay; eyes fluttering or opened wide. Dark circles, an edge of desperation, she rotated the stool, adjusted her shoulders. Ready. Action.

The women in the peep shows were the people who had made the journey, Margaret thought. They came from the stock of wayward ones, plodding across the country — through the Great Plains, across the West, and over the Sierra Nevadas. They birthed babies and buried husbands and pushed and pulled through terrain that never ceased to undo them with its beauty and its spite. It took a certain type to make the journey, or survive it. The later wave of travelers boarded sooty trains and waved so long to everything they loved. Wheels lurching away from the wooden platform, a basket at their feet: onion sandwiches wrapped in crisp newspaper, a jug of beer.

Having traversed thousands of miles, the moment of seeing the ocean again on the other side must have been a true miracle. A comfort. An end.

Margaret had made the journey in her mustard-yellow Datsun, with the luxury of road signs and truck stops and a decent car stereo. But like those other pioneering women, hers too was a fragile rebirth. She went to the Musée Mechanique each week, like visiting a shrine. Before she left its dark, dank interior to enter her bright blue world of office temps and hipsters, she put fifty cents into "The Magic Typewriter," a black cast-iron hulk encased in a glass and wooden box. Margaret turned the big, Bakelite dial on the front to her zodiac sign, Cancer, rested her hand on its side as instructed, and pushed in the coin slot. Without fanfare the box whirred and the typewriter, with a faded ribbon and faulty keys, diligently, mysteriously, haltingly tapped her future. The metal crank returned one, two, three, four times, and a curling sheet of white paper floated from the shoot, sometimes drifting to the floor before Margaret could grab it.

This fortune guided her life until she returned the next week, a blank slate, no future, no past—ready to be told what to do. Margaret needed to remake herself with the help of the Magic Typewriter and the startling beauty of a fresh new coast. She knew it was ridiculous, but it was all she could think to do.

Back on the beach, squinting to spot a seal on Seal Rock, prying up sand dollars and shells, she was happy to go forward into her life. She was young and couldn't see the future, couldn't know that even these thoughts could get old. Margaret saw only endless days unfolding. Contentment and happiness were things relegated to the theoretical, relegated to the future—to a time that would come when it was handy. She remembered thinking she never wanted this life to end.

But it did. Margaret couldn't stay. She had to get in her car more and more, looking outside the city, aimless, up skinny roads skirting the coast, in toward the steep mountains and expansive desert. Wandering. Margaret didn't understand that life had a timeline, that decisions were more important as the line stretched, that a person couldn't travel forever, that each result narrowed choices.

Margaret picked a lemon from the wooden bin at the produce stand on Valencia Street. A miraculous, dimpled yellow, it radiated sun and heat. The stinging smell when she nicked the skin with her fingernail made her want more. She loaded eight into her bag, thinking, *lemon tart.* Walking out of the Mission District, toward her apartment, through the Castro and Duboce Park, she tipped her head to the sun, the shops' glinting storefronts, the leather-clad men walking their poodles, buses zooming by, everyone engaged in their lives as Margaret floated through.

As she clicked the front door closed, stray notes from Kevin's guitar trickled down the hallway. She jostled groceries into the fridge, and he joined her. "Good, you're home. What're we doing?"

"We're making dinner, playing cards? You're soup. I'm dessert. Ready? Go," Margaret said.

Kevin handed her a slim apron lined with red polka dots, while he put on a frilly blue number with roosters. Chopping, slicing, sautéing—a well-oiled machine. Fred's keys jangled in the front door as they traded jokes about thyme. They were out of it and Kevin wanted more. "Thyme and thyme again," Margaret said as Fred walked in the door, tossed his read-through newspaper onto the floor.

"It's just that I've wasted so much thyme these past few weeks. If I'd only considered thyme management," Kevin said, searching through the spice cupboard in vain, his voice muffled.

Fred came to the kitchen door but didn't enter. He said, "You guys are talking about me." He was in a mood. Jealous of Kevin, of the world, of something he'd read in the paper on the train home. Longing once again for everyone to acknowledge the wrongs only he could see.

Kevin shut the cupboard door with a click. He laughed, "No. We're talking about thyme. That's it. We've been talking about it for about the last ten minutes, actually. Kind of pathetic. The herb. You know. It's a joke?" Kevin glanced at the floor, then at his bare, knobby feet poking out from the bottom of his frayed jeans. He smoothed his apron. Pulled once, compulsively, on his patch of goatee. "A pun?"

"I don't like it when you guys talk about me," Fred said. He turned abruptly from the doorway—oxford shirt, tie, khakis. Soon the band Dinosaur screamed from the darkened living room.

Kevin said, "So it's going to be one of those nights." He sprinkled some marjoram into the simmering soup, closed the jar, opened it, dropped in another pinch.

Margaret smiled. She was in charge of Fred, having brought him and his hundreds of record albums into their happy, platonic home. "Right," she said. "I'll get on that."

"I'll watch the tart for you," Kevin said optimistically, blowing on a spoonful of the steaming soup, slurping the thin broth through thick puckered lips.

Margaret made her way to the living room where Fred fumed in the overstuffed green chair silhouetted by the streetlight through the window, an explosion of red and pink geraniums on the low table at his side. His legs were spread, his feet planted on the floor. He looked at Margaret with disgust, his lips pressed firmly together.

As Margaret turned on a tiny light beside the stereo, she said, "Hey," pulling off her apron.

Fred glared. "You *were* talking about me," he said.

Margaret smiled, smoothed his hair into place, even as it fell back into his eyes. Grabbed one of his fingers. "We were, honestly, talking about thyme. The herb. It was a stupid conversation. Although we do talk about you sometimes," Margaret said, sitting at his feet. "Sometimes we say awful things. You know we do." Fred took off his glasses. Set them on the table. Margaret said, "Did you have a bad day, Fred? Is that it? World out to get you again?"

The music boomed through the room — electric guitars blocking the thoughts that might have otherwise disturbed this encounter. The carpet scratchy on her knees, Margaret rested her head in Fred's lap. She didn't mind. They would all have a good evening. She wedged her hands along his thighs, held him, even though he didn't deserve it. He was getting hard. She rubbed her face across, gave his crotch a quick kiss. She mumbled, "To the bedroom?"

She would do this for Kevin who knew he couldn't talk her out of this relationship no matter how many times he tried. Margaret edged up to Fred, along the tangled sheets.

When she returned to the kitchen, Kevin looked like a catcher squatting in front of the oven door. His apron dragging on the tile floor, he watched the tart like he was waiting for a curve ball.

He didn't look at her. "This is really wonderful," he said. "Come see."

She squatted beside him, their shoulders touching. They stayed like that for a long time. Margaret's heart pumping, then settling into itself again, secure. "It is," she said. The crust on the tart was browning, and its pale yellow top had baked itself into a galaxy of tiny, flecked paisleys.

Kevin hesitated, whispered, "Mission accomplished?"

"Bingo." They looked at the tart a while longer and then Margaret stood to grab the oven mitts. "Why don't we call Dawn and Rachel? See if they want to eat and play cards? "I'm sure Fred has something better to do," Margaret said.

Kevin looked weary as he double-checked her stability, assessed her stamina with a long stare.

They'd met a year before at the Franklin Temp Agency, not long after Margaret had arrived in the city. His thrift-store argyle vest, too-short dress pants, and half-shaven head. Kevin was the only other person who seemed to be struggling to achieve the proper corporate look. His left foot bounced a tiny tap dance as he confided to her across the hushed, carpeted waiting room that he'd just failed the typing test for the second time. Margaret asked him if he wanted to drown his sorrows. Weeks later, after that first beer, she taught him to type sixty words a minute without mistakes. When his roommate failed to return from a weeklong Boston trip to visit his girlfriend, Margaret moved from her rotation of couches into his place. Then Fred stormed into her life, and finally into her room with the bay windows and sliding French doors, the coveted bedroom off the living room.

Margaret opened the oven door, just as the timer dinged. She said, "It isn't that hard to be happy, Kevin. Everybody needs something different. Fred has some flaws, sure, but he can be very sweet, too. Remember the bouquet of flowers he brought home last week? Remember when he recited his grade school poem around the bonfire? So he wants blow jobs. Hey, some people want crack."

Kevin said, "Some day you're going to lose your mind. For now, I'll ride Fred's wave. Just know that I worry about you. I believe in your superiority. I'm waiting for you to come out of this in one piece."

Soon Margaret's long walks took on meaning. After work — stockings, skirt, freshly ironed white shirt, pumps, typing numbers, answering phones — she continued for blocks. The cement stretched out in front of her, and it was effortless. All it took was one foot in front of the other. It was the inside world that couldn't be traversed.

4

Margaret listens to Peter's breathing, a slight whistle on the exhale. The morning light, so distinct as it settles across the Great Plains, creeps in as the clock blinks 7:00 a.m. The steady weight is at her chest again, pushing gently but firmly on her lungs, keeping her from pulling in enough air. Panic hovers nearby like a lost dog.

For the past hour or more she has listened to Vivette shuffling throughout the house from bedroom to kitchen to bathroom to front porch to car — creaking floorboards, the click of doors. Tapping, stomping. The tiny, determined motor of the coffee grinder whining. Silence.

It's Vivette's second morning. Margaret likes to give guests private time, because she knows it's what she'd want. Time to think, to digest the previous day's explorations and conversations. Margaret needs time away from people to understand them. She wonders what Vivette, a person who seems to only live for the moment, thinks about her. Yesterday, in the kitchen, when she wore Margaret's jacket and was humming that silly song, for Margaret it was like gazing across years and seeing herself: young and cocky and mocking the world. Cynical, judgmental, Vivette humming and bored, standing there waiting for coffee.

The pressure continues, now a wide rubber band squeezing Margaret's chest, pulling in her ribs. She tries to breathe evenly. Focusing. In. Out.

The anxiety attacks began out of the blue when she arrived in Lincoln. At first she thought she was having a heart attack, but then she realized this thing that had her lying in a darkened bedroom panting in physical misery was emotional — a mini nervous breakdown. Nothing to worry about, the doctor reassured her. Very minor, he said. Margaret's mind and body decided one day she didn't like to have people in her house. That she needed to worry about both big and little things.

None of this existed in her previous life. She could go anywhere, meet anyone, make her way without second thoughts. Margaret now needs to monitor her contact with people the way others ration alcohol intake. If she binges at a party, socializing without a care, she pays for it the next day, curled in bed, door closed. She has to clear her mind. Think happy thoughts.

Margaret's life contracted over the years. In and in. Repercussions. Compromises. Obligations. She read somewhere that anxiety is just unprocessed fear. But she fears the unknown, so where does that leave her? Before she was simple and the world was in disorder—everything unknown a challenge, something new to discover and explore and put together. Now she's complicated, a puzzle to herself, and the world around her is flat.

Growing up Margaret never felt connected to her hometown in Ohio. It was just the place she was from. Once she'd resettled and claimed New Hampshire, the connections she felt there, needing a place so badly, the ocean and her friends, felt like a trap. They scared her. Leaving was easier than coming to terms with that kind of happiness. Portsmouth was just one place, and she needed to be a part of everything all at once. For a long while, floating above it all was the most consolation Margaret could find.

Now she loves her life at the farmhouse, loves Peter. He isn't like most guys she's been with. He talks about clothes and books and movies they should drive into Lincoln to see. He doesn't have strange fetishes or unrealistic expectations. Their life together is straightforward, and this realization is shocking to her. She wonders how she has managed to travel from there to here, leaving tangled, broken parts of her old self as she went, creating a new Margaret she doesn't recognize some days.

She twists flat onto her back with her hands behind her head. Big inhale. A long sigh. Breath in. Breath out. All the unnamed trouble circling, taunting. Memories from her old life join noises in the kitchen: Mixer. Bowl. Measuring spoons against ceramic. Glass. Vacuum. What's going on out there? A crashing noise and the coffee grinder again.

Sometimes Margaret resents that her edges don't show. She wishes people came with a list of ingredients, like the cookies she knows she shouldn't buy at the grocery store. A list people could read before judging her that shows what messed-up stuff has been added to get her to this place, to make the person she is today: four affairs, twenty lovers, three long-term relationships, forty out of fifty states, baker, temp, compulsive list maker, obsessive personality, demanding father, controlling mother, only child, the need to run away, softball team, cheerleading squad, cigarettes, whiskey with no ice — short glass. People would understand that she'd paid her dues, that happiness was a deliberate decision. They'd understand she'd learned the hard way.

But this is the Great Plains where secrets are kept buried deep inside and words are scarce as trees. Less said is more said. She has a good idea how she ended up here, but what kind of person chooses this place?

"Pioneers were pioneers because they didn't want to carry around all that baggage," Peter said, crossing his arms over his chest, leaning in the doorway of the living room.

"What do you mean?" Margaret said. "They were all about baggage. They carried goddamn cast-iron stoves. If that isn't baggage, I don't know what is."

"Mental baggage, Margaret. Mental baggage. They didn't want mental baggage."

She went back to knit, knit, knit, purl, beside the fireplace, then stopped. "But still. People left whole families behind. Houses with heat and fine furniture. Towns with culture and stores. There was a lot of mental baggage by the time they hit Nebraska. Add that to the cast-iron stove, and it's a wonder anyone made it across."

Peter was annoyed. He wanted this to be one of his lectures, not a discussion. "Margaret, you never let me make my point. You take off like it's a relay and you've got the baton. It isn't a relay. Give it back."

"Okay. Fine. Whatever." Margaret checked her stitches, found a mistake, decided it was Peter's fault that it looked crooked.

"They headed out, because they didn't like the crowds, the organization, because they wanted less, and poof, they could be anyone they wanted to be. It lessened the mental, albeit not the physical, baggage. People just take people for face value out here."

"Except for Barbara Kovel, of course. She's the most judgmental person I've ever met," Margaret said, smiling.

"Yes, of course, except for Barbara. No. That's not right," Peter said, "Barbara is no exception: what you see is what you get. That's all there is to it. You have to remember, these people are here because they didn't make it the whole way. Their wagon broke down. They ran out of money or got lost or lost heart, whatever. Somewhere back in the past someone set out for nirvana and instead ended up here."

"Except, of course, the people who came here and liked it. The Russians, for instance. It reminded them of home. Of the . . . What do you call it? The Russian tundra. You know, those Russians in Cather's novel, *O! Pioneers?*"

"You mean the ones that almost starved to death eating those gnarly, dried-up potatoes?" Peter asked. "C'mon, Margaret. There's no glory. There's no ocean. There's no finish line. I think the people here have internalized that. They understand they're halfway. I mean, given the choice, wouldn't you rather be in California? Who wouldn't rather be in California? Why would anyone choose to live here? It's an inferiority complex. We're living in an inferiority complex. The people who live here believe they can't live in California."

Margaret was ready for Peter to leave her alone again. "Okay, Dear," she said. "Yes, that's a good theory. Thanks for making me feel like a loser. Now please go away so I can knit in peace."

The fact is, Margaret likes knowing she's not at the finish line. Nebraska is too big and empty and overlooked to ever truly be discovered. The middle — potential framing each side — rippling off into endless horizons. That's her life now. No fortunes needed to get through each week.

There must be others like her who traveled to both the Atlantic and the Pacific and then stopped halfway because they wanted to. Every trip doesn't need to have rolling waves at the beginning and the end. Some people long for beauty in the unlikely, in the rising and falling grasses of the plains. Not a lighthouse in sight to give warning. No need.

Margaret nestles in further under the sheet to bring the quilt up higher over her shoulders. Thin, blue, morning light changes to deliberate orange as the branches strung with tiny green leaves outside the window vibrate triumphantly in the spring wind — the big, blank horizon stretching beyond. She tucks the blanket up over Peter too, who always sleeps a crazy, dead-to-the-world slumber until the sound of an alarm or a couple shakes from Margaret.

7:30 a.m. The mixer again. Oven door. Metal on metal, can that be right? Refrigerator door.

Margaret has already been up and out, feeding the animals before Vivette stirred from the guest room. Selfishly, stupidly, she carried her jacket back to the bedroom with her today, and it now points a sleeve of accusation, crumpled in the chair by the closet.

Early mornings aren't difficult for Margaret. These days she doesn't need an alarm to get started. The big, flat land doesn't provide any dark shadows, like the hills back east do. She adapted an attitude to match the geography, and wakes up ready to go. Today after walking through the yard to feed the animals, after letting Sparky out to bug the sheep, she felt compelled to crawl back beside Peter, to give Vivette a chance to have the house to herself. The creak of the oven door. Water full-blast into the sink. A cupboard slamming shut. Finally, the smell of coffee and — is that bananas?

Peter shifts slightly, his nasal cavity vibrating into a full-on snore. Mouth open and slack, the rise of whiskers on his chin makes him look like an old man. Margaret nudges his shoulder. He reaches out instinctively for her and instead of turning on his side in the opposite direction, pulls her close, an arm around her belly, spooning into her curved spine, resting his nose against the back of her neck. Instantly, he's asleep again. Short, small breaths. In and out, soft little secrets against her neck.

When people come to visit from Margaret's past, Peter is needy. Something he'd never admit to if asked. Normally a quiet, independent man with only a hint of desperation wedged under his calm exterior, he sits closer to her on the couch, checks on Margaret when she's talking alone with a friend. She wonders if Peter thinks she's capable of just up and leaving this life the way she left her old ones, that these visitors drift in from her past to tempt her away from shore.

Could she? Where? North or south? Canada or New Orleans?

Does she have it in her? When she senses this small amount of possessiveness and Peter pulls her close to keep her there to remind her she's loved, Margaret lets him. She lets him pull her back with his firm, beautiful arm. She closes her eyes, holds on, unsettled and resigned.

5

Vivette, Nebraska

Vivette bolts upright in the too-early light. A slippery dream scuttles away before she can catch it. The gray haze makes everything in the room around her silver—the picture frames, the wooden bureau, the braided rug, rocking chair, scattered clothes, yawning suitcase, capsized shoes. She shuffles into Margaret's kitchen, determined, without forethought, to make bread with the browning bananas she noticed yesterday in the glass bowl next to the fridge. It's a compulsion, a mechanical and perhaps neurological urge to bake, programmed into her early-morning consciousness by Penhallow Bakery. She creams the butter in the tabletop mixer, adds sugar and eggs. The paddle diligently scrapes at the metal bowl until the grainy, yellow sludge transforms to smooth silk. Vivette wonders if she's dreaming—moving smoothly through the kitchen she finds ingredients without thinking twice. A dash of vanilla, some grated orange rind, a handful of currants, walnuts. This recipe from heart, she mashes the soft bananas through her fingers. Their perfume hangs above the bowl before they drop into the eggy slush. Vivette measures flour into a separate bowl, fingers down into its cool center for a moment before adding the other dry ingredients, pushes up her pajama sleeves.

The bread now baking in the oven, the smell of warm bananas and roasting walnuts, she takes up vigil at the kitchen window.

After watching the sheep a while, she pulls a postcard from her bag slung over one of the coat pegs.

Dear Grandpa Joe-Joe. Creaming butter and sugar together, it's like gravity. The law of baking. You can't change it. I learned this the hard way. So far I find my stay here disturbing. But the car looks great hitched up out there by the watering trough. It's the kind of car every cowgirl dreams of. I wonder if you dream. Vivette

She scribbles his address and throws on a stamp. Vivette has never talked to Joe-Joe like this. In fact, she's always been a little afraid of him—his smell, his slow, constant, incomprehensible work at lighting his pipe. But this is her new life, and she feels bold and changed.

She realizes that she can't ask Margaret or Peter to mail the postcards. They'll read them. It's the temptation when handed a postcard addressed to someone else. Vivette will hoard them until she finds a drop box. She tucks the card back into her bag. A secret. Grandpa Joe-Joe can wait.

As the day clears, the static lifts from her head. Vivette washes the dishes, continues checking on the progress of the sheep, makes the coffee too weak, dumps it out, starts again, spills the grounds on the kitchen floor, finds the vacuum. Breaks a juice glass. Vacuum again. Finally, coffee in the pot where it belongs, at a legitimate octane.

Margaret stumbles in from the hallway, rumpled and nervous. "My God. I'm at Penhallow all over again," she says, fiddling with a drawer knob, then promptly drying the bowls propped in the drainer, putting them away. She lets each cupboard bang just a little each time. Vivette winces as these noises disturb her peaceful morning. She wonders if Margaret is feeling sick, or maybe trying to wake Peter.

The two loaves finally pulled out of the oven to cool on the counter are denser, smaller than Vivette anticipated. Margaret puts her hand over each one, as if baptizing it. She declares, "They're a little small. Did you remember everything? I just don't think these are quite right, Vivette." Margaret turns a loaf on its side, frowns at the browned bottom.

Vivette is sleepy. This new world will not let her do things right. "I don't know. I tried Penhallow's recipe from heart. The funky banana bread with all the stuff in it? It seems like I should know that by heart," she says. "Must've forgotten something though. Baking soda? Though I pulled it out of the cupboard, I don't remember putting it in." She looks at the tops of the withered loaves. "Shit."

"That's probably it," Margaret says, stretching her neck left and right. She inhales slowly. "No biggie," she says, pulling two metal travel mugs from the cupboard, looking outside to gauge the weather. And then in a voice pushed up a touch to suggest cheeriness, she says, "Let's go for a walk. It'll be nice in the fields this morning. Want to? We can finish the coffee and talk." She looks at Vivette, reluctantly confiding, "The walls are closing in on me."

The abandoned loaves are an unspoken offense. Their tiny vapors of steam, accusations in the air. Peter will eat one loaf standing at the kitchen sink before he drives into town. Vivette will polish off the second one late night, alone in the kitchen, cutting one thick slice, then another, the interior chewy and sweet, the crunch of roasted walnuts, tiny currants. Sparky's nails will click in conspiracy on the tile floor, and she'll feed him the last piece.

They walk the property line — a rough, three-mile circle away from the farmhouse outlined with crooked barbed wire fence, four-foot posts propping up each section. Margaret is out the door, ahead of Vivette at a brisk pace. The cool breeze at her back pushes her forward into the smell of earth and spring shoots. It's this kind of opening up that Margaret lives for. Rounding a corner that overlooks a rutted part of the pasture, cows graze lazily through a meadow dotted with old cars and outdated farm equipment. A thick rope of tail swishes the side of a light-blue '72 Cadillac that has prairie grass jutting up through rusted floorboards. Margaret pushes her legs into longer strides, forcing the silence away. Her mood shifts north with each impatient step.

Up an even grade, past Mr. Smith's old barn, caved in on one side as if leaning on a cane. Cows nibble the short, scrubby grasses from last year's planting. Calves following mother cows scamper into a playful run to test their skinny legs. Each brown field is ridged into rows, ready for the summer's corn and wheat. The dark soil is rich and luscious, like cocoa. After a while Margaret feels a ripple of comfort descend, and with it she stops to look around, waiting for Vivette to draw closer, panting at her side.

Vivette says, "Wow. Do you always walk that fast?"

Margaret puts her hands on her hips and says, "I wonder sometimes how the pioneers who landed here from the East Coast could have ever doubted this place." Margaret had read somewhere that the strange, treeless landscape made some of them believe that the dirt itself was tainted. They overlooked the grasses and flowers and were dead set on failed plantings of apple orchards with maples and oaks and pines. They wanted New England, what they'd left behind. The longing for texture in a place so big and flat must have been overwhelming. Wanting a wooden house where there wasn't any wood must have been a strange itch to scratch. Margaret tells Vivette this, then mulls it over as she sips her coffee.

Vivette doesn't bother to keep up with Margaret, whose bolt through the front door is confusing. Bringing up the rear, she daydreams what she'll do in Des Moines. Will she meet people, make the same kinds of friends she just left behind? Will she get herself into the same kinds of trouble? Will she finally change? Will there be bands? Is it possible she'll turn around and head back? Is that possible? She can already feel the humiliation that will come if she has to ask for her job back, find a new apartment. Admit that yes, yes, they told her so.

Vivette catches up with Margaret who launches into a lecture about pioneers. When Margaret is done Vivette asks, "Does it ever change? Do you think your life has really changed out here, or is the old Margaret just in hiding?" When Margaret doesn't answer, Vivette hesitates, but decides she needs to know. She asks again, "Hey, Margaret, do you think you've changed?"

All these years later, is she the same person? Margaret imagines the old patterns covered up, but seeping slowly to the surface, stones rising, lying in wait for the plow to come along and dent its blade with a magnificent spark. Or do those old patterns wear out, sag, and drop away? She doesn't know.

Walking more slowly now beside Vivette, Margaret shrugs and says, "Yes, I've changed." She pulls on a long stem of grass and stumbles a bit. "I don't know if that's true. Maybe the Margaret you met in New Hampshire wasn't really me, maybe that's when I was pretending. I'm not sure. I think shit happens in life and there's no erasing it. Once your heart is broken, you can't really go back to a time when you didn't understand what it felt like, you know? Once you lose your innocence, you see the big picture, you see what's coming more and more and you react to it, change course, instead of just blindly crashing into it. Or you know what's coming and you decide to smash into it. Big difference." Margaret stops, takes a sip of coffee, thinks about what she's saying, decides it sounds like good advice and continues, "I think that kind of thing—big emotional things that fuck you up—they make people care more about getting hurt. It makes people kinder. It makes them cautious. But it also makes people into little bastards sometimes, too. I mean, there has to be the potential for change, right?"

Vivette says, "I guess." She brushes her fingertips along the tops of the grass, settling them before the wind pushes the tips away again. Plucking a long stem, she tries to balance it on her fingertip. "I'd like to change into the kind of person, the kind of single person, that married guys stay away from. That's one of the things that nudged me out."

"Who did you have an affair with?" Margaret asks.

Vivette hesitates. She needs to be more careful. She can't talk about Robert because Susan is Margaret's best friend. She thinks fast, decides Wesley will take the fall. "This guy named Wesley? Do you know him? We got together," Vivette says.

Margaret's chest pulls tight. "Wesley Parks?" Of course, she thinks. Vivette and Wesley. Why hadn't she thought of that? Margaret eyes Vivette suspiciously. She says, "I dated him."

"Large coffee, wheat roll? You dated him? They call him 'the beautiful person'? Oh, wait a minute, I do remember something about you and him." Vivette is already regretting her lie. "Was it hot and heavy?"

"That was a long time ago," Margaret says. "He wasn't married then. Just a guy." Margaret's travel mug hangs limp at her side. Irrational jealousy builds from the tips of her fingers, edging up toward her neck, her mouth. "He's making moves on someone half his age now? God. What an asshole."

"Well, I made some moves too, unfortunately. He's married now. You knew that. To 'the beautiful woman.' At the bakery, we all call her that. And they have a baby girl."

"So," Margaret says, gently prying a burr from her coat, smoothing the material with her fingers, "you screwed?" She looks off at the horizon, starts walking again, abruptly taking the lane down toward the Kovel's red barn. "That's kind of crazy."

Vivette drops her stem of grass, hurries to catch up along the rutted lane, unsure of what to say. "Just once," she says.

"Her name is Olivia," Margaret says. "Olivia Kingsley."

Vivette continues, beyond her control now, "He took me to the river one day. And just the day before I'd seen him walking with his beautiful wife and beautiful baby in an antique wicker pram, looking all happy, perfect New England couple. I mean, I saw them. And they looked so content, smiling at each other and the baby—stopping to talk with friends. I was sitting there on the park bench envying them. I just couldn't believe he would actually risk fucking that up. And with me. With me of all people." Vivette stops to stare at the irrigation system in the field below them. It looks like a giant centipede. "God, I get so worked up about this," she says, crouching down to look at a piece of dried wood. "This is kind of interesting. It would look good on your porch. Should we bring it back with us?"

Margaret stops to look at Vivette's find. "Sure. I can't promise you Sparky won't drag it back out here though." Margaret turns and shades her eyes from the sun with her hand. "What did he say to you?"

Vivette wedges the weathered piece of wood under her elbow like a newspaper. "You mean the proposition? He said, 'Hey wanna see some otters?' Maybe that's his standard pick-up line. But there were otters. They were cute. His wife is so stunning. That's what blew my mind. Jesus. Maybe he thought there wasn't the chance of fucking it up, though; maybe he thought I was a safe bet? I don't know. Maybe he's just a jerk."

"He has a baby? That's so hard to believe. I wonder what he was thinking. With a baby and a wife. What a stupid thing to do. He was always an irrational man. Anyway, you just slept with him once; that just sounds like a mistake. What other married guys are pursuing you?"

"I don't want to talk about it. It's way too depressing," Vivette says.

"You're a calculated risk, Vivette. Not sure how you can change that," Margaret says, "except maybe get some perspective. Just say no?"

Vivette laughs, "Sounds easy, doesn't it? It's so incestuous there. I just felt misunderstood. A lot of people see me as this wild bakery woman. This loose, easy girl. I was so lost in the middle of that tiny town. Fucking Wesley was just one cog in the machine. I needed new geography. Space. Momentum. That's when I finagled the Buick from Grandpa Joe-Joe. I knew I needed out. Out, out, out." Vivette raises her arms above her head, stretches, closes her eyes, rocks up onto her toes. "You know her? Olivia? The beautiful woman? Kind of short? Perfect fair skin, nice lips, long, black, flowing hair, nice body? Kind of dresses like a New Yorker so she stands out. You know, all-black expensive clothes that don't look fancy but they cost a fortune? And she's so happy when she comes into the bakery. The baby sleeping like a perfect cherub. She's charming. She's always perfect. I mean, I like her. She's super nice to me, anyway."

"Yes, she is charming," Margaret says.

"Do you know her?"

"I knew her. Olivia. And she is beautiful. She's a painter."

"Right. So I guess, actually, I should thank Wesley for getting me out of that rut. For nudging me onto the next phase. I should look at the bright side and not want to ruin his life, right?"

"No, and I don't think anyone ever needs to thank Wesley. You did it all on your own. I mean, I don't know if Des Moines is the answer," Margaret laughs, "but the thing is you're up and running. It was time to leave. You're thinking about the big picture, looking for adventure. It's best to do that on the road and not in a little town. You're a cowgirl riding off into the sunset."

Margaret tests her arm around Vivette's shoulders, pulls her in close, smiles awkwardly. "You're going to be just fine. You just need to find a cute, single guy. Wait. I'm not sure that's what you need. I think what you need is to be alone for a while. Stop letting other people figure out who you are and do it yourself. It's much easier that way."

"I hope," Vivette says. "It actually seems really scary to me."

"We should head back," Margaret says, her own sharp loneliness nudging at her stomach. "I'm starving."

6

Vivette, New Hampshire

Birds nervously anticipated the sun as Vivette's shoes hit the pavement, the air cool and oily against her cheeks. Darkness faded, and the town leaned toward daybreak. Leaves rang out the tiniest applause from their branches.

The North Church clock read 4:55 a.m. The old men would be waiting. Efficient and silent, they were there with umbrellas when it rained, parkas when it snowed. Each day through fog and wind and world events they formed their queue of four. The old brass lock needed jiggling, the handle pulled up hard, and then the door swung free.

Penhallow Bakery at 5:00 a.m. was pure and sweet with a little edge for good measure. The old men radiated quiet, understated sadness, with their hats pulled low, their woolen blazers and heavy black shoes. At first Vivette tried to make small talk, but these men were at the bakery at this hour for a reason, and it wasn't because they wanted her company. She imagined they were widowers whose wives had once made them laugh, cooked them breakfast, held their hands on walks beside the river, and watched them dance the limbo at Hawaiian-themed parties where they sported brightly flowered shirts.

Now they were lost, and the bakery served to comfort them as they ordered black coffee and bought newspapers. On a rare day one would mutter a sports score to another, but mostly they stared silently out the blackened wall of windows as daylight overtook the town.

Vivette stocked the case with muffins, brioche, scones, and danish, set out plates of cookies — chocolate chip, ginger snaps, pecan clusters, raspberry squares. She filled the metal pitchers with milk and cream and made more coffee in anticipation of the seven o'clock rush. Towers of large and small cups beside their lids. Warm wheat rolls nudged off sheet pans into baskets. Everything alive — fresh and warm.

Vivette sliced the carrot and coconut cream cakes, warming the knife with hot water in between each swift drop of the blade. Ten perfect slices. Taking a break, she leaned on the counter with a cup of coffee drizzled with honey. Meanwhile, beyond the windows of the bakery, the town threw covers aside, dressed, and rushed into its busy life. Vivette waited.

But she was no fool. There was more to being happy in this world than well-sliced cakes and pots of coffee. This thought grew, nudging at her in dreams each night, but she wanted nothing to do with it. Avoiding the future *was* her game plan. Settling down wasn't on her to-do list.

She tired of running into regulars at the post office or bookstore. They asked her to list the ingredients in the raspberry squares, reminded her that she had agreed to save them a loaf of pumpernickel. Although Vivette loved working at the bakery, the center of the town's pulse, she didn't want these customers to believe they knew her when they didn't. They couldn't. But the locals wanted to join in, claim her along with the bread, the music, the cookie they bought at two o'clock for a special treat. They asked what video she was renting, said they'd seen her out dancing the night before, wondered about the book she was reading, asked what Thursday's soup of the day was. Jeans, T-shirts, coffee, muffin — that's what they knew. Sure, Vivette made small talk, but there was always a counter between them. Even when she ran into someone walking down by the railroad tracks, there was an invisible counter, an expectation that Vivette could satisfy some need like a food therapist. Other days she imagined she made it all up.

In fact, the day Wesley propositioned her proved to be something out of the ordinary. The idea that the women at the bakery saw a lot of action was more theory than practice as far as Vivette could tell. She'd been watching Wesley the day before with his lovely wife, pushing their baby girl down the sidewalk, looking proud and financially secure, right out of the pages of an L.L.Bean catalog and past the fountain at the entrance to the park.

At the end of her shift, Vivette cut across the bank parking lot. Wesley smiled. They chatted about otters, of all things. His short, wavy hair graying at the temples, his cotton shirt and shorts rumpled in a pleasing way. Expensive hiking boots. Wesley casually asked her with nothing much behind it, it seemed, if she wanted to go see them at the river. The otters. His green eyes. She smiled, looked up at the clear sky, swept her hair over her shoulders, brushed some flour from her jean shorts, and said, "Why not?"

His car was right there in the lot, a six-pack in the back seat. Vivette caught a glimpse of the stiff metal helmets as she leaned in. She imagined Wesley and his wife sitting in matching wicker chairs on the front porch of a renovated Cape Cod, drinking imported beer and talking softly about worldly things after putting their baby to bed.

Once parked on the gravel berm, Wesley grabbed the beer. The six-pack swung by his side, an unanswered question as they crept down the bank of the river. He opened one, a soft sigh, handed it to her, and took one for himself. The otters performed. Jovially in and out of the water, coasting on their backs, then up the bank, sliding in with quick, little splashes, like applause. Vivette laughed, said she felt like a peeping Tom.

Wesley leaned toward her and whispered, "Now is the part where I kiss you."

It wasn't a simple, happy day about otters after all. Of course not. As Wesley's hand came to rest at Vivette's waist, her body felt electric. She set her beer carefully on a rock the shape of a coaster, and said, "No," in a playful voice, "It isn't."

Wesley tipped his head. "No?" He smiled. A charming smile, perfect teeth. The hand was a warm, steady announcement at her side, fingers confident, unmoving, as if he and Vivette would get up and dance a waltz along the river road. His other hand brushed her cheek, a gesture that made her involuntarily love him, just for a second. In that second she imagined Wesley's unbearable unhappiness. That he'd been done wrong, his wife had had her own affair. A torrid one, Vivette thought. In that moment Vivette believed, yes, she would kiss him and live happily ever after.

A handsome man and, Vivette suspected, a safe man. Wesley was a regular at the bakery who wasn't going anywhere, who needed to maintain a reputation. But still. To her, he was an old man. She had never thought of kissing him. In fact, he'd never entered her thoughts much beyond his wife and daughter and the large coffee and wheat roll he ordered each morning. And now out here by the river, all alone with the otters.

Vivette said no again. Not smiling this time, but not unfriendly. His hand lifted from her waist, leaving a phantom in its place, an afterthought — the real hand already back at his side.

Wesley waited a moment, and then said, "I suppose you have a boyfriend."

Vivette said yes too quickly.

Guardedly he asked, "Do you live together?" He opened a second beer, neatly placing his finished bottle back into the cardboard holder.

Already she had lied about the boyfriend, and because any life was possible now, Vivette said, "Yes, we do. Just recently. His name is Todd."

Wesley stood, walked up the bank, Vivette trailing behind. He paced in the fine gravel beside the river road. He said, "I bet he's the condescending type with fashionable eyeglasses, isn't he? Todd. No. I bet he played lacrosse in college, wears lots of sloppy looking Patagonia clothes."

Vivette said, "Sounds like you're describing yourself. What do you have against Todd? You don't even know him. Plus you have him all wrong. No glasses, kind of nerdy, though. Into music and motorbikes. Very macho, actually, in a geeky kind of way. I like the conflict." Vivette did like the idea of this imaginary Todd.

"Oh, what does it matter?" Wesley said, immediately deflated. "I'm married." He looked older than the man Vivette had run into in the parking lot an hour before—wrinkles around tired eyes, bony knees. He paced a little more, then he said, "Although that does make us even. I have a wife, you have a boyfriend?" He looked up expectantly. He said, "You know, you remind me of someone I used to know."

"You're kind of nuts," Vivette said. "Do you know that?"

Wesley said, "Do you want me to take you back now?"

The memory of his hand wouldn't let the day end so easily. "Fashionable eyeglasses? What do you have against eyeglasses? Let's walk for a while," Vivette said. "Finish our beers." She continued down the lane ahead of him, the light shining in her hair, her thin legs tan and muscular. Her half-finished bottle hung casually by her side. Wesley followed.

In the blinking light with the hollow sound of the river below, Wesley complained about his overachieving but beautiful wife—her lack of interest in him now that baby Nicole had arrived. How some days she talked about her depression like it was a pet. How his in-laws now gave stern advice on financial planning. Bright green leaves shook themselves open all around.

Wesley dug the toe of his hiking boot into the gravel. "You just can't imagine what it's like," he said. "You're on the other side of it. I used to be where you are now, you know. You can't imagine growing old, because it totally takes you by surprise. You'll think you're the exception—but you're not." He fixed first one sock, then a shoelace, flexing each bicep on purpose, Vivette was sure, as he continued. "You always look like you're having fun at the bakery. So carefree. You looked open, you know, to suggestions?"

"But you know that I know that you're married with a kid. I mean, I *see* you guys all the time. I wait on your wife. I just waited on your wife this morning. Almond brioche, small decaf, leave room for cream."

Wesley laughed. "Sometimes I don't think at all. I didn't have a plan. I swear. I just thought you were interesting, thought it could be an adventure for you. What do you care if I'm married? I thought you were single, that it could be a little bit of unexpected excitement. I thought you'd like the otters." Wesley looked up into the leaves, the speckled sunlight. He touched her shoulder.

"On principle, I don't sleep with customers," Vivette said.

"Well, I know that's not true. What do you do, import your lovers? Everyone in town is a customer."

"Okay, I don't sleep with regulars, then. Look. I don't need to talk with you about this."

"But you are. You do want to. Come on. You like me. I can give you advice. You've been thinking about me for weeks."

"Honestly, I didn't really know your name until we were talking back there in front of the bank," Vivette said. "At the bakery we call you and your wife 'the beautiful people.' That's all I know."

Wesley laughed, "You refer to us as the beautiful people? That's kind of shallow, isn't it? I can't wait to tell Olivia. She'll be handing out her vita to the entire staff next week."

They continued along the river road. Vivette told stories—some true, some false. They pulled leaves off low-hanging branches, kicked stones in rounds ahead of them. Vivette knew this kind of interest was a kind of flirting, too, a kind of teasing. She liked harmless attention. She confided in him private stories about other customers, their separations and affairs—people who snuck in together in the early morning, bleary-eyed and mussed, having lost sleep, ending their romance over a cheese danish.

Below the steep bank to the river's edge, crisp, clear water smuggled itself around flat rocks. The smell of moss and pine. They skipped sharp gray stones one after another across the buckling current. Wesley said maybe they could do this again some time, just talk. He said maybe they could be friends. "I'm sorry to have misjudged you," he said. "No harm done, right?" Raised eyebrows, hands to his sides, Vivette knew this was her last chance to prove him right, the last offer on the kiss and the six-pack and the possibility of wild sex in a musty hotel room.

7   *Margaret, New Hampshire*

The first time Margaret visited her friends Susan and Robert, she drove to New Hampshire for a long weekend, a way of cutting the strings with her college years. In her phone message confirming her visit, Margaret said, "I'm in need of spontaneous geographic relocation. See you tomorrow." She applied Rum Raisin lipstick, wore a Clash T-shirt that her roommate had given her for Christmas, and laced up the Doc Martens boots she'd bought with graduation cash. With Robert and Susan at work, Margaret wandered out on her own that first day, down Portsmouth's sunny brick streets and around the town square.

People gathered on park benches and around outdoor café tables. A guy in a baggy, plaid cardigan sweater and thick, black eyeglasses looked up at her and smiled. Margaret asked him for directions to the pier. Later he would be her friend, Scott.

She arrived at Susan's place with no real plan, but feared she'd end up back in Boardman, Ohio, in her childhood bedroom with its assortment of teddy bears and pink ruffles, slowly suffocating, waitressing at the local diner with her communications degree stuffed into her back pocket. Jocks she went to high school with would demand more coffee, then try to look down the front of her uniform as she poured.

She ambled the narrow streets speckled with sunshine. The Piscataqua River swirled below her with sailboats and tugboats moving along, the drawbridge sliding up with bells and whistles. Photography studios, bookstores, galleries, and biker bars all shouldered each other along the tiny, crowded blocks. Where State Street intersected with Penhallow, she came across a bright pink building. Along the front were two park benches, and beside each one was a flower box—herbs and pansies, an abandoned pinwheel spinning in one. The early afternoon sun hit like a spotlight across the gold letters that spelled out "Penhallow Bakery."

The wooden case boasted jumbles of scones and rolls and twenty different kinds of cookies, each in their own basket with a hand-made sign. Behind the counter a metal rack propped up the day's bread selections: onion dill, anadama, oatmeal molasses, crusty white, and whole-wheat baguettes.

A warm sesame-wheat roll came with Margaret's split pea soup. The sun filtered through the front windows. The bakery was vi-brant: the smell of simmering soup mixed with music and the tabletops covered with Mexican tiles. Women with strong arms and kind faces moved swiftly behind the counter, chocolate and flour smudged across their aprons. They worked through the lunch rush, taking turns eating bowls of soup on the big wooden table near the ovens. They propped their feet up on colorful plastic barrels labeled FLOUR, CORNMEAL, and OATS, and yelled good-bye as customers ran out the door.

A whole new idea for Margaret's future took hold that day, one that had nothing to do with a career track or the board game Life that she'd played as a kid where you spun a dial and married, then added little pink and blue baby pegs to a blue or green or red sedan as it drove toward retirement.

Margaret spotted a handwritten sign on a cheap paper plate that read, "Counter person wanted, needed. You won't know what love is until you put one of these aprons on and step behind the counter." Hand-drawn flowers circled its rim. The stick figures in the center wore blue aprons, smiled, waving hello.

Margaret bought two baguettes, nine cocoa-butter hearts, and three pounds of wild-mushroom linguini for the dinner she planned to make Robert and Susan. The woman behind the counter had brown curly hair in a makeshift bun kept in place with various pens and pencils. When Margaret asked for an application, leaning against the back counter, drinking coffee, the woman said, "Sure, give it your best shot." She handed Margaret a brown paper bag and a pen. "Tell us what you want us to know."

"Hi, I'm Margaret," she said.

"Gert. Good luck."

Back at her table Margaret drew a quick sketch of herself in an apron with a bubble coming out of her mouth that said, "I love food. I really want this job. Please don't send me back to Ohio and my childhood room filled with pink gingham, Holly Hobby sheets, and half-used Love's Baby Soft bottles." She scribbled Susan and Robert's phone number at the bottom.

Two years later Margaret carried an overloaded garbage bag out to the dumpster in the alley beside Penhallow Bakery. She swung the bag up, around, and in like a discus thrower and turned to race through the bakery's back door, when suddenly she was nose to nose with Wesley—so close she could have counted his freckles. Handsome and nice. He commented on her future as a shot putter, gave her an 8.5 for overall performance. Margaret said, "You should see my figure skating," as she let the screen-door slam behind her.

Soon they were walking near the piers together almost every day and meeting for picnics in the park. Wesley offered her a dresser from his parents' cottage, said they'd be happy to see it go. Later as he pulled up in front of the old house where she rented the attic apartment, the bureau stood upright in the back of his pickup like a parade queen. Veneered wood with round 1950s Bakelite handles in deep maroon, a brass center on each knob. He squeezed it up the two flights of stairs, resting the dresser in the middle of the braided rug on her living room floor.

"Looks good," he said. "It fits right in with the minimalist kitsch you've got going on here." Wesley stretched his back, ran his fingers through his black, wavy hair.

Margaret propped herself against the door frame, leaned toward Wesley despite herself. "The style is bohemian with a touch of Midwest," she said. "My own personal accidental blend of grandma and beatnik."

"I like it. It suits you," he said. "The hippie beads with the doilies over there? I don't think I've seen that done before."

Wesley pulled on the edge of Margaret's shirt, tugged it just once and dropped his hand at his side.

Margaret reached out to touch the bottom of his cut-offs, pulled her hand back. "Okay, then. I guess I owe you dinner."

"I guess you do," he said.

"Tomorrow, then. Seven o'clock," Margaret said.

"Tomorrow it is." Wesley grinned and slipped down the stairs. She heard him whistling as he opened his truck door, a metallic whine and then it clicked shut. That night she pushed the dresser into her bedroom, its tiny ceramic wheels a quartet of squeaking mice.

The next night Wesley came to the door with a bottle of Jim Beam and a bunch of wildflowers. He said, "Your favorite, right?" Margaret had never cared for whiskey, but for years afterward Jim Beam was her brand. Straight up, on the rocks, with soda, with lime. She couldn't know it then, but later she would drink it to spite him, to suffer, to overcome his charm. No going back. She took the bottle, the flowers, led Wesley into the living room. Two jelly glasses on the low coffee table, and she poured strong drinks. Jim Beam. Ice.

They barely made it through dinner.

Through the green bean and sweet potato turnovers, the salad with homemade tarragon vinaigrette, the heat settled in. He kissed her beside the stove and then between bites. She put her hand on his face, on his thigh. Still holding the apple tart, they edged down the hallway. They pinned each other, hot and awkward, onto her futon.

At three in the morning he made coffee with her grandmother's sputtering percolator. He said, "You spend all your time taking care of other people, don't you? I think you need someone to take care of you for a change."

Margaret sat back against a pillow smashed against the wall, exhausted, listening to him move around her tiny kitchen. Taps and bumps. A spoon in the sink. Coffee with milk, sugar, and whiskey steamed between them as they talked through dawn.

They fell asleep hunched against each other, Wesley's hand just touching her breast, Margaret's thumb through a coffee cup's handle.

In the morning Margaret's heart was one big, complete world — untouched, intact, pounding. As Wesley got up to leave and she pulled him close to give him a kiss at the door, she rubbed his shoulder and grinned.

He said, "I don't even have your number," pulling a slip of paper from his pocket, grabbing a pen from the coffee table. As Margaret recited the digits, she believed she still understood up and down.

A small snow globe perched on the landing outside her door when she left her apartment that afternoon, raw and showered, alive with exhaustion. Inside the globe, a plastic San Francisco cable car flopped on a wobbly track, a sunny city scene pasted in the background. Too-big flakes of snow, a kind of precipitation that city never saw, drifted near the tracks. The snow globe weighed down a note that read, "Thanks for dinner."

Margaret put the snow globe on her kitchen windowsill. It glowed there, and she smiled every time she looked at it. Eventually, it led her to San Francisco and followed her to Nebraska where it rested deep in a trunk in the barn.

8 *Margaret, New Hampshire*

The North Church clock tower struck 4:00 p.m. The deep bell moved from side to side and echoed off the brick buildings around the square. Subarus, Volvos, BMWs, and Volkswagens lined up as passengers worked crossword puzzles or read tattered novels, idling on State Street, waiting for the drawbridge to ease back down.

Margaret felt uneasy. Wesley hadn't shown, and real life, unwanted, poured in through unguarded edges. The sun slanted across Margaret's suede jacket as she pried up a crinkled packet of butter from the sidewalk and threw it into the garbage can beside her. The wind, the sun, the jeans hugging her thighs — all an intrusion.

Panic. It was irrational, she knew. But Margaret needed Wesley there beside her, craving her. She liked the world void of details. She longed to be monopolized. Margaret wanted fuzzy — not all this Technicolor complexity with traffic signals and glittering litter.

A quick breeze of violet perfume and Susan materialized beside Margaret, catching her in a hug.

"Fancy meeting you here," Susan said. "Let's go get a beer."

"I'm waiting for Wesley," Margaret said. "We had plans. He must have forgotten." She tapped her feet on the cement, picked a chunk of dried flour off her red Chuck Taylors.

"That guy you've been hanging out with? White pickup truck? Pretty sure I saw him heading out of town while I was walking this way," Susan said. "Not positive though. Don't worry. He'll catch up one way or another if he knows what's good for him. But you've got to leave some room for your friends, right? I haven't talked with you in ages, haven't *seen* you in ages. I haven't even met this new Romeo stud muffin. This Wesley. C'mon, Robert is out with the guys tonight at some hipster Ping-Pong tournament. I'm so happy I found you."

A dull hunk of emotion since she met Wesley, Margaret now found everyday banter a mystery. Conversation, gossip, friends, all unfamiliar territory. Her body was raw. She didn't want to talk or think. She wanted to flirt and fuck. She'd had boyfriends in the past—sex, dates. More cautious and by-the-book than anything else. But nothing like this. Nothing that changed her chemistry. Her body hummed. She landed back in her head. Blushed.

"Look at you. C'mon, let's go to the Fish Kettle," Susan said. "The new deck should be clear. It's too early for the dinner tourists. We can watch the sun set. My treat."

Settled into a corner table overlooking the harbor with two sweating beers and a basket of crispy fries, Margaret took a deep breath and said, "Okay. Yes. This is nice. Thank you. It's just that I'm a bit oversexed these days." She addressed her beer as she said, "Susan. I'm in love." The tugboats leered nearby. A buoy clanged.

Susan cautiously said, "No, you're having sex. Sex isn't love. Sex is lust."

"Why do you say that?" Margaret whined. "Are you and Robert the only ones who get to be in love? You have no idea. I think he's the one. The one." Margaret waved to a customer, who waved her way, smiling. "I really do, Susan."

Susan grabbed Margaret's outstretched hand, pulled it to her chest so Margaret would look her in the eye. "I want to meet him. You've been hiding. That's what happens. The boyfriend comes, and you disappear. Robert and I are living together, and look, I'm still around." She tapped her beer bottle. "Sometimes you lose perspective. From what I've heard, this guy is a traveled travel writer."

Margaret whispered, "Like I'm pristine? Have you been doing reconnaissance? I can't believe you. Wesley is cool. He's different. He's devoted. He's sexy. I think he comes from money, and I find that a little exciting, too. I love that he has a real job. He goes to exotic places. That's mysterious." Smashing two fries together, she dabbed them into Susan's puddle of ketchup and threw them into her mouth. She wanted Wesley there beside her, his hand sneaking up under her untucked shirt.

"Okay. I'll reserve judgment," Susan said, tapping the table firmly with a finger. "You be careful though. Just remember you had your doubts when I met Robert. It's our job to be suspicious. It's what friends do. And mysterious, by the way, isn't a comforting description." She waved at the waitress, raised two fingers, and pointed at her empty beer bottle.

A woman came into the bakery the next morning, far too refined for Portsmouth. Long black hair, bright red lipstick, dark brown eyes, black T-shirt, black work pants, black boots. She pulled a few bills from a pink leather wallet.

"Are you Margaret? I'm Olivia. Olivia Kingsley. Wesley's friend? He's probably told you about me. He said you had pretty blue eyes, so I figured you had to be the one." She poked forward with a thin, pale hand, shook Margaret's.

Margaret's intuition went on red alert. It said CAREFUL, reminded her she'd chosen to wear a shitty thrift-store housedress to work that day and that her hair needed tending. Margaret pulled on her bangs, looked at the Chuck Taylors at the end of her pale legs, nudged away her gut reaction. Elbows on the counter, she said, "I'm having a few friends over this Friday. Do you want to come? If you're new here, you could meet some nice people."

"Well, sure. I'd love to," Olivia said. "Here's my number." She handed Margaret a business card. "I'm staying at my parents' cottage out near Rye? I'm in from New York for the spring, trying to get some painting done. The city was just doing me in." Olivia looked beyond Margaret at the bread rack. "Could I have a baguette and one small chocolate-chip cookie?"

Margaret bagged the bread, wrapped the cookie in a piece of waxed paper. She handed them to Olivia. "That's a dollar fifty. The cookie's on me. So, you and Wesley go way back?"

Olivia looked at her, smiling as if they had an inside joke. "You are nice, aren't you?" She handed Margaret two dollars, waved as she rushed out the door.

"So who's Olivia?" Margaret said into the phone as soon as she got home from work.

"You met Olivia? Oh good. Good," Wesley said. "I thought that might happen. We went to prep school together. Everybody called her O.K. back then. You know, her initials? Anyway. She's a good egg. My parents know the Kingsleys, that kind of thing. She's a little *needy* right now so I've been helping her get settled."

Margaret could hear water running, dishes clanking in Wesley's sink. She knew his hands, competent, imagined them skimming through the bubbles.

"I gave Olivia some furniture my parents had in storage," Wesley continued, "helped her get the utilities set up, stuff like that."

Margaret shifted the receiver to the opposite shoulder, her eyes burned as she looked out the window at the waning evening light, a rusty, orange glow filtered through the trees on her street, thick like applesauce. "Why didn't you tell me about her? Do you give all the women you know furniture? Why did you blow me off yesterday? We were supposed to get together."

"I gave you the best dresser," Wesley said.

Margaret didn't respond.

"I didn't think our plans were firm, Margaret. You suggested stopping by. I said I might. Look, don't get upset." The water stopped. Silence.

"You're right. You said you might, but you always do," Margaret said. "She's gorgeous."

"Olivia? I guess so, if you're into that sort of brooding style. Hey, I like you, remember? I'm not into the whole New York thing. Don't get jealous. Let's go visit her out at the cottage so you two can chum it up."

Caution, Margaret thought. *Caution*.

Olivia's cottage, set back into a small dune, was a quaint place built in the thirties, so unlike the overbuilt, new beach houses jutting up on either side. White wooden whales spouted on each blue shutter. The first floor was filled with cheerful light. The small kitchen had a worn wooden counter, a stove, and a fifties refrigerator. A window seat heaped with multicolored throw pillows lined the wall facing the ocean. Bookcases spied from every other wall. A small, enameled, wood-burning stove sat squat in the corner of the living room. Wood smoke combined with mothballs and oil paints. Olivia already had easels up and finished paintings hung in the hallway—bright, intense patches of color vibrated off the canvases. Olivia immediately offered Margaret one for her apartment.

"Are you serious?" Margaret asked. "They must sell for a lot of money."

"Well. Not that much, not yet, but you aren't going to sell it, right?" Olivia asked. "You're going to put it up, which is more than what most people do. I swear, they buy my work, and then I never see them again." Olivia looked at Wesley, touched his shoulder. "I really like her. Can she join our gang?"

9

Vivette, New Hampshire

Susan was in Connecticut settling her recently widowed, recently transplanted mother into her newly purchased condo the night Robert retrieved the half-full bottle of tequila from under the kitchen sink, put away the summer before after a failed attempt at margaritas. A bunch of friends had wandered over to Robert and Susan's place after hours.

Out of beer, with scrunched-up faces they sipped tequila from juice glasses, which glinted in the dull yellow porch light. They passed around a container of salt for the licked fists that followed the shots. No limes. Robert had found an orange in the back of the refrigerator, a bowl of apples on the counter, but everyone refused. They toasted to the moist, humid night. They toasted to the array of empty brown beer bottles lining the porch rail. Eventually the hot evening air scooted out, and a cool breeze and twittering birds suggested morning. The others waved goodbye one and two at a time. Robert and Vivette pushed at the swing as it creaked a response, Vivette's feet barely touching the floorboards.

Robert said, his voice a slur, "C'mon. Inside. You'll sleep on the couch, or you'll get run over by a car."

Vivette laughed. Stood up. Sat back down. Squinted, "You're right. How'd this happen? When'd this happen? Where'd everybody go? Am I obnoxious?"

Robert slung his arm around her small frame and pulled her up off the swing. They leaned into each other for leverage through the front door.

Vivette curled forward onto the living room couch in a fetal position, her face smashed into a scratchy, woolen pillow that would leave a zigzag pattern on her skin long after she awoke. Robert stumbled up to the bedroom, trailing his shoulder along the wall for balance as he tipped up the stairs.

In the morning Vivette made her way down the dimly lit hallway, stopping for water and aspirin in the bathroom. In the small beveled mirror that swayed above the sink, her thin face was creased with sleep and hangover, the mess of her hair tucked half into her t-shirt, its neck pulled half over her shoulder. She tried to keep both eyes open at the same time but couldn't. The humidity and heat needled through the closed blinds.

Then up the stairs and against the doorframe of Robert and Susan's bedroom, Vivette sucked air into her lungs, thick and filmy. Her eyes burned. She thought, just briefly, *So this is Robert and Susan's bedroom*. She'd never had a reason to walk into it before. She didn't have a reason now. Lavender walls with pale green trim. A big, oval rug in shades of black and gray spread out like a trivet under the antique bed frame.

"I'm hungover, and it's your fault," she mumbled as she dropped beside Robert into the creak of bedsprings, her arm across her face. "Bad influence," she said.

Robert moaned, pulled at the thin, yellow sheet tangled around him. He twisted on his side to face Vivette, eyes half closed. "Who drinks cheap tequila after high school?" he asked. "Oh, Vivette. I'm too old to do these kinds of things." He tapped her softly on the temple. "Could have been worse. Peppermint schnapps."

Vivette whispered, "Thank God for that."

Robert said, "Let's get a really greasy breakfast. That'll make everything better. Do you have to work?"

"Me? No way," Vivette said.

Time passed both slowly and quickly. Neither of them moved. Side by side, they stared at the dim ceiling, the dust-filled glass fixture cradling two crispy flies.

Inertia fixed them to the bed. It was silent except for the tick of a branch against the window, the muffled gossip of birds out on the electric line, the roof bracing itself against the oncoming sun. Robert patted Vivette's arm, then her head again, his finger tickled over the zigzag pattern imprinted on her cheek. Tracing, tracing. He said softly, "Look what happened to you."

They lay in silence, their shoulders touching, a strange, new current vibrating into being. "This isn't breakfast," Robert said.

Vivette arched her back, stretched out her short length along the bed, turned to look at him. "Not sure," she said.

And Vivette wasn't sure. She wasn't thinking anything at all. Wasn't trying to get up or stay. This was Robert, her friend, and she simply floated in this pastel world. On the opposite wall, one of Robert's industrial landscape paintings with three vacuum cleaners, green, gray, and blue, standing in a field, an ominous sky in the distance.

Robert slid his hand over toward hers, intertwined their fingers in the still-neutral ground between their bodies.

To drown out the voices that would soon reason through this — the ones already starting up in her head to convince her to go with Plan A: breakfast — Vivette rolled on top of Robert. Her small breasts smashed into his chest. She wanted comfort, silence. They lay like that for a few minutes. Then she kissed him. Then again. His tongue darted out, a little dab of lightning. Robert slipped off her t-shirt, her shorts. It was so simple to be naked. She pulled at the sheet, his boxers.

Later Vivette strolled home across the sunny, oblivious town and through her front door. On her couch, she clutched a tall glass of water to her chest, then let it roll along her collarbones. There was her shiny, awful reflection in the blank TV screen. Robert had made her breakfast while she stood in the kitchen doorway. They'd ignored the bedroom scene. Only once, when Vivette asked — "Have you been thinking about that for a while?" — did the obvious come up.

Robert said no. Shook his head, looked at her as if for the first time ever, smiled, and said, "Well. Of course the idea might have trailed through my thoughts once or twice. Sure. Why not? But no."

"Fantastic," Vivette whispered, crouched, watering the plants on the living-room floor. The word hung in the air like steam that refused to evaporate. Her jade plant, the ivy, the stack of overdue library books — witnesses.

Vivette waited for regret, but it didn't come knocking. She willed herself to be done with Robert and his married ass. The energy that had sparked back in their bedroom ran a low, dim course through her body — Robert stroking her, Robert inside her, Robert and the idea of deceit egging her on. As she sat on her couch, as her head tipped back, she fell asleep, mouth slack with exhaustion, her glass of water spilling — a trickle at her side.

Much later she dialed Robert, making each digit a long, hard tone under her fingernail. He answered on the second ring, an anxious hello.

Vivette lay back and closed her eyes, pinching the short bridge of her nose. "Okay. Hi, Robert."

"Vivette, how are you?" he asked softly. Too softly.

"Fine, fine, fine, fine." Vivette's voice trailed off. She played with the fringe on the edge of a throw pillow beside her, a crazy green-and-pink plaid number she'd recently found at the dollar store. "How are you? Is Susan home?"

"I'm okay. How are you doing? Really." Robert's voice unraveled, smooth and caring, his compassionate-friend voice, his I'm-older-than-you-and-can-give-good-advice voice.

She wanted to yell, *you!* She wanted to poke a finger into his chest. Instead, she said, "I just don't want to do that again. It was fantastic, don't get me wrong, but that can't happen again. Is Susan home?"

Robert said, "I didn't expect you to be so calm."

10

Vivette, Nebraska

The morning hours and the whole afternoon zip away. Peter had planned to make roasted fancy chicken and buy some wine. But it's already nearing four o'clock and too late for any of that. Monday is Peter's day off and his only weekday to tackle chores. By 10:00 a.m., he was mending fences along the property line; he meant to spend just a few hours re-stretching the barbed wire and straightening posts, but Mr. Kribeck talked pheasant hunting at him and then Barbara Kovel wanted to show him Lady Jane's new litter of pups, six little balls of fur, tiny tails already wagging.

Peter smoothes out a rumpled electric bill and sketches the second garden he has planned for beside the garage. The sky warns gray. He props himself beside a crooked cottonwood. The potatoes and spring mix are sprouting. He thinks about the eggplant and broccoli seedlings waiting on him, along with the corn, kale, carrots, and brussels sprouts. Heavy clouds roll somberly forward, tugging their shadowy selves across the fields. The wind picks up, the temperature shifts. Peter loses track of everything at the farmhouse. He gets absorbed in the idea of digging in the dirt, making plants grow from the tiniest seeds. Progress. It can't evade him here.

Hamburgers and baked potatoes, Peter's traditional Monday night dinner, will have to do. Cookies for dessert, the chocolate-chip kind Margaret taught him how to make last Christmas. He isn't surprised he's solo with Vivette today. He's past getting upset about such things. Margaret has a habit of ducking out when her friends visit. Initially baffled by these disappearances, Peter eventually learned just to give into them.

It seems that when Margaret's friends like Peter, Margaret gets along with everyone a little better. He knows he's proving himself in these moments. Usually he ends up liking Margaret's friends, and in the process of spending time alone with them he learns more about Margaret, too. He guesses that's what she's shooting for — using these people to fill him in, to help him understand the parts of Margaret beneath her silences, the times he finds her staring absently across the room or down the lane. All the unspoken words.

The wind tangles in earnest at his feet as he nears the farmhouse. The rain, miles off, is a gray flannel sheet hanging down from the clouds. Meadowlarks loop crazy circles, and Sparky has crawled under the porch. Peter hopes Vivette, who set off exploring on her own earlier that day, isn't out roaming too far.

Ingredients on the counter, the recipe attached to the toaster with a little black magnet. Like a worried grandmother, Peter checks the lane every few minutes, the storm fiercely at hand now. Droplets of water cling to the screens, which vibrate like drums on the other side of the closed windows. The wind sniffs around outside the house, offers a low, faint howl. Every few seconds the droplets tap themselves loose from the screens, zip away, and are replaced as a new troupe rushes into place.

Peter tells himself that if Vivette doesn't round the lane in five minutes, he'll go out in the truck looking for her. He flips on the porch light. It'll be dark soon, and she'll never find her way back if she gets turned around in one of the fields.

He imagines himself out there searching for her under bursts of lightning, prairie grasses blowing crazy in every direction, rain pelting the darkness.

Just then a yellow-and-pink flash crosses from the lane into the yard, and the door slams, air shifting as the wind tips in and back out of the house. Vivette stomps her feet and peels off her rain slicker. The backpack is a soggy, yellow marshmallow. She holds it away from herself as it drips onto the hardwood floors.

"Oh my God. What happened? Oh God, sorry about the floor. I really am," she says, dabbing the backpack on the braided rug in front of the door. Peter throws a kitchen towel her way, heads to find a bigger one in the bathroom. Vivette shouts, "I'm walking down the lane. I see an amazing-looking upturned tree and I sit down to read my book, write a few postcards. Completely ideal." Peter drapes a purple bath towel around her shoulders. "And next thing I know, I look up and there are the clouds. Huge. And I'm in those opening scenes of *The Wizard of Oz*."

"Things can come on fast out here," Peter says, awkwardly trying to keep her on the welcome mat and off the wooden floors. "You have to keep your head up."

Vivette pulls her hair up into bunches and wrings it out into the dishtowel, wraps the big towel around her waist to sop up water from her jeans. "It's a good thing I keep that little pink rain slicker in my backpack. I felt prepared, you know? To a degree." Vivette notices the abandoned baking pan in the kitchen and the ingredients lined up in a row. "Oh, and you cook too?" she asks.

Peter shuffles back into the kitchen. "You should get into dry clothes. Do you want to take a bath? There's the claw-foot tub. Towels in the dresser—well, I guess you know that by now. Help yourself though. Margaret has all kinds of smelly bath stuff, third drawer down. Fizzy things and bubbly things. Candles too."

After Vivette kicks her boots into the corner, she thanks Peter, and squeaks down the hallway, damp socks on shiny floors.

Peter lines up Vivette's abandoned boots on the rug and uses a dishtowel to wipe the floor dry—a few quick pats, and then he throws the dirty towel under the sink. He hears Vivette's belt buckle hit the tile floor, the dresser drawer creak open, the bath water start up, and then muffled through the door, Vivette's voice. "Jackpot," she says.

Peter smiles. He likes Vivette's spunk. He takes the largest nesting bowl from the bottom of the set, measures the flour carefully into the tin measuring cup, checks the recipe, measures the baking soda, salt, and sugar. Mixes the dry ingredients with his hands.

Margaret says he has to feel the ingredients, love them. If she was around, he'd make fun of her—use a spoon. Alone, the silky feel of the flour rubbed between his fingertips reminds him of childhood. The butter squeezed in his hands before he puts it into the other mixing bowl to be creamed reminds him of summer.

He preheats the oven. A fire in the fireplace is his next task if the storm keeps up—and popcorn once Margaret gets back from town.

He knows he hasn't always been patient or kind. At times people from Margaret's past egged on a meanness in him that bubbled up without warning, with their one-word inside jokes and endlessly overlapping stories. They come to visit less often these days. Peter feels bad about that. But maybe that's what happens. People drift apart, live different lives, move on. He can see how fragile it is even between him and Margaret. The chances of them being together forever or the two of them falling apart can barely be measured. They flail and mess up and lose balance and cling to each other. He knows that's all they can do. That with regrets or progress. And then there's love.

The deep, old tub is painted violet with a few tiny gold stars flecked along its side. Vivette fills it to the brim. Tiny tethers of steam gather in the room. Eucalyptus bath salts and a jar of ginger scrub at the ready. Candles flicker in the corners. Vivette's feet burn breaking the surface. Pins up her calves as she forces them in. Next her thighs, butt, stomach. She props herself up by her elbows, then dips her arms and tips her head under in one quick burst, water slopping over the sides—a tidal wave onto the tile floor. Fully immersed in the scalding water, something happens—her brain resets—and the reality of her new life frightens her.

Resurfacing into the dim room she cries big, snotty tears. Panicking. Rain beats against the window. Steam rises. Trying to pull herself together doesn't work. The water and heat confuse everything—inside and out. Vivette is nauseous. She wonders if it's obvious to everyone that she's lost, that these are pointless, restless times. "What," she whispers, "am I doing here?"

She curls her neck back onto the smooth curve of the tub and lets the tears slide down her cheeks, into her mouth a trickle of salt, and on into the sea of water. She tries to conjure sunflowers against a barn, but the fact is this slowing down isn't working. Isn't working at all. Vivette wants more than the world can possibly offer. And she knows there's so much out there, and here she is deep in the middle. Why this urge to leave Portsmouth and Penhallow Bakery just when she had everything? Why plow forward into a blank future? Why the longing to undo? She doesn't know yet. She only understands that she needs to keep going now that she's shoved off. And she hates herself for it. Hates outgrowing her easy life. Here she is. All alone.

After a long soak, the water in the tub cools. Vivette pulls herself together, eases herself out. Her limbs feel impossibly heavy— waterlogged. She gathers her seaweed hair up into a knot, secures it with barrettes. She throws on jeans and a flannel shirt, scrunches her wet clothes into a ball in the corner of her bedroom.

Her bare feet are pickled pink when they hit the tile floor of the kitchen, fingers puckered, eyes red. Head pounding. The timer ticks as Peter awkwardly forms hamburger patties at the counter. His big hands clap the meat flat. Potatoes wrapped in tin foil just came out of the oven.

"Beer?" Peter asks, tips his head toward the fridge.

Vivette stretches, touching her toes. Then she swings her arms straight up into the air, her flannel shirt rising up off her belly. "Amazing tub," she says, rolling up her sleeves, grabbing two beers. She sets Peter's on the counter as she asks, "Any bars nearby?"

"You eat meat, right?" Peter asks. "Margaret doesn't eat meat, so I make burgers on the Mondays she's not here. I forgot to ask. There are a few little-town taverns not too far away."

"Guilty carnivore. Don't worry. I love meat," Vivette says. "I just thought maybe after dinner you could take me out? Go find some dimly lit place, smoke some cigarettes, play some pool. I'm kind of in need of a bar. I'm feeling kind of . . . defeated."

"Well, we can't have that on my watch," Peter says. "You make the salad. I'll finish these up, build a fire. And then maybe Margaret will be back and want to come. That would be two bars in one night for her, a record. Margaret will probably wrap up the gossip session with the guys early with this storm. Driving in the rain makes her sad."

Sitting on the floor in front of the fireplace, greasy beef smell mixes with wood smoke. They shove their plates up on the coffee table away from Sparky's nose. An impatient wind makes the house moan as the sky turns from bruised blue to jet black.

Sparky races to the window, braces his paws on the sill, and then whimpers at the creaking trees as rain pelts the doors and windows, bombards the roof. Somewhere off in the house, a constant drip, drip, drip sound. "Gutter," Peter mumbles. "Good thing I put on that new roof last fall, or we'd be doing the pots-and-pans dance right now."

Vivette leans back against the couch, pressing the last bite of burger into her mouth. Everything about this house is comfy and perfect, she decides. There has to be more to it though. Peter. Margaret. This effortlessness. She wonders if these people ignore the edginess in the corners because it's just easier that way. She wonders if that's even possible—to will yourself into a holding pattern—everything smoothed too taut, corners neatly tucked underneath. She wonders if this is all a show.

Peter pokes at the fire. "It's nice having guests who like it here," he says. "Other city people who come to visit won't even get their shoes muddy."

"Well, I'm not a city girl. A Pennsylvanian turned New England girl, you know. I understand mud and rain." Vivette walks to the window. Squints at her reflection. Pushes her nose up to the cold glass to see the streaks of rain, slash marks through the sky.

"When did you move to New England?" Peter asks.

"When I was sixteen, with my mom. We moved away from Wilkes Barre where all my crazy relatives live. After the divorce my dad vaporized, and my mom just up and moved, me with her," Vivette says, pressing her ear to the window to hear the wind. It's an eerie growl like the inside of a gigantic seashell. "Then I up and moved from Keene to Portsmouth under the guise of going to college. It was a great move, though, away from everything and into a big mess of happy people."

"It's nice you're here," Peter says, standing beside Vivette. He offers her another beer, and then reaches to fix her shirt collar, tips the end down that rises up like a flag. "Why are you here, by the way?" He pats her shoulder, then turns to poke the fire again, pulling Sparky over beside him to pet his sides in short, quick thumps. "Oh wait, let me make some coffee to go with the cookies," he says. "I've got it all ready to go, just have to press start. If we're going out, I'll need some."

Vivette fixes her collar again, feels her naked body shifting under the shirt as she leans against the doorway, arms crossed over her chest. "I felt the need to move," she says. "I was ready to slip into something somewhere I've never been before, meet some strangers, you know? The world was nudging at me. How did you and Margaret meet? In Lincoln?"

"I think she'd just gotten into town the first time I saw her," Peter says, "all decked out in a short skirt and dingo boots, a cute little T-shirt, with a scarf in her hair. I thought, 'That one's not from here.' I saw her in line at the movie theater. She was two or three people ahead of me. I was just getting out of this really stupid thing and didn't think much more about it, until I saw her a few months later at the Hinky Dinky. That's a grocery store," Peter says laughing. He pulls two bright blue mugs from the cupboard, hands one to Vivette as the coffee pot gurgles to life.

"What happened?" she asks.

"She was ahead of me, talking to the cashier about tofu. She had on a bright green suede coat and a pink scarf. I wanted to say something to her, but couldn't think what. So I left my buggy in line, walked right up to her and said, 'I like tofu.'"

Vivette says, "That's a pick-up line you don't hear every day."

"Yeah, I know," Peter says. "I'm surprised she ever talked to me again."

Vivette moves beside Peter at the sink to look out into the black night, but all she sees are her own swollen eyes and Peter's determined reflection in the window. His rugged chin, broad shoulders. "So you met praising bean curd? That's crazy. But cute. Definitely cute," she says.

Peter swivels the pot back and forth under the stream of coffee, cuts the cookies into squares. "When I finally convinced her I wasn't a freak, I asked her out for dinner. I took her to this restaurant outside of Lincoln called the Soy Hop. They had it made up to look like a 1950s diner, except all the meat stuff on the menu was made from soy? They grow soybeans all around here, so someone decided to bring it to the people."

"Can you show it to me?" Vivette asks.

Peter carefully transfers the cookies to a plate, stacking them in a pyramid. "Well, unfortunately it isn't there anymore. This is a meat and potatoes world. That night there were a couple confused farmers looking at their plates like they were exploring the moon."

Vivette nibbles the edge of a cookie.

"I took her out there for dinner as a joke," Peter says. "We got some strange mock country-fried steak with gravy and a soy burger. They had shakes and stuff too, made with real ice cream. It was pretty good."

"And then?"

"That was it. We just fell for each other. I married her and we lived in town until I found this land and dragged her out to the middle of nowhere."

Steam puffs as the coffeemaker finishes brewing. Peter clumsily places a creamer, sugar bowl, and the plate of cookies on a tray, balances it precariously on one hand as he heads toward the living room. "This is all Margaret training. I even know where the cloth napkins are if you want one," Peter says.

"I'm impressed," Vivette says. "I was wondering if you had a brother I could check out. I would gladly start with a basic model. Break him in."

"Oh, you don't want my brothers," Peter says. "They're much different models than me. It's all training though. Guys need training for these things. Sad but true. It took me a first marriage and a whole lot of trial by error to appreciate that. But I've shown Margaret a few things, too, like it's okay to turn the radio news off every once in awhile. Like she doesn't need twenty-two pairs of vintage shoes."

"It sounds like it works out for you guys," Vivette says as she places her hand on his shoulder to lower herself onto the floor again, the fire at a low, constant flame.

"Some days . . . some days it seems fair, that's true," Peter says. He takes Vivette's hand off his shoulder, briefly smothering it in both of his and then resting it on the floor beside her. The fire pops and settles back into gentle flames again.

"I feel like a stupid teenager around you guys," Vivette says, grabbing another cookie. "You're so . . . grown up. It's good to know that somewhere in this world there are people who love each other and cohabitate for all the right reasons without revving themselves into completely weird shit."

"Well, we're a lot older than you," Peter says. "We both got ourselves into some crazy stuff before this came along." Peter rubs his hands together, grabs another log. "I guess when a good thing came, we knew enough to grab it and hold on because love just doesn't show up every day. We did our best not to blow it." He throws the log on and another, although the fire doesn't need it. It's warm and raging now, turning their cheeks pink and flush. "I think when you're young you mess around with relationships because you think your options are endless. At some point, you say to yourself, do I want to try and change, or do I want to live alone forever?"

"Yeah, that's good," Vivette says. "Maybe some people need to hit bottom before they shoot to the top."

Peter tips the rest of his coffee down his throat. "You can fool yourself into believing just about anything is good for you. Definitely."

11

Margaret, Nebraska

The monthly all-staff dinners at the All-Right Trucking Company started after owner Larry Schultz attended what was for him a life-changing conference on small-business management hosted by Hallmark Cards in Kansas City. The conference stressed getting to know employees "away from the desk" and offering opportunities for positive, interactive discussion between departments. The first meeting had everyone sitting around a bunch of tables pushed together and loaded down with fried chicken, mashed potatoes, and peas. They talked about their favorite TV shows and how many kids or pets they had.

Along with ten pepperoni and two cheese pizzas, this month's agenda includes, "Trucks help the environment," "Remember to turn off lights to save electricity," and "Don't forget to add your own inspirational jokes and quotes to the new employee quote board." When Mr. Schultz opens the floor up for questions and comments, no one says a word. The room holds its collective breath, hoping for an early dismissal.

Although Margaret has tried talking Larry out of these employee dinners, he says, "Sorry, Margie, sometimes I have to listen to the smart little voice in my head." And it's true that voice has made him a successful man.

Tonight, however, Larry looks tired and ready to call it quits.

He seems to know the highlight of his pep rallies is when they all escape afterward to catch the end of happy hour.

At the Zoo Bar on a musty bar stool between Joe and Allen, the loading dock guys, Margaret gets the scoop on who's sleeping around with whom and who was quietly fired. The guys have their ears finely tuned to the vents. Margaret has no idea if their information is accurate, but the gossip keeps the job interesting. She feels purged by the end of the night and okay about another month's employment at the All-Right Trucking Company.

The Zoo's narrow doorway and long, L-shaped bar lure people in. The opening band has just finished a sound check, and the jukebox is backlogged with enough tunes to last until the music starts in earnest. Margaret sits mid-bar, waiting for Joe and Allen. John Lee Hooker's "Boom, Boom, Boom" starts up, and Nick the bartender sets a Jim Beam and soda in front of her and a glass of water, no ice. The bar top is glossy slick, bright red where it has just been wiped down, and her glass shimmies to the left along a slimy water trail. The wooden floor, rough and dirty, squeaks as people walk by to their tables or slide onto another stool in the long lineup. Meaningless bubbles of conversation rise up and disintegrate around her: a debate about the University of Nebraska women's volleyball team, the story of the homeless guy who recently won $500 at pull-tabs, a toast to a new grandkid. Margaret sips her drink, thinking that surely Joe and Allen didn't get laid off in the last round of craziness. Someone would have told her. Although now that she thinks about it, fishing season might have started, and she doesn't remember seeing the guys lurking at the back of the pep rally as usual. She'll wait it out through one drink.

Margaret appreciates the alone time, away from Vivette and her full-on energy. Pulling a napkin from the square tray, she folds it slowly in half, over again, more folds, and then pulls the wings across, puffing up the body between beak and tail. She props the origami swan against the napkin holder for Nick.

A handsome balding man with a neatly trimmed beard a few stools away gets her attention by waving two fingers in a tick-tock peace sign. "I can do a frog," he says. The man pantomimes folding while shrugging his shoulders. "But not with a napkin — too flimsy. Real paper, and I'll have a frog like that," he says snapping his fingers. Nick, ever the eavesdropper, hands him a flyer for Magic Slim and the Teardrops, next week's headliner. After a little fumbling and a lot of folding, the man blows into the frog's end, puffing up its middle. He hops it once toward Margaret, then rests it on top of the napkin dispenser.

"That's good," Margaret says, unimpressed. "When you're homeless you can make those on the street corner for quick cash."

"Wow, do I look like that's where I'm heading?" he asks, rubbing at his beard. Nick nudges the frog into his hand, looks it over, and sets it on top of the cash register beside the swan.

"Sorry," Margaret says. "I came with the wrong filter. I think something, and there it is. Thought I'd fixed that in recent years."

The man pulls a pack of cigarettes from his leather bag, takes one, stretches to tip the box Margaret's way.

"Thanks," Margaret says, surprising herself. She puts the cigarette in her mouth, the dry paper a consolation against her lips. The man rises from his stool, silver lighter extended. Margaret asks, "New in town?" as she bobs her cigarette into and out of the flame. She takes one tiny drag and rests it in the ashtray.

"It's good to relax after an intense origami session," he says. "Married?"

Margaret smiles at him, in spite of herself. "Yes. Married.

Stopped wearing a ring a while ago," she says. "Don't like jewelry. Gets in the way. And, you are new in town, because around here you don't ask a stranger a question like that, you just ask Nick."

The man rubs his beard again, pushing the stiff hairs the wrong way then smoothing them right. "Good to know. I'm new. Teaching at the university next year. In early to find a place to live. I was married, but never homeless." He switches to methodically rubbing the lighter's smooth chrome.

"I found this bar by accident. It's amazing where aimlessly bored can take you," he says, looking around. "You know, I always thought I'd get a tenure-track position at one of the big schools in a city. I never expected this." He holds up his skinny fingers, wiggles them at the walls and ceiling.

"This is a great bar," Margaret says. "All the Chicago jazz and blues guys used to hit it on tour. They still get some good gigs coming through. It's nostalgic for the old-timers, although I usually have to leave pretty early because there's no ventilation. Some days I think they actually add smoke. You'll like Lincoln. It's cheap so you can travel a lot in the summer. I'm sure that's what everybody in your department has told you."

"Ha, yes, that's exactly what they said." He studies his drink on the bar. "If I'm still here in five years I'm going kill myself." He takes a long drag off his cigarette. Margaret checks the door for the guys. Tomorrow at work she'll have to ask about them. They should've been just behind her. B. B. King's "The Thrill is Gone" starts up. Someone down the bar softly sings along.

"Waiting for someone?" he asks.

"My buddies from work," Margaret says. "I don't know what's keeping them, or maybe I lost track of fishing season. I hope it's fishing season — they're the only drinking buddies I have."

"Do you mind if I sit here until they come? I'll be your tem-

68

porary drinking buddy. It's nice talking with someone who isn't a real estate agent or a prying colleague. A real person," he says, as if it's a novel concept.

"Sure, sure. Sit away," Margaret says. "Free world and all that." There's a whiff of musky cologne as he shifts onto the stool beside Margaret. "Welcome to the Great Plains," she says holding up her glass. "I'm Margaret."

"Good to meet you, Margaret from the Great Plains. I'm Bailey Johnson from the other side of the moon."

Margaret feels obliged to buy the lonely professor another scotch in exchange for the cigarette she has left unsmoked in the ashtray. She knows Peter will be fine as solo host to Vivette. It'll be good for him to have a young woman fawn over his cooking. Margaret deserves something unexpected, a bit of randomness. How often does something like this happen to her, meeting someone smart and good-looking from out of town? Never, she thinks. She smiles, raises two fingers at Nick. "Every guy I ever dated until my husband I met at a bar or in front of a dumpster. I don't recommend it," she says, studying her empty glass. "They were all maniacal and insane, but I loved every one of them for a while just the same."

"Where'd you meet your husband?" Bailey asks.

"At the grocery store," Margaret says.

"I'll keep that advice in mind," Bailey says. "For now, I'd just like to find a house within walking distance of campus without a yard. Everything here has lawn. I don't do landscaping at this stage in my academic career."

"I live on a farm, which I guess is all about yard," Margaret says. She checks the door one more time.

The next thing she knows the jukebox is off, and they're both swaying to the band and on to their third drink. A haggard-looking bleach blonde belts out a desperately loud "Proud Mary." They yell over the music.

"So then," Bailey says, "after she convinced me to finish my degree and supported me financially and emotionally while I finished it, I divorced her. I took the first job that was offered, because I had to get away from the mess I'd made. I mean, she kept organizing my closets and cleaning the cat boxes. She wanted to dig up the yard and start a garden. How can you leave someone who's willing to clean the cat boxes? The garden thing just seemed like the wrong direction for me. I don't know. She's devastated and pissed off, and I'm not sure what I'm doing. Penance, maybe? I think I'm doing penance."

Margaret doesn't recognize anyone in the bar. It's like she's shifted into another time, living a night of her past to get a fix before returning home to the steady and predictable. The professor nudges her shoulder. He moves away, then closer.

Margaret yells into his ear, "You stayed with her because she cleaned your cat boxes? Oh, come on. You could just hire someone to do that." She asks for another cigarette, lights this one herself with matches from the ashtray and then holds it aloft in her splayed fingers, liking the idea of smoking, the ritual.

But her eyes sting and a tight clothesline tugs at her lungs. Suddenly, she's scared. "Crazy," she mutters. "I have to go." Grabbing her jacket from the bar stool, her bag, she leaves a handsome tip for Nick on the bar, smiles his way. Bailey walks close behind. She can feel him. Hopes to lose him at the door. Turning quickly, face to face with his scraggly beard, his small moist eyes, brown flecked with green. She says to his mouth that seems to be puckering into some word or another, "Bye then, Bailey."

If she lived in a big city this wouldn't be a problem, but it is. Margaret is angry. Her world is small, and there isn't room for

Bailey Johnson in it. Already, she can hear Nick's insinuations the next time she steps foot inside there.

The pouring rain and wind beyond the glass door are a relief after the heat of the packed bar. The storm that had been brewing all day on the horizon is at hand. Margaret wheezes, just a little. Her skin is suddenly too small for her body, and no thinking through it can stop this now. Under the bar's small awning she scrambles through her bag for an inhaler, an umbrella, feeling the smooth plastic, anticipating relief, despising her own efficiency, how practical it is that she has the inhaler, that she's prepared with an umbrella of all things. Shaking the canister, inhaling, she releases the puff. Instantly her lungs are hers again. Big and open. Easy. Like new. She presses the button on the umbrella and directly she's dry, too. She points it into the wind. Simple solutions. The rain pelts down accusations, but she's dry. Dry and breathing and free. Margaret is startled from her interior world when she hears Bailey's voice behind her.

"You really shouldn't hang out smoking in bars with strange men if this is what happens to you," Bailey says. A faulty gutter nearby splatters water onto the sidewalk. He stands unnaturally still under the awning with his hands shoved into his pockets.

Margaret is annoyed. The sky is shouting, *Who do you think you are?* Who does she think she is? Prissy. *Prissy*, she thinks.

Bailey says, "Can I walk you to your car?"

"My car's right here. Right there. That's it," Margaret says. "The beauty of the Great Plains. You can always get a good parking spot. But thanks."

As Margaret steps off the curb, Bailey steps forward, away from the protective awning, the rain soaking him. "Can I get a ride? I didn't bring an umbrella, and I need to walk to my hotel from here."

Margaret needs to sober up, calm down. She flips her soggy umbrella into the back seat. "It's open," she says.

Margaret snakes through the lettered and numbered blocks, stopping in front of the Holiday Inn, not far from her first job in Lincoln, at a coffee shop called The Beanbag. Peter used to wait for her after her shifts on Fridays, walk her home, hold her hand. A little wave of nausea pulses at her heart.

"Hey, thanks," Bailey says, patting her shoulder in the idling car. "I had fun. I'm not an asshole by the way. Just freaked out and lonely."

He leans over to, what? Margaret doesn't know. She kisses him. Without warning or forethought. She kisses him long and hard, and he kisses her back. His soggy arm drapes around her, nudging her forward, and for a moment they're a high school make-out session in front of his hotel. Their breath steams the windows. Arms, tongues, noses nudging in furtive exploration, stark and angular.

Up for air, he looks at her suspiciously, reclines against the car seat, hesitates, and says, "Room 345. I'll be here for a couple more days before I head back to Baltimore." Bailey leans on the arm rest, edging toward her again, and then he's gone, pushing himself out of the car into the heaving storm, the heavy metal thud of the door a stiff period at the end of a sentence. Margaret's tongue tingles as if she has just tasted a new spice. One small bite. The pressure of his lips on hers. Margaret's body is ready for anything. Next, she figures, she'll rob a bank or start a religion. Anything's possible if such a thing can happen after years of faithful marriage. The world is so fragile. Edging her car away from the curb, she looks three times for oncoming traffic on the slick, deserted street and pulls out cautiously. She makes her way to the interstate, hood pointing toward home. She thinks she might throw up.

The rain erases the blank, dark plains, the gusts of wind rumbling forward and then subsiding and then hooking in from another direction. They push at the prairie grasses until their neurotic little heads quiver above the ground, pop back up, and over again. Mailboxes vibrate down to their wooden posts. Plastic lawn chairs cartwheel end on end across the road into gullies. The cottonwoods sway, reaching out blindly to touch something—one way and then another—groping the dark sky.

Her own headlights are the only dim light Margaret sees for miles—two tiny cones barely illuminating the way through the black expanse. Pencils of rain pour from the sky, and Margaret's car snakes away from Lincoln along the fields. She leans forward, closer to the windshield, squinting, turning up the radio. For once the blues on KZUM don't bug her.

The wind and the clouds converge, beautiful and ominous, for no one to see, and they won't let up, rushing over the land, whistling a high pitch, then moaning a big thick hum.

And soon Margaret isn't in her life at all. Instead, she's rolling around in deep nostalgia, wondering aloud how long Wesley had been sleeping with Olivia while he still dated *her*. Wondering what their first night together was like, knowing Margaret was near, feeling heartbroken and lusty. Did they sense her behind each kiss?

Could Wesley have known that Vivette planned to travel out here to visit her? Could he have seduced her because he suspected Vivette would tell her all about it? Or is Margaret herself crazy for wondering if Wesley thought about her at all? Can it last this long? His need to complicate her life? And why, she asks herself, does she care? She's happy, married, spending her life with a sane, kind man who isn't capable of being awful. A man who, with only the slightest prompting, builds her a fire, learns to bake cookies.

"Paranoia," Margaret whispers. "Paranoia. Drop it, Margaret. Drop it, drop it. Get your shit together."

The nostalgia tugs her back into its dark spirals, though. A split-second memory: It's early morning. Margaret in bed, still sleepy. The yellow curtains blow in the wind through the half-open window. In the kitchen, Wesley whistles along to Hank Williams. Margaret rolls off the futon, planting her feet on the floor. She stretches. Wesley's shirt hangs on the doorknob. She grabs it, puts it on. The sleeves hang past her hands. She wanders into the kitchen, her hair a scattered mess, yawning.

Wesley has the coffee percolating. Milk heats in a saucepan, the way Margaret likes it. Whistling. The kitchen in the little apartment is bright and cheerful with its old enamel sink and white wooden cupboards, a pantry along the one wall. The floor sags and the wallpaper is peeling, just a little. The smell of coffee rises into the room. Wesley hasn't noticed Margaret standing in the doorway.

He looks up. "Hello there," he says, his voice filled with the kind of contentment Margaret feels.

Their favorite music plays, and Wesley has made her coffee, and he's whistling as if this is his kitchen too, standing there in his boxer shorts and T-shirt, his bare feet on her faded linoleum floor.

And Margaret holds him then, from behind, her arms around his middle. She holds him, and they sway to the music. Their music. Wesley holds her arms in place, even after the milk starts to boil. He holds her there and says, "I'd love to spend every single morning of my life with you." And Margaret believes him. She still believes him. It clings in her throat, and now her heart breaks all over again. She believed him.

And, who is this man, this Bailey Johnson? His wife believed him, too. She wanted a garden and he up and left. Margaret shakes her head, dull still from the whiskey. It's hard on a night when sad memories seem to be spilling from the sky itself. It's hard to live in the present, when the past seems so vivid, so accessible, so just there for the taking.

What would she do if she saw Wesley, if they lived in the same town and he asked her to go watch the otters play down by the river? Would she kiss him? Fuck him? Would she?

She thinks about the one time, the one and only time, she had sex with Kevin in San Francisco. Did she do it because it played into Fred's greatest fear? Did she break Kevin's heart because hers was already cracked in half? Did she know that Fred planned to come home early from work? Did she make all that happen? And why? Was there satisfaction in seeing Fred's face stretch in assurance and rage, seeing Kevin happy and then hiding under the sheets? Was she satisfied getting back together with Fred, watching their previously balanced household tip and settle and tip again? Getting in her car in the middle of the night and leaving the two of them together in that apartment? Leaving them to work it all out without her?

But it's true. She was proud driving out of the city that night, as she hit the mountain passes. Margaret remembers being quite pleased with herself, feeling smart and free, feeling like she'd made the right decision, with the long, empty darkness rushing toward her. She remembers, and she knows this might not be right, but she remembers laughing with delight. But surely she wasn't that cruel? It happened, though, laughing and plugging Blondie into the tape deck. She remembers it like it was yesterday.

Margaret continues to accelerate down the waterlogged road, but soon realizes she's lost, actually lost. Lost in Nebraska, a state whose street systems are built on the largest grid imaginable, a place where it's impossible to lose your way. But she doesn't recognize anything. The rain is confusing and somewhere, somehow, she made a wrong turn. Margaret pulls over. Her windshield wipers hyperactive and ineffective against the onslaught. Beyond, nothing but darkened, howling fields. She'll turn around, head back to Lincoln, and start over again. Once she's lost she knows it's the only way to reset her radar. She sits and pounds her hands against the steering wheel. "This is," she says, "Vivette's fault."

Margaret retraces her steps, both hands on the wheel, returning to Lincoln. She's near her starting point, close to Bailey's hotel. She drives into the lot without thinking twice. She parks her car, rushes into the lobby, snaps her umbrella closed. The elevator to the third floor, and she's knocking on his door.

Bailey sheepishly opens it, a look of both surprise and expectation on his face. A reading lamp softly glows in the background, a trickle of classical music.

Margaret has traveled too far into her past tonight to stop.

"Who," she asks, "do you think you are?"

"What are you talking about?" Bailey asks.

"I mean, she wanted a garden, Bailey. It isn't asking so much, you know. Couldn't you have just done it? I mean, you broke her heart. For what? My advice? Get a yard. Cut some grass."

He looks down the hallway both ways. He wears reading glasses and a cardigan, his finger wedged midway into a thick book.

"Hey," he says quietly, "you're insane, you know that? Who do *I* think *I* am? You're the one out kissing complete strangers."

Margaret walks away, pushes the big plastic button with an arrow pointing down. An embarrassing sense of both defeat and victory hem her in as she heads home for the second time.

Finally her farmhouse rises up in the distance, a bright pocket of light jumbled in her streaked windshield. Her car rocks and splashes down the lane. Flooding her shoes as she pushes open the door, the rain pelts her face. Already she smells the wood burning in the fireplace. She rushes out, diving headfirst, slamming the car door behind.

But only Sparky is there to greet her. The embers in the fire have a painful glow. The house is empty. Margaret drops her bag by the door and looks for a note.

That night after the fire has died down and Vivette is in bed, Margaret hugs Peter tightly in front of the fading ashes. She hugs him again beside the bed, kisses him once before they curl back the covers. She traces his lips, his eyelids, his lips, over and over. The dim bedside lamp is a soft yellow afterthought. "I love you. You know that, don't you? I'm sorry I was so late," Margaret says.

Peter smiles, rubbing his hands along her thighs, "You don't have to apologize again. It was good for Vivette and me to hang out." He kisses her nose, her forehead, her hair. He nuzzles her neck. "Everything okay?" he asks.

12 *Vivette, Nebraska*

In her short skirt and snug-fitting velour shirt, Vivette assures Peter she knows they aren't heading to a hipster bar. They race into the·rain. Windshield wipers shove aside the onslaught as Peter backs up the truck and maneuvers to the main road, the rocky lane laced with newly formed rivulets.

Soon they're seated across from each other, in a stiff wooden booth at Lucky's bar, Hickman, Nebraska. Rainwater drips from Peter's chin.

"You know, you kind of look like this guy from New Hampshire," Vivette says. "Do you know Wesley? Did anyone ever tell you that? You're taller than him, though, and a lot nicer."

Peter rubs at his jaw. "Wesley? No," he says. "I know a little something about him, I guess. Sounds like a real piece of work."

Vivette rests her head in her cupped palms, watching Peter like a TV set. "Do you mind if I smoke?"

Vivette buys a pack from the vending machine in the corner, coins dropping into an interior metal tin followed by the whoosh-pull of the lever. She feeds dollar bills into the jukebox, selects Springsteen's entire *Born in the U.S.A.* album.

"You're right. This place is dead," she says, scooting back in. "Don't know what I was shooting for, but this'll do. A suggestion of humanity, the potential for bustle — beer signs, pool table. I'll smoke, drink too much. It'll be fine," she says as if to console Peter. Vivette sips her shot, sips her beer in equal measure. "Where I grew up, in Wilkes Barre, P.A.? You're required to love Springsteen," she says. "But it's not hard because the music is just sort of in your blood. I try to ignore it, but I know all the words. Fair warning."

Peter's tiring of Vivette's confessions. Her banter is a smoke screen, he knows it. Yet with Margaret not around, he's tempted to turn the conversation back to Wesley. "So," he asks, "do you know Wesley well?"

"Me? No," Vivette says. "He's a regular at the bakery and looks super together all the time. Super New England superhero. Him and his wife, Olivia, they just have all the equipment, all the get-ups, you know? All the right *knowledge*. They're very nice, and Wesley does seem smart, although tricky and smarmy and definitely aloof. He propositioned me once, you know, out by the river? And all I could think was, 'but you're . . . old.'

"Oh, right," Vivette says, laughing at Peter's expression. "Sorry. I mean, mature. I thought he was mature. Anyway, it was gross. After I told everyone at the bakery, they started overcharging him. You know, you also remind me of my Grandpa Joe-Joe.

He's the one who sold me the Buick? He's kind of firm and quiet like you."

"Wesley, Grandpa Joe-Joe," Peter says, "anyone else you see in here?"

"I'll keep you posted," Vivette says, tapping her index finger, quietly keeping time to the music.

"Are you close with him?" Peter asked.

"Wesley? No. Joe-Joe? No. No one is close to him. I'm writing him postcards on this trip, though. Joe-Joe, that is." Vivette pulls a postcard from her bag, lays it face down on the table. "It's payment for the car. I think I've written like ten or fifteen so far. I hope I'm not freaking him out."

The rain pelts the roof; the wind nudges the walls. Two more customers enter through the wooden door, shake off their coats and hats. A deep, rumbling thunder booms in the distance as Vivette hums "My Hometown."

"Why would your postcards freak him out?" Peter asks, pulling a cigarette out of Vivette's pack.

"Joe-Joe?" Vivette says. "I don't know, exactly. I kind of want my life to change so I'm trying to shake it up. Move out here. Tell Joe-Joe my inner secrets. Spend time on a farm. I don't know. I'm not sure what's next, and I thought maybe Margaret would give me some advice. I mean, that's not why I'm here on the Great Plains, just why I'm here — you know — staying with you guys. I thought it might be informative."

"Sort of like an educational field trip," Peter says.

"Sort of," Vivette says, fiddling with the label on her beer.

"How's it going so far?"

She angles the paper off the bottle in one long slice. "Don't want to tell you," she says.

"Really?" Peter asks.

"No, definitely. Don't think I want to be honest about that right now." Vivette scouts out the bar anew. "What's a fried pickle? There's a sign over there."

"Wait a minute. You're disappointed?" Peter says, laughing. He taps his cigarette into the ashtray, leaves it there to idle. He picks up the postcard to see its front, a big-headed sunflower with the words "Love Ya Nebraska" across the bottom.

"Well, Margaret has definitely changed," Vivette says. "It's like she's a new person altogether." Vivette waves smoke out of her eyes, sways in her seat to the music. "I mean, she used to be so different. Kind of blunt, saying the craziest things to people, and doing crazy things, too. People still tell 'Margaret stories' at the bakery all the time. Like, you know, 'Do you remember when Margaret worked here, and we all poured beer into to-go cups during Friday afternoon baking shifts?' Those-were-the-days kind of stories. They call the years she worked there the Golden Years. Yeah. She was really different. Not necessarily better. Just different."

"That was a long time ago," Peter says.

"Hey, let's play pool. I bet you're a good pool player," Vivette says. "I'm good. My Uncle Sammy taught me. I don't play like a girl, I swear."

Peter is amazed at Vivette's twentysomething energy. It's like she's about to burst. He wonders where Margaret is and what held her up in Lincoln. They waited, but she didn't show before Vivette got too antsy, so they left a note. He knows Margaret will never drive back out to meet them once she's home.

He knows Margaret has changed. Some days he can't help but miss the Margaret Vivette is searching for. But he loves her more every year, the Margaret who wants to make a home with him instead of the one always searching for something just beyond her reach. The one who stays instead of going. "I'm up for it," Peter says, watching smoke waft under the light suspended above the pool table. "Whatever you want to do. This is your night on the town."

"Okay," Vivette says. "Let's put some quarters up on the table. Those guys who just came in, they look like they might want to play. We can do teams."

Peter looks over at the two big men leaning on the bar engaged in a shoulder-hunched conversation, flannel shirts tight across their backs, mustaches hovering over bottles of Miller High Life. One man pokes a finger to the bar top to make a point. "I don't know, Vivette," Peter says, "they don't look interested to me."

After the men decline Vivette's multiple requests to join them, she and Peter square off over the pool table. Vivette hitches up her skirt for long shots, banks balls in with a quick jab of her stick. They're evenly matched three for three when they run out of quarters. Peter buys another pitcher of beer and gets change from the bartender.

Vivette talks too loudly, makes jokes, eventually buys the guys at the bar drinks, lures them over for a couple games of eight-ball, two against two. Peter talks less, watches more. Everyone in the place, including the six other stragglers who blow in from the rain, know Vivette's name, say good-bye, wish her luck in Des Moines, and sign her postcard to Joe-Joe by the time they lean against Lucky's door to leave.

Vivette turns to Peter once they're buckled into the truck, contemplating sobriety. "That's what Margaret used to be like," she says.

13

Vivette crawled back to Robert on the weekends Susan drove out of town. And with her mother nearby Susan was away more and more. Vivette never had it in her head to continue the affair. Instead she told herself she was just passing by, just dropping in to see a friend, just returning a book she'd borrowed. Nothing more. Nothing wrong with that. Friends scattered all across town every day mixed and matched in a variety of ways, relaxing, drinking a beer or two. No problem.

Vivette would linger, and Robert would ask her if she wanted to stay. They'd fall asleep like an old married couple pressed between flowered sheets, cuddling through the night. In the morning, though, a different story unfolded. Going at it, throwing blankets off, staring each other down, naked and needy. They couldn't get enough. Each time they re-created the first time — over and over again.

Concentric circles. Rippling and rippling, but in or out? For Vivette, for a long time, it was fresh and new and electric.

But then late one Saturday afternoon, as the sun trickled around the drawn blinds, Robert said, "It's just so fun. This." He ran a finger up between Vivette's breasts. "I love that you're so easy about it. I totally separate the two worlds. You walk in, and it's only you, until you leave and my real life pops back. Look how compact you are — so tiny. Perfect."

Vivette rolled her back to Robert so his hand rested on her shoulder. With each breeze, the rippling sunlight snuck through the window blinds onto the floor, creeping toward her, them. Their window blinds, of course. Not hers. Until now, she simply hadn't felt like she was doing anything wrong. "Do you honestly think Susan has no clue about us?" she asked.

With his voice low and firm, Robert said, "The truth is only based on the facts that are presented, if the affair never exists outside this room, it'll never be a problem." He propped himself up against the backboard with a pillow, one hand cupping his hairy belly, a tiny paunch above the edge of the sheet. He cleared his throat. "The fact of the matter is, one day you're going to leave me in the dirt." Robert mussed Vivette's hair, this way and that, walked his fingers across the top of her head, ran a finger down her spine. "But I'm ready for that," he said. He kissed her shoulder blade. "You'll outgrow me."

Vivette stared at the wall, stretched a thin arm toward the ceiling, and closed her eyes. She liked being watched. She liked being kissed. She rolled to face Robert, ran a finger over his rounded nose, his thick black eyebrows, smoothing them into place. With that, she twisted herself out of bed, grabbed her clothes from the jumble on the floor, and got dressed. Robert watching, waving.

Vivette closed the apartment door, the latch's click signaling the beginning of her other life. She roamed the alleyways and side streets, followed the sidewalk past the furniture store and the sandwich shop, the war memorial park with four soldiers pointed north, south, east, and west, their hats like inverted salad plates on their heads. The moist air carried with it remnants of the ocean — seaweed, musty seashells, and brine. The sun a brilliant white, flickering between the shadows. Her body felt smooth and graceful under her clothes. The hum in her head said, *Life is simple.* Vivette eased on through, believing that some day she'd break Robert's heart into a million pieces. She just didn't know when or how. With that knowledge came a kind of assurance that sent her brazenly into the world and then back to him.

Later that day she wandered into Rocket Records on Main Street, chatted with her friends Suzanne and Melinda as they flipped through albums. Between gossipy declarations they sang along to a new Pavement song pounding over the sound system. The fact that she hadn't been interested in anyone but Robert for a long time hit her hard in the brief heartbeat-thud between tracks. Melinda asked her who she was seeing these days. Vivette twisted her hair around a finger, checked for split ends, shrugged.

"You know, I don't think I've been out with you since that crazy night of tequila drinking at Robert and Susan's," Melinda said, flipping a double album open to read the lyrics. "Anyway, as usual, people are asking about you. What's your status? I mean, I don't care. Whatever you want to do is fine. Single is fine."

Robert, Vivette thought, over and over again. *Robert*.

At the bakery, Gert had been in a long affair with a married man, waiting years for him to divorce his wife. Now, nearing forty and single, she said she wasn't interested in the game anymore. Vivette knew that wasn't true. Gert feared the future, the crazy passion hidden behind so many doors, that married guy, all guys, herself.

Vivette didn't expect Robert to divorce Susan. That was completely unreasonable. They were happy and perfect. Everybody thought so. If anyone knew she was sleeping with him, the entire town would hate her. She tapped her fingers on the worn wooden record bins, stared out the plate-glass window. "I'm a free agent," she said to Melinda. "Not much interested in complicating my life right now though. Who's interested? Send him my way. It's not like my phone is ringing off the hook." She could see the top edge of a car's bright-yellow hood as it zipped by.

Suzanne joined the conversation, edging closer to Vivette and Melinda who hovered over the P's — Parliament, Pavement, Pearl Jam, The Pixies, The Pretenders, Public Enemy. "Hey, do you guys think you'll settle down here? Buy a house someday, if we ever have any money? Maybe we'll all have babies together. You know, take them for walks on the beach." She tossed a few strands of loose hair over her shoulder and fidgeted with her bracelets, looking nervous that this kind of talk came near to selling out.

"Babies aren't dogs, Suzanne," Melinda said. "You don't walk them on the beach. My God. I hope you never have kids."

Suzanne moved over to pout near the new releases, with Melinda following after her. Vivette stayed glued in place. No one she knew was married, except Robert and Susan. Even older people she knew were single. Being married was still some kind of future fantasy no one took seriously. Why Robert and Susan? If they were just going out things would be different. People broke up all the time. Only boring people got married. But Robert and Susan had known each other forever. It was okay for them to be married, just not having affairs.

Something that had been settled in Vivette broke free.

She saw Melinda hand Suzanne a stick of gum as a peace offering. They walked back over toward Vivette. "Two years seems to be my limit. Two years and I need to break up with the guy because it's obvious he's a dork," Melinda said.

Robert and Susan should be merely living together, yes, that was it, then they would break up. Robert would be Vivette's boyfriend, sleeping over and making her breakfast—he'd paint pictures of her. There'd be dates and sex and arguments, like normal couples.

The goth posters on the walls leered. Teenagers dressed in black denim, spikes, and leather gathered in the other corner of the store. A boy wearing eyeliner and black boots laughed too loud, braying like a donkey. Vivette's friends in their faded jeans and Converse sneakers now hummed along to Cracker. Simple. Carefree.

Vivette's life screeched. Her future had arrived. Complete indecision glided off into infinity. Until that very moment she had believed she was happy, but why?

A weak wave good-bye, a promise to join them the following week for the Belly show in Boston, and a little bell rang above the door as Vivette stepped onto the sidewalk, took a deep breath. The moist undercurrent of evening clung to the edges of the breeze.

And then, right there, two blocks away: Susan and Robert. Dull sunshine between the two buildings highlighted them sitting on a bench outside the camera shop that had thousands of empty film canisters filling the storefront display. They ate red shoestring licorice, their knees touching. Happy. Ecstatic, it seemed.

Susan's hand on Robert's shoulder, she squeezed his arm, whispered, and then he laughed. And there at their feet, a puppy tugged on its own bright blue leash, tail wagging. Robert had obviously bought a dog after having sex with Vivette that morning. A beagle. Vivette watched Robert's perfect, picturesque life, knowing it had nothing to do with her. The puppy barked twice and a family of tourists turned to smile at the lovely young couple.

Vivette walked the other direction, away from town, taking the longest route she could think of to circle back to her apartment. The breeze turned chilly as the sunshine escaped the street. Even after she pushed herself inside her front door, she couldn't warm up. Vivette wrapped herself in a blanket from the bed. For the first time in a long while, she didn't know what to do. The old floorboards creaked when she neared the darkened kitchen, paced through the brightly lit living room, the blanket a reluctant cape. Back and forth. She thought, *A puppy*, over and over again. *Of course. A fucking dog.*

Vivette admitted to herself, with only some trepidation, her attachment to the glorious label of "the other woman." She was the mysterious stand-in, the secret, the conspirator. Uncertain danger captivated her, its undercurrent, its ambiguity, but how would she ever get on with her life?

She listened to friends leave messages on her machine: the beep, click, voice, whir. The beach? Dinner? Movies? Vivette tilted up a wooden shutter in her bedroom cluttered with books and magazines, empty to-go cups, T-shirts, socks, and shoes. Two thin candles swayed in a metal chandelier over her futon. Robert's sketch of a rotary telephone resting on a park bench lifted from the wall as she walked by. An ivy plant withered in a bright red pot in the corner. She looked out onto the empty alley — bare cobblestones with weeds peeking up between. She was in hiding, busily transforming into a revised Vivette with fewer feelings, more plans, and a heart that could withstand anything. She paced until midnight, and then fell into a deep, blank sleep.

The alarm screamed after each snooze. Big, empty houses with endless rooms filled her dreams. Lulled her back to sleep.

LATE, was her one and only thought as she switched on her bedside lamp. Vivette threw on yesterday's T-shirt, pulled jeans and a sweatshirt out of a half-open drawer. Brushing her teeth, turning on every light as she went — socks, shoes, and she was off, running, stumbling through the dark. The North Church clock finished five bells, and she was still blocks away. The cool air teased her cheeks, filled her lungs so she could see her breath in the streetlamp's glow.

When she rounded the corner, the men from the early-morning club were peering in the windows, hands in pockets. "Sorry," Vivette said, unlocking the door, breathing hard. The men walked face-first into Guns N' Roses blasting from the stereo. "Oh, Francie, God," Vivette mumbled. The newspapers, corseted with thin white plastic strips, were splayed along the dewy sidewalk. She heaved them inside toward the rack in twos, keeping the door wedged open with one foot. She found the *Globe*, opened it first, nudged it into waiting hands.

The front interior was dim and dark and sleepy as the men shuffled to the counter, oblivious, somehow, to the music screaming, "Welcome to the jungle!" The lights above the baking table spot-lit Francie with her permanent frown and Harley-Davidson T-shirt, rolling out lines of skinny baguettes. Half-pound mounds of dough settled around her in a semicircle. Kneading them once, twice, they turned forward, forward, forward, into long snakes the exact length of a sheet pan. Francie popped the air out of each end with a quick karate chop then shifted them onto a dusting of cornmeal. All the while, she stared at Vivette. Steady eyes. Waiting.

Vivette clicked on the front lights, punched off the Guns N' Roses, allowed a moment of humming, brilliant silence before pressing play for Joni Mitchell. She mumbled, "Thank you, Francie," when she saw one full pot of coffee gleaming on the front burner. She took each man's money. Smiled. Rang them up in the old crank register, stacked filters in high towers with a scoop of coffee in each one, started a new pot, unwrapped the cakes, the cookies. Mumbled, "Thank you, Francie," when she saw the scones in baskets. She poured the cream and the milk into their metal pitchers. She took the bowl of butter pats out of the cake case and set it on the front counter. Finally, she poured herself some coffee. Hovering over the mug like a little campfire, she took a deep breath. Walked back to help.

"You're late," Francie said. Her dark eyes glimmering.

"I slept in. Honestly," Vivette said, "how often do I blow it?" Vivette held her hands up and out at her sides in surrender.

"You're messing with my system," Francie said. "You don't do my job, I don't do your job, remember?" Her short hair had been dyed so many shades of auburn it now had a permanent punk-orange glow to its stiff edges.

"Okay, okay. You're right. What do you want me to say? I'm sorry," Vivette said. "I overslept. Honest mistake. I'm having a weird life right now."

"Weird life, whatever. If I had to keep track of all the troubles in this place, I'd lose my mind," Francie said. "Comb your hair. Your shirt's on inside out. Don't make it a habit."

Vivette looked down at the wrong side of her Elvis Costello T-shirt, the tag straight up, a cowlick at her throat. "Okay. Wait a minute," she said. "I've got to fix this or I'll never hear the end of it." Vivette rushed to the bathroom. She could hear Francie bark a laugh. She turned her shirt around, and splashed some water on her face, staring herself down—a million miles away, tracing the dark circles under her eyes, tapping each cheek to bring some color to the surface. "Get it together," she whispered. With an elastic from the box under the sink, she pulled her tangled hair up into a bun. A test smile, her thin lips, even teeth. She knew Francie was nocturnal. She had no tolerance and held grudges. Big sigh, and then, "That'll do." She could hear the front door open and close with a swoosh.

Large coffee. Danish. $2.25.

Vivette tried to make up with Francie, rolling loaves, stirring the hot chocolate, weighing pound-and-a-half chunks of bread dough between customers. Francie didn't speak kindly to most of the staff—especially the counter shifts—but somehow, over time, Vivette had broken through.

She gingerly placed puffy chunks of freckled dough on the scale—a teardrop weight at the pound-and-a-half mark, small black disks weighing down one end until the other floated level.

Francie plopped loaf after loaf into a long line of oiled metal pans. Silent. Brooding. Vivette oiled more, the brush slurping against the metal. She lined them up evenly along the counter. When Francie started talking about her other job, Vivette knew the road to forgiveness had opened up.

"It's just what happens. It's a job like any other job," Francie said. "Why do people get so worked up about it?"

"About what, Francie?" Vivette asked, cautiously.

"Killing dogs," Francie said as if this had been the morning's conversation all along.

"Well, you know. I don't know," Vivette said.

"If people are so upset, they should adopt a dog. I mean, people kill things every day."

Francie worked at the Humane Society on Tuesdays and Thursdays after her bread shift. Her job was euthanizing the dogs, and it created in Francie a deep intolerance and disgust for humanity that increased each year as she valued animals more and more.

"I mean. I'm nice to them before I put them down. I am not mean to those dogs," Francie said, snapping the oven door closed. After pulling her leather jacket off a wooden peg by the back door, she walked quickly up to the front counter to retrieve a cassette, and with that she was gone. Just the tap of the door and Vivette left to un-jumble the pumpkin and bran muffins that Francie had purposely mixed together as punishment.

Bran, bran, bran. Pumpkin. Bran. Pumpkin, pumpkin.

Suddenly 10:00 a.m. and silence, except for a group of jogging housewives and two housepainters with speckled eyeglass frames scribbling out the details of a project on an outstretched napkin.

Vivette leaned against the bread rack. "Can you imagine how long it would take to get to ten o'clock if we didn't have anything to do?" she asked.

Gert walked over to the aging stereo to flip the cassette, Crosby, Stills, Nash, and Young.

Vivette pulled a coconut cream cake out of the case.

"You know," Gert said, "you aren't always going to be able to get away with eating cake before noon. Someday your body will let you know you aren't young anymore." She eyed the cake and readjusted her glasses on the tip of her nose.

"But cake is so good," Vivette said, "and I am young."

"You're right. I'll have a bite," Gert said. "Just one."

Jeanine, the 10:00 a.m. to 6:00 p.m. baker, came in the back door, either mumbling or sobbing. In the midst of her messy divorce, they'd all learned to ignore her unless spoken to. Gert and Vivette ate cake and sliced baguettes for lunch. Vivette moved closer to Gert, away from earshot of Jeanine. She'd been waiting for the lull to ask a few questions. "So, Gert," she said. "How did you know when your affair with that guy was over?"

"Jeffrey?" Gert asked.

"Yes, Jeffrey. How many affairs have you had?"

"I'm just stalling for time. I don't talk about him too much anymore," Gert said. "Let's see. I knew it was over after he promised me for the hundredth time he was leaving his wife, and then I saw him down by the waterfront buying jewelry for her, and then I saw them out to dinner, and she hung on his every word like she was in love. Which, I now realize, she was. I knew when I found myself strolling by their house late at night, knowing what room they were in by what lights were on. I knew it was over long before it was over, but I didn't want it to end, so I let it continue. And when he bought me a piece of jewelry, I thought, so there, see, I get jewelry, too." Gert wiped stiff, round circles on the counter with a towel. "And when he visited my place, I purposefully left the curtains open in the bedroom window and a light on and imagined her walking by, like me with her, and seeing our silhouette. Except, important point, she didn't know I existed. I thought it was kind of sexy and dangerous instead of what it really was: mean and pathetic. I lost perspective. The truth is, I didn't break it off with him. He broke it off with me."

Gert moved toward the sandwich bar, her face red and the freckles at the base of her collarbone growing prominent. She flipped open its silver lid. "I never would have left him," she said. She looked at Vivette. "I consider his ending it a favor." She spooned mayonnaise vigorously into a small plastic tub. "I was young and stupid and hadn't seen enough soap operas growing up, I guess, so I made my own. Now I understand there's something inside me that attracts these messed-up guys. It's in me, so I don't go out with anyone anymore. I'm much happier this way. Fuck sex. It isn't that great."

Vivette smiled.

"Oh, I know. You think it's the best thing ever. You're young. You'll understand one day when you're older and sick of being toyed with. You'll think back and understand what I'm saying," Gert said. "You'll think back to right now when I say you need to be careful."

Vivette smiled, confused and cautious. She asked, "What do you mean? I'm fine." She knew she would never choose to be alone like Gert, that for most people it wasn't a choice. It just happened.

"Good. Keep it that way," Gert said. She went into the bathroom and didn't come out for a long time. When she did, she'd smoothed her hair, retied her apron, and plastered a fresh grin on her rubbed-red face.

Like clockwork, Wesley came in at 11:00 a.m. He sat at the table next to the door, serious, with his graying hair, his button-down shirt and jeans, his *New York Times*. Slim. Confident. A quick smile.

Vivette gathered up the broom and dustpan. She edged her

pile of crumbs and napkins near his table, asked, "How are the otters?"

Wesley hesitated, lowered his newspaper, took a sip of coffee. "They're fine. I go out to see them every so often. It's nice out there, by the river," he said, as if speaking a secret code. He fiddled with the edge of a page, bending the corner over and smoothing it flat with his long fingers: over, smoothing flat. "How are you?" he asked.

She leaned toward him, the shift imperceptible to those behind the counter, and said she'd like to see the otters again. She asked him to dinner at a little fish stand out by the river.

"A friendly dinner?" he said.

"Yes," she said, "Friendly. I need a break from my real life."

"Okay," Wesley said, ruffling his paper. "I'll be your pretend life. Just let me know my lines." After Vivette swept her crumbs away, he read intently as if she'd disappeared.

14 *Margaret, Nebraska*

Margaret meandered up and down the aisles of the Hinky Dinky, looking for oats. She wandered by the breadcrumbs, cider vinegar, and shiny jars of prepackaged spices. She had been in Lincoln two months, and she wasn't blazing trails on the people-meeting front. Lonely and discouraged, the novelty of setting up shop in a cowboy town was wearing thin. She found that big empty spaces and conservative ideas filled up the middle of the country. The little discoveries she made couldn't sustain her, like the blind organ player belting out off-key pop tunes at Lee's Fried Chicken, the sixteen-foot chicken statue outside its front door, the thrift stores packed with western shirts and cowboy boots, the used book shops that weren't picked over, the Vietnamese restaurant on 28th Street.

Every other weekend she drove her trusty Datsun six hours to Minneapolis, sometimes ten hours to Chicago. But once she got there, she only wanted to escape back to Lincoln. Her life had become a series of U-turns. Margaret missed San Francisco like a valuable possession she'd left behind on the bus, but jump-starting that city would only send her spinning into orbit again. "No going back," she wrote on the pale yellow Post-it she stuck on her atlas. She'd clock a year in Lincoln if it killed her.

A scruffy-looking guy carefully cradling two boxes of crackers in aisle four checked the lists of ingredients with his index finger on first one box, then the other. He switched to squinting at the shiny labels attached to the shelves, labels listing costs per ounce. Margaret thought: interesting. Cute. She assumed: married. Crazy.

At the downtown bars, Margaret had flirted with several men who said things like, "I'm not really good at pick-up lines." These men could barely make eye contact. Recently, she'd taken to sitting alone in the movie theater downtown, whispers of friendship and love trickling around her, the darkness a consolation. After the lights dimmed, Margaret would see an arm wrapped around a shoulder, a head nestled into the crook of a neck. She knew now that was the kind of love she wanted. Movie-theater love. Not the complex scenarios of the actors on the screen but a life of patiently waiting in her seat, holding hands, biding time until the next show began.

A tub of tofu and a bunch of broccoli. The bright lights made her numb with false optimism. If she stayed there too long saying hello to complete strangers she'd be locked forever within a Hinky Dinky hum. Margaret edged her squeaky cart toward checkout, diverting only to get ice cream and a magazine.

Bette, whose nametag had a pink teddy-bear sticker in the corner, held up the tofu after beeping it across the black scanner. The springy blue band wrapped around her wrist jangled keys with each movement. "Now what do you do with this?" she asked with caution.

Margaret explained that some people ate it raw, others sliced it into chunks and sautéd, fried, or baked it. She then talked about marinades and how tofu was like a sponge soaking them up. Margaret ended by saying, "Tofu is good for you."

"I've heard that," Bette said, jangling. She dipped the container into a thin, plastic sack. "Sounds interesting, but I wouldn't know what to soak it in."

Margaret pulled on her short bangs, tipped her long hair behind her ears. "Here. I'll give you a quick marinade." She smiled at Bette, dug in her bag for a piece of paper and a pen. Margaret smiled at the man beside her, at his fat-cheeked daughter wedged into the front of the cart, holding a pack of gum. Everyone there, including Margaret, knew Bette was just trying to be polite, that she didn't care one bit about tofu marinade, but Margaret couldn't stop herself. She scribbled, "orange juice, soy sauce, olive oil, and garlic." She said, "Just let it soak in there for about twenty minutes before you cook it. It'll be great."

Bette looked skeptical as she took the piece of paper from Margaret and pushed it into her pink smock pocket. She said, "Okay. Thanks."

Margaret smiled. "Maybe I'll see you again and you can let me know how it went?" She paid with a wilted twenty, held out her hand—still and obedient—for change. She declined the bag boy's attempt to carry her sacks to the car, wrestling the filmy mess into her cart. "It's okay," she said three times as he tried to hug her bags into his earnest spaghetti arms.

She smiled back at Bette, who had moved onto the man's reassuring pork chops and frozen corn.

A tap at her shoulder, and the crazy guy with the crackers said, "I like tofu."

"Great," Margaret said as she jammed her cart into the rack with the others. She walked out the automatic door toward her car.

A rush of cold, brutal air met her outside. Margaret knew that this was just the beginning of winter. The middle would bring more wind, ice, and twenty-four degrees below zero. Jim at the Jiffy Lube told her all about it last week as he pushed their over-priced winterization package.

A tap at her shoulder again. Margaret's teeth chattered from the cold. The cracker guy zipped his wool coat up around his neck, saying, "Hi. Me again. I mean. I like all kinds of food. What I mean to say is, I've seen you around town, and I thought you might be new around here. Actually, I saw you once before." He laughed nervously. "I'm not a stalker. I thought it was nice of you to give the checkout lady the marinade recipe. The bright green coat is a dead giveaway. For being out of town, that is. It's too thin. I like it. Very cool with the pink. It looks good. Oh man, I'm just not good at introducing myself. Are you at the university? Peter." He stuck his hand toward hers. It was red and rough.

Margaret pulled the thin suede coat tighter, touched his hand after shifting bags. "No, I just moved here. I don't know why exactly," Margaret said. "I went to school in Ohio, lived in New Hampshire so I should know cold weather, should know better about the coat. Kind of stupid. I moved here from San Francisco to get away from it all for a while."

Peter was handsome, close to her own age, wrinkles around his eyes just starting, little crow's-feet that showed he smiled a lot. His arms were empty. She hugged one paper bag, and the other two plastic bags hung like pendulums, at her side.

"Here. Let me be your bag boy," he said.

"Um, no thanks," Margaret said. "I'm right over here. I didn't realize I'd gotten so much stuff. I live alone so I don't know how I filled up these bags. Guess I should just give in and let the bag boys do it, but it's just too much. I mean, it freaks me out that they're so enthusiastic about wanting to carry my grocery bags to my car."

Peter walked alongside. "It's a conspiracy," he said, "to control every aspect of your grocery shopping experience." He leaned in close as he said, "experience," laughing maniacally.

Margaret looked for a wedding band.

"Hey," Peter said, propping his hands on his hips, then abruptly letting them hang by his sides, "have you heard about this place out on highway 34, I think, a restaurant where they only serve soy? No meat. It's supposed to be on the edge of some actual soybean fields. I've been wanting to check it out." He stopped short of asking her to go. Margaret could see the hesitation, his smile receding. She put her bags into the back seat, slammed the car door—a tiny whack.

"Sounds like an interesting place," Margaret said.

Peter creased a sad smile. He shrugged. "Okay," he said. "I'll see you around."

Margaret couldn't tolerate the idea of losing contact with a person who wasn't required to talk to her. Even if Peter was crazy and not wearing his wedding ring, she needed to stop the banter with cashiers, her landlord, and the postman. "I go to the Zoo Bar on Thursdays," she said. "Maybe I'll see you there sometime? Margaret. Margaret Jackson. Nice to meet you, Peter."

Peter pulled a striped stocking cap from his jacket pocket and yanked it low on his head. "Yeah, maybe I'll see you Thursday," he said. "That would be nice." He walked back into the Hinky Dinky, long, lanky strides, his hands in his pockets, head down as the automatic door swung wide. Margaret got into her car and plucked a pair of pink gloves out from between the seats, watched

Peter through the broad plate-glass window. First to Bette's line where a tall man with a puffy mustache pointed to the candy rack. Peter nodded thanks, found his cart, pushed it to the rear of the line, and out of Margaret's view.

Margaret imagined her heart, that stiff lump of flesh in her chest, pitter-pattering just a bit. "Nice, nice, nice," she said aloud to herself. "Crazy, crazy, crazy." She put the car into reverse chanting, "No, no, no."

She turned on the radio. The community station's nearly constant bluesy guitar music crackled out from the cold speakers. She turned it off and drove home in silence.

That evening, snug in her apartment, wearing flannel and wool, a cup of tea at her side, Margaret wrote the first letter to Kevin since leaving San Francisco. She filled him in on the crazy Nebraska guy who walked up to her in the middle of the Hinky Dinky. Later he'd send her a postcard that simply read: *Get back here.*

The next day she made an appointment with Jim to get her car winterized. Snow was coming. It was time to stock up, think long and hard about her heart.

15   *Vivette, New Hampshire*

Vivette sat on the curb, the cement rough and cold through the material of her thin, cotton shorts. She had her back to the bakery, her pink-flowered bag at her feet. Her plan to arrive late so Wesley would wonder if she was going to show had backfired, it seemed. She figured he'd come and gone, but couldn't determine if she cared and wasn't sure what she was doing dragging him back into the picture anyway.

The bakery flitted its energy, pulling like a magnet. Jeanine, midway through her shift, would appreciate some company, Vivette thought. Leftover mushroom barley soup, good conversation, and she could be on her way home for the night to get some sleep for a change.

As she stood up to go inside, Vivette thought she saw Robert round the corner. It wasn't him after all, but when the man walked by she imagined candles lit on Robert and Susan's dinner table, a bottle of wine, the new puppy snoring softly in the corner, curled into a plaid puppy bed. Robert would think about Vivette, want to call, maybe he would call, but she wouldn't be home. Vivette was anticipating his whispered message, the quick hang up, the empty room once his voice was gone when Wesley pulled up in his Volvo.

The sunglasses shielding his eyes made him look even richer and more distinguished than usual. "You're late," Vivette said, squinting at Wesley and seeing her own reflection instead. She fixed her hair.

"Oh, come on," Wesley said, "get in."

They drove to the river, "Your Cheatin' Heart" by Hank Williams looping along in Wesley's tape deck. He turned it up. "I love classic country," he said. "It's so true. Hank totally knew what was going on." Vivette absently tapped her fingers on the armrest, distracted and antsy. She never understood the attraction. To her country music sounded old and twangy and wrinkled.

At the river road, waning sunlight filtered through the trees, making long, dark shadows in the cooling air. Vivette and Wesley searched for the otters, but they were nowhere to be found. Just the mottled river and its big, unwelcoming stones. Gray and cold. Soon it would be dark, the air around them heavy.

"Let's get out of here," Vivette said.

They pulled into the thick gravel lot of Hester's Fish Stand and seated themselves at a small, rickety table adjacent to the take-out window. Wesley said, "So. What're we doing here, Vivette? Why the renewed interest?"

"Good question," Vivette said. "but don't you need to have initial interest in order to renew it?"

Wesley smiled. "And yet."

"I guess I just felt sorry for you and that wheat roll sitting there all by yourselves every day," Vivette said. "I don't know." She sifted through the sugar packs, separating the pink sweeteners from the white sugars at opposite ends.

"Hmmm. I don't think that's right," Wesley said. "Something's eating you. I can tell. You're feeling guilty, aren't you? What is it that you can't tell anyone, but you're going to tell me?" Wesley pulled the container of sugars away from her.

"I resent that," Vivette said, grabbing it back, lining up the pink and white packets every other one.

Wesley laughed. "But it's true," he said. "Isn't it?"

Vivette's face tingled pink. "Look at your menu," she said.

Nearly empty, Hester's had reached the end of its tourist season, a time when the locals came out of hiding. Another couple claimed the far end of the place. Eight tables lined up along the knotty pine walls, each with a mishmash of wooden chairs. Calendars from twenty, thirty, forty years earlier spotted the interior, each sporting an earnest-looking girl licking an ice cream cone, the pages curled with age. Vivette smelled greasy-sweet fried fish and ketchup.

She ordered a lobster roll, Wesley fish and chips. Two beers. The waitress, tan and fit in shorts and a university sweatshirt, bounced away with her hair pulled up high in a ponytail, bundles of plastic silverware in her wake.

"Well, you know it's funny," Vivette said, unsure what she was about to say. She smiled at him, leaned a little closer. "I am a bit involved."

The story of her affair, out loud for the first time, sounded slutty and rude. Vivette gained momentum as she went. Just to be safe, she changed Robert's name to Terrance. The first night on his porch, sex in the morning, meaning for it to end, but then doing it again and again in his bedroom, sleeping over, breakfast, casual phone calls, furtive glances, back to his bedroom.

When she finished, Wesley leaned his chair back on two legs, assessing Vivette anew. "I knew it," he said. "That's kind of crazy. I mean, you always go to his place? Isn't that risky?"

"I want you to help me get some perspective," Vivette said, trying to guide him toward a more substantial point.

Wesley met her gaze and whispered, "Yeah." Then slowly, "We didn't do anything. I'm clean. Remember?" He raised his hands in the air, raised his voice. "This guy kept his pecker in his pants."

The couple near the window looked up like startled birds. Wesley lowered his chair to the floor.

A storm came on, pressure rising as the wind nitpicked at the remaining leaves on the tree outside. Soon the rain pounded like little tack nails on the restaurant's tin roof.

"It's clear you have no idea what you're doing," Wesley said after looking out the window for a long time.

Vivette knew that was probably true, even though she felt fine, in control. Her life just kept pounding against her with no effect.

"It's dangerous. It's building inside you," Wesley said. "I've seen it before. You'll look old and haggard by the time you're thirty if you keep this up. You'll be one of those women wearing bad-looking clothes, running after a guy on the sidewalk. You'll smile as he rushes ahead of you, always giving him the benefit of the doubt. You'll think you're in charge, but you know why he's rushing? Cause he doesn't give a shit, Vivette. He does not give a goddamn about you."

"Who are you," Vivette said, suddenly unreasonably angry,

"to tell me that? You don't even know me. God, you're so pretentious."

"Look, you're the one who doesn't know me," Wesley said. "And I know you better than you think. You asked for my perspective. I'm just trying to fill you in on the facts. Everybody settles down. It's just what happens. You need to get on the inside track before you're miserable for the rest of your life and constantly justifying your actions with lame excuses that don't hold water. You said yourself you know this guy isn't leaving his wife. So what're you shooting for here, except some debatably decent sex and a theoretically well-planned deception?"

"What about you?" Vivette said, arms crossed tightly over her chest.

"Hey, I wanted a one-time fling," Wesley said. "Something we'd both throw out afterwards like the trash from a good take-out meal. Loved the meal, now it's over. Zing. In the basket. I never suggested something long-term. That's nuts. Talk to Gert at the bakery. She'll tell you how messed up it can get. I remember when she was with Jeffrey. Look at her now. I knew Gert back then. She'd leave parties packed with perfectly decent single guys totally interested in her to meet Jeff out behind his office for a quickie in his car before he went home to his wife."

"It isn't like that," Vivette said. "I just. I don't. It isn't like that. It's more like just being friends, but closer. I mean. I knew him beforehand. I know Susan. It isn't like a quickie behind his office kind of thing."

"Oh, I see. Your affair is more refined," Wesley said. "Susan? Wait. Are you talking about Robert?" he whispered. "Oh my God. You're having an affair with Robert Gooding? That is so . . . unlikely."

"I told you his name is Terrance. There are a lot of Susans in this town. It isn't Robert Gooding," Vivette lied.

Wesley looked skeptical. He said, "Okay. But you aren't doing it with anyone else. That's the problem. What about this boyfriend you told me about? Todd."

"Imaginary," Vivette said.

"Okay," Wesley said, "Okay. No Todd. That makes sense. If you want my advice, I'd say you need to branch out, at least. You also need to be very careful. Who knows about this?"

"No one. Well, now you. I think Gert suspects though," Vivette said.

"Once you start talking, it just keeps coming up. I know how this goes. It can get freaky. Stuff lingers. People feel the need to leave town, that kind of thing. If you can't keep a secret, just get out now."

"But I can keep a secret," Vivette said. "Absolutely."

"But you can't," Wesley said. "You see, you've just told me."

Their baskets were empty, and fresh, sweet grease lined their mouths. Drops of rain danced up from the gravel puddles in the parking lot as they finished their beers.

Vivette longed to be out in the middle of it. "Let's go watch the storm somewhere," she said.

They left a tip, drove to Rye Beach through the tiny pelts of rain. There the waves crested gray and angry, combining with thunder and lightning all around to make the air electric. Wesley rolled down all the car windows to let the thick air whip through. Soon they were soaked.

"I love this," he yelled, suddenly awake and alive and laughing. "God, I love to watch the storms." His graying hair wet, goose bumps on his arms, Vivette remembered the tiny bit of love she felt for him months before as his hand rested at her waist.

"We used to have a place out here," Wesley said. "A great old cottage that Olivia's parents sold. I loved sitting there and watching the ocean. This makes me nostalgic."

Vivette leaned her seat back, closed her eyes. "It's pretty intense," she said. "I forget to come out here. I get so caught up I forget the ocean is nearby."

"You must think I want to live in the past," Wesley said tapping her shoulder until she opened her eyes. "That's not it. I guess it's just remembering. I want to remember where I've come from, what I've done. But it feels like it's slipping away."

The windows steamed while the wipers crept up every so often, set on delay. Wesley and Vivette fell into silence. Wesley turned the defrost on high. Gray beach, the sound of waves wild and pounding. The fog lifted, and they could see again. The rain pattered to a stop.

Wesley put the car into reverse.

They drove through the silence that emanated from the small clapboard houses, the cemetery, the streetlights beginning to blink on. People on the sidewalks shook their umbrellas and folded them neatly shut.

Wesley dropped her off in the bank parking lot. He said, "Sorry. Not sure what you needed to hear, but I probably didn't tell you the right thing. If you want to get together sometime, I'm still into it. Nothing crazy, though. Nothing long-term. I can't afford to screw up my life right now. I have a baby." With that, he drove away.

The town caved in around Vivette in the blips and pops of leftover rain dripping from every corner. Loneliness soaked the edges. For the first time she wondered if she could leave this place. Just get up and go. The impulse was there, like a heartbeat, a solution. She just needed to follow through. A car, a plan, and a place to go. She remembered Grandpa Joe-Joe's Buick, how it crouched there in his oily garage like a dinosaur, dust collecting on the windshield. The seed of a plan, but where to? It was suddenly obvious to her that she had overstayed her welcome.

She had to make plans, get a car, but already Vivette missed the bakery. She peeked in the front windows as Jeanine pulled double-crust pies from the oven. Three little golden orbs in the bright bakery lights. Vivette tapped on the glass. Jeanine looked up as she coaxed the tins off the wooden peel onto the cooling racks. She motioned Vivette inside. But Vivette pointed behind her, toward home. Shrugged. Waved.

Water dripped from the trees and gutters and awnings. Vivette splashed through every puddle she could find, let the muddy sludge stick to her calves and fill her shoes. She knew this kind of late-summer thunderstorm cleared everything out. Tomorrow the sky would be startling, frightening, and new.

16
Margaret, New Hampshire

Margaret walked up the creaky stairs to her apartment. Her hair and clothes smelled of flour mixed with butter, sweat, oil, and old coffee grounds. Eleven p.m. and she'd just finished up a baking shift. She loved making pies and cakes after hours, taking her time washing up the sheet pans, sitting at the big wood-block table to mark up the produce order for next week's soups and salads. No customer questions to break her train of thought, none of that endless acoustic music droning on the stereo. Tonight she blasted Sonic Youth and then the Velvet Underground. She was still humming along when she got home.

She pulled off her shirt and unzipped her jeans as she pressed play on her answering machine. A message from Wesley and Olivia, out at the Fish Kettle. Susan wanting to borrow her Galaxy

500 album. Olivia: "Margaret, dear, give me a call when you get in. I have an excellent plan."

Margaret opened her closet door and threw her clothes into the basket. Bakery smell. "Laundry," she mumbled, closing the door quickly.

She pulled on a clean T-shirt, filled the kettle for tea. Curious, she called Olivia as she pulled on clean underwear.

Olivia picked up on the first ring. "Margaret," Olivia said. "How are you?"

"Great. Twenty pies under my belt. Three birthday cakes. My arms feel good and limber. You and Wesley went to the Fish Kettle?"

"Underwhelming. I dragged him away soon after we called you. Glad you didn't show. I wonder if you'd like to go exploring with me tomorrow? Investigate a diner I've heard about in Rollinsford—the Agawam? I thought we could stop at Salisbury Beach, at that little boardwalk, and take some photo-booth pictures? Then, I don't know, maybe head on into Boston if we feel inspired, if we aren't sick to death of each other by then?"

Margaret wasn't sure if an entire day alone with Olivia was a good idea, but she had a hard time saying no to people over the phone, so she suggested Wesley or Susan, wondering aloud if they'd like to tag along. Margaret opened and closed kitchen drawers, looking for a tea bag.

"Oh, actually, Wesley said he has some big writing meeting. He's tied up." Olivia said, "So let's just do a you-and-me thing. It'll be fun having you to myself. I can mine you for details."

Margaret didn't want to be mined, but she agreed to meet at the bakery at 11:00 a.m.

After the phone conversation, Margaret sipped her tea, assessed the new painting dominating her living room: *Untitled New Hampshire #3*, part of Olivia's recent series. Before Olivia, Robert was the only successful artist Margaret knew. She'd had his paintings and sketches tacked on her walls for years. They fit well into her homey décor. But this piece from Olivia radiated what Wesley called legitimacy. The thin, multicolored lines drawn on vellum, one after another, freehand, converged into an organic glow, a heaving energy. Layered on top of a painted canvas with larger swatches of horizontal color and stretched tight over a box frame, the painting looked backlit, but it wasn't. It drew Margaret in, made the room fall away. Her funky couch and antique floor lamp, the braided rug and hippie beads, the postcards, quotations, and photographs thumbtacked here and there, all seemed insignificant in comparison. The painting begged for clean white carpet, a glass coffee table, and leather sofa. It reminded Margaret of Olivia herself, how lost she looked standing in her parent's funky cottage. Margaret liked to stare at the painting as she lay on the couch, but she thought she might move it to the bedroom.

Deciding to get the laundry over with, she stuffed her pile of dirty clothes into her backpack and dragged her bike down the stairs. She rode to Laundro-Suds on River Street, her tea transferred to a travel mug wedged in the bike's front basket alongside a bright blue bottle of detergent. Usually she bugged Susan and Robert, who had the extravagance of a basement washer and dryer. But with tonight's clear sky, she was in the mood for a ride to the freaky Laundromat to watch her clothes tumble in the big machines. The edge of a breeze whispered fall as it tangled her hair. She was happy. Her life felt neatly stacked and collated.

She thought about Wesley—his energy. Wesley in bed. His smell. Still, after all these months, it was absolute lust. Her body felt hard and strong, well-tuned. She couldn't get enough. She thought about calling. Maybe surprising Wesley, waking him up when she finished her laundry. His bed. His neatly arranged apartment filled with books and a row of lopsided pottery bowls an old girlfriend had made him. Bits of rock from the places he traveled gathered in a fish bowl on the coffee table. He could tell a story for any piece she picked out. A few weeks earlier he'd given Margaret a key, but she hadn't used it yet. She could already feel the crisp sheets, her hands running over his chest.

Margaret coasted through town. The tower struck twelve. She flew past the bakery. Francie would be inside mixing the first batch of bread. Margaret guessed she would have Mötley Crüe playing, standing there in the bright lights of the bakery in her black T-shirt, red hair, as her powerful arms shifted the gears of the big Hobart mixer. The mass of dough forming, slow and elegant, until it pulled away from the edges of the bowl. Francie would lug it over to the table, cradle it in her arms, and cut and roll, staring straight ahead at Penhallow Street. A dim streetlight outside the front windows open to let cool air in. Francie rarely looked down at her hands. Each loaf quick and sure. She'd flip the tape to Ozzy Osbourne, fill up her water bottle, egg-wash the baguettes, push on into morning when everything seemed too bright, too easy, too rushed — then she'd slip out the back door, heading for her car, while the next shift took over what she'd begun. Francie slept while everybody else started their days. As 3:00 p.m. neared, she woke up to start all over again. She once told Margaret that each afternoon she made a pot of coffee and sat in her rocking chair looking out her big back window at the empty lots sprouting up weeds and wildflowers. Francie said she daydreamed about living in a place like Nebraska, away from absolutely everything. Margaret brought in a road atlas to show Francie, but she wouldn't even look at it.

"There aren't even any towns out there," Margaret said.

"Good," Francie said with a grunt.

Margaret locked her bike to a meter outside Laundro-Suds and peeked in the window to make sure there weren't too many crazies.

Last time she'd stopped in, the cigarette smoke made washing her clothes pointless. Tonight it stood nearly empty, except for Wesley, of all people, staring at a dryer going round and round. His clothes rose and fell, a light blue shirt leading the way for pairs of white boxers.

A small buzzer screeched as Margaret walked in.

"I was just thinking about you," Wesley said with a tired smile.

"Wow. I hope not," Margaret said. "Through the window you looked pretty depressed."

"Oh, no. Just worn-out. I have a big meeting tomorrow. Realized I needed some clean clothes. Didn't have time to take anything to be laundered. Come here," he said. "Have a seat."

"I was just thinking about you, too," Margaret said. "Boy, was I thinking about you." She sat on his lap, facing him, straddling her thighs over the pink plastic chair.

"Hmmm. What were you thinking?" Wesley put his arms around her waist.

"This." And Margaret put her hands under his t-shirt, rubbed his chest, touched his nipples. She pushed herself up against him, whispering, "I wonder what the bathrooms are like in this place?"

Wesley laughed. Pulled her into a big bear hug. Kissed her quickly on the lips, then pulled away. "The bathrooms are gross here. Trust me. Plus, I've got to get some sleep tonight. I'm worried about my meeting. They don't usually call me this close to deadline."

"Oh, c'mon. Let's try. I'll take a towel in; we can wash it afterwards. I promise to be very, very quiet," Margaret said. She wasn't tired at all. Her body was buzzing. She knew Wesley could have sex all night and be just fine for his meeting. They'd done it before.

Wesley followed her into the cramped, airless room. With the door shut behind them and the light off, a stale darkness closed in. "Here," she said, "I'll sit on the sink." She pushed her sweatpants down, nudged herself onto the cold enamel. She heard a zipper, Wesley's breathing, his sudden urgency after his reluctance. He didn't say a word, was just against her, in her, and her legs wrapped around his back—her strong legs squeezed him in closer until she was up off the sink and he was standing, holding her against him, pulling her in and in toward him.

True to her word, Margaret didn't make a sound, just grabbed at his back, gently bit into his shoulder. And then a lusty shuddering and Wesley shuffling forward, tipping her back toward the edge of the sink, his belt buckle clinking along the floor. He wiped at her with the towel, moved to wipe himself. She heard his zipper rising, and still he hadn't said a word. He groped, found her face, pulled it to his chest. She heard his heart pounding, felt the strength of his arms. Then he flipped on the light and the buzzing fluorescence ended it all. Tan vinyl floor, moderately clean toilet, a bottle of bleach, a mop in a bucket, and a sink with a crusty bar of soap.

"There, now I've had sex in a Laundromat bathroom," Wesley said. "I can check that off my list."

"It was great," Margaret said. "You were awfully—" She hopped off the sink, pulled up her sweats.

The door creaked on its hinges as Wesley opened it, fixing his hair, stopping in the doorway to eye the line of dryers.

"Awfully what?" Wesley asked.

"I don't know. Quiet. Weird."

"It did seem a little weird to me, a little anonymous," Wesley said over his shoulder. "I forgot it was you there for a second. I'm just not myself tonight."

"No one's out there, Wesley," Margaret said, pushing him forward, suddenly wanting out of the bathroom. "Well, it certainly seemed like you."

Wesley returned to his chair in front of the dryer.

Margaret pulled her clothes out of her pack, shoved them into the washer, and fished around for quarters. She drizzled some detergent in, sipped her tepid tea. Started humming a new Vic Chesnutt song from a tape Robert had given her.

"Aren't you going to put water in first?" Wesley asked, suddenly at her side.

"Nope. I just do it like this," Margaret said, rubbing his arm. "It all works out. Comes out in the wash, as they say."

Wesley looked into the machine's interior and the dry clothes covered with a zigzag of liquid lines, blue puddling in the fabric's crevices. "You know, Margaret," he said. "You really need to get some systems in your life. You can't be so freewheeling forever."

"We're talking about my laundry, here, right? It's laundry," Margaret said, "not a huge priority. I'm not taking any radical risks, not like, for instance, sex in the bathroom."

"Margaret. I'm not kidding," Wesley said, folding his arms across his chest, stepping away from her touch.

"Are you lecturing me? I don't care about these clothes," Margaret said. She lined up the four quarters in their metal slots, shoved the stiff steel in, then out. She loved that part. Water poured onto her clothes, and a soggy brioche smell rose up from inside the washer.

"How often do you wash those things?" Wesley said. "My God, you don't even sort for color."

Panic started, a ping at the base of Margaret's spine as she said, "I don't know. I wear them a bunch of times. I throw them in the washer. Why do you care?" Margaret faced him, straight on. She could feel the heat rise to her face.

Wesley focused on the water pouring in, not her. Margaret slammed the lid. He said, "I guess it's not that big of a deal, but, you know Margaret, the world is about systems. You should focus on getting some procedures straight instead of trying to be bohemian all the time."

"Bohemian? I didn't realize I was *trying* to be bohemian, Wesley. I just happen to have my own personal style that doesn't involve having fifteen all-cotton button-down dress shirts laundered for me."

Wesley said, "Laundry. You put the soap in, put in the quarters, the water starts, then it makes suds, and then you add your clothes, sorted by color for the appropriate water temperature." His voice rose with each sentence.

"What in the fuck are you talking about?" Margaret said. "You sound ridiculous. You understand that, right?"

Wesley was unmoved. He said, "Look. Okay. I just think you need to stop being so scattered. You just need to get your shit together. I mean, what are you going to do? Work at Penhallow Bakery forever? Wash your clothes at Laundro-Suds for the rest of your life?" As he spoke, Wesley expertly picked his clothes out of the dryer, tossing socks, underwear, and T-shirts into a basket on the floor — stopping to smooth each dress shirt and carefully wrap it around a hanger. Margaret knew he'd wear one of those shirts tomorrow — pressed clean and smooth with the iron he set up in his kitchen. He'd wear his khakis, perfect fit. He'd look handsome and together. He always looked handsome and together. Wesley folded a few towels, bundled the socks, folded the T-shirts, put his boxers in a neat stack. The Laundromat silent except for Margaret's washer as it clicked into its first cycle, the mechanical shift of the agitator beginning its monotonous rotation. He said, "I'm concerned about you, Margaret. Very concerned."

Margaret double-checked to make sure there was enough water in her machine, put the lid down gently, then lifted it back up again and let it settle with a bang. She sat on a plastic chair against the wall, both feet resting firmly on the worn linoleum floor. She said, "You aren't my father, Wesley. Take your concern back to your own fake bohemian life, Mr. Pick-up Truck. I've got my own situation under control over here."

Wesley threw his shirts over his shoulder in one graceful motion. "I've got to get going," he said. "I'll call you tomorrow." As he bent toward Margaret, she turned so his kiss hit her cheek.

The electronic buzzer screamed behind him.

Earlier in the evening, Margaret had baked twenty pies: five apple, five peach, eight pecan, and two rhubarb. Fifteen orange pound cakes, beautifully browned at the edges, moist in the center. They were cooling on the racks right now. She had decorated three birthday cakes with perky violets and yellow rosebuds and written *Hannah, Jane,* and *Cecily* in perfect, loopy script. She did all of this, without missing a beat. Sure her shoulders hurt, her back was a mess, but she restocked the flour, lugging out the fifty-pound bags for Francie, and pulled ten pounds of butter out of the freezer for Gert. She even had time to rearrange the walk-in fridge, making sure soups were labeled and the box of produce was up off the floor.

Systems? Procedures? Margaret had so many the last thing she wanted was more. So she couldn't do laundry. "Big fucking deal," she said, tapping her feet to the rhythm of the washer, staring up at the cracked pressboard ceiling, the neon Laundro-Suds sign buzzing. Stupid name, Margaret thought. Shitty night.

The washer nudged into its rinse cycle. Little jets pumping against her incorrectly washed clothes. It spun and vibrated like it would explode. Margaret watched it with her arms crossed — daring it to.

She jammed everything into one dryer and put in all the quarters she had left. They tumbled as she sat where Wesley had been. Around and around, then there was the brief moment when the dryer clicked to a stop and the clothes hung suspended, weightless, and then flopped to the bottom.

When she opened the door and edged her hands through her still-damp clothes, she thought she might cry. She was out of quarters and didn't have any bills on her. The pack heavy on her back, reeking of sex, she raced furiously back through town.

Once home, she threw T-shirts over the backs of chairs, hung her jeans from the corner edges of the bedroom and bathroom doors, decided the underwear and socks were dry enough and poured them into her top dresser drawer. Later, they would smell musty as she pulled them on.

Margaret sat on the couch surrounded by the injustice of her laundry. Its fresh, spring scent mocked her. With the TV at a low murmur and the town silent, she fell asleep, stiff and upright and angry on the couch.

Margaret woke without remorse. She had flopped over in the middle of the night, curled into a tight fetal ball. Now a wool sweater that she'd pulled from the back of the couch scratched her bare arms, and her stomach remained tense and tight. A morning news show chirped enthusiastically from the TV. Margaret snapped it off.

"Procedures," she said, shuffling around the kitchen. Margaret turned on the shower and checked to see if the clothes had dried during the night. Cold and damp.

"Fucking Christ," she said, pouring coffee into her travel mug after dumping last night's tea down the sink. She stepped into the shower with the mug in both hands, holding it outside the stream of water. Margaret let the water pour down, bakery smell and sex rising up, seeping out of the pores in her skin. Brioche.

Danish. Muffins. Cakes. Pies. Coffee. Tea. Heavy cream. Butter. Flour. Salt. Sugar. Molasses. Honey. Walnuts. Pecans. Oil. Coconut. Cinnamon. Cardamom. Pepper, the smell of Wesley, sex, her world. It all ran down the drain. She leaned out of the hot water—burned her tongue sipping the coffee. She sat down in the tub, let the water pour over her eyes, nose, and ears—let it drown out her thoughts.

When the hot water turned cold, Margaret pulled herself out of the shower. Better, almost normal. She thought, *Fuck Wesley.*

She let the machine get the ringing phone, turning down its volume in case it might broadcast an apology, because she wasn't done being mad just yet. Margaret checked the time on the kitchen clock: 9:00 a.m. The machine clicked and whirred. Margaret watered the plants, cleaned up her clutter, rearranged the living room, moved Olivia's painting to the bedroom, changed the sheets, made her bed, ran the vacuum, emptied the dish rack, and gathered up recycling.

As she dragged her bike down from the second-floor hallway out into the bright day, she decided to ask everyone at the bakery to weigh in. Margaret knew they'd say, "Systems, my ass."

By the time Olivia arrived, Gert had set up a chart above the register to record laundry responses. So far it favored, much to Margaret's dismay, water first.

On the back counter facing the baking table, Margaret had her legs crossed and eyes closed as she followed Gretchen's precise movements without actually watching her. Gretchen, an avid fly fisher, talked about plans for her next excursion as she worked. The metal whisk made a sloshy chop-chop, clip-clip-clipping sound as she whisked eggs and cream, added bits of roasted ham, some green pepper, scallions, and sage. When the tapping stopped, she poured the mixture from the big metal bowl into the three pie crusts lined up and waiting on the baking table. The creak of the oven door. The rattle of the soup lid and dull thud of the wooden spoon once, twice, on the side of the pot.

Olivia's voice. "Hello, is Margaret available?"

Dreading her day, Margaret opened her eyes nonetheless. Gretchen finished discussing the priority of properly tying mid-sized mayflies as Margaret pushed herself off the counter and waved good-bye.

Gretchen smiled halfheartedly. Gert waved from the phone where she whispered to Jeffrey, who often called around eleven to make plans or break them.

They tipped themselves into Olivia's car, a bright-red convertible that Margaret found a little embarrassing. Olivia reapplied lipstick and donned sunglasses. Margaret wrapped her hair into a bun as Olivia squealed out of the bank parking lot, the attendant already walking over to yell at her for parking there.

Nearing Salisbury Beach they could smell the ocean, brittle and sharp. Seagulls hopped along the old boardwalk scattered with waxy 7-Up cups, discarded ketchup packets, and cigarette butts. Inside the arcade, a black-and-white photo booth stood beyond the legions of pinball machines and video games, their hot electric smell skirting the big room.

Margaret and Olivia's quarters fell into the booth's interior with a tiny clap. The red light blinked on. Posed. Red light. Posed. Red light. Outside the booth, exposed in the dusty fluorescence, they waited impatiently for their moist sheet of photos to slip down the worn metal shoot.

When it did, the thick, damp paper smelled of chemicals as Olivia held its edges. There they were, dark lipstick and upturned eyes—demure and devious.

"We look good together," Olivia said. "Let's do one more." She pulled Margaret into the booth. "Topless," she said. "Want to?"

"Hmmm. Okay," Margaret said. "But only if we go incognito. Sunglasses on."

Margaret adjusted the swivel seat, made sure the curtain was fully closed. Their staccato striptease began as Olivia pulled at her shirt and Margaret squealed, "Up!" They barely had time to unhook their bras before the last flash.

"I hope I had the seat adjusted right—would hate to lose the striptease," Margaret said, stepping out of the booth, sliding her bra strap over her shoulder.

Olivia almost walked right into the elderly woman waiting outside the booth, holding her grandson's hand. They entered next, pulled the curtain closed, no giggling, no laughter. Just coins dropping, four flashes, a mechanical chugging noise, and then they waited along with Olivia and Margaret for their photos to drop from the shoot, slimy and newborn. Margaret rocked on her heels, looked at the ground, tried to remember if the photos slid out face up or face down.

They weren't perfect. Olivia was too close in the foreground and a little blurry in the first shot. Margaret's mouth stretched into a lopsided pout in her effort to unhook her bra in the second. They both laughed hysterically in the third and fourth frames, Olivia holding each of her small breasts up as if for display—perfect nipples, creamy skin, bright, bold, toothy smile—with Margaret laughing to her left, her larger breasts round and obedient, light bouncing off her cat's-eye sunglasses. Her hand rested gently on Olivia's bare shoulder.

As they zoomed toward the diner, Margaret said, "So, how's the painting going?" She fiddled with the radio, turned it off. Air pushed little currents around her nose and across her cheeks.

"Tapes in the glove box, if you want to pick something," Olivia said. "The painting? Good. I'm feeling a bit lazy, though. Now that I'm here, I miss the city. There's nothing to do — zero energy, really. Here, after ten o'clock everyone's in bed or out drinking beer. Not super inspiring. But then I see my work, and I know I just need to keep going. I'm really picking up on all the ocean colors."

"Can't you just go back?" Margaret asked, shuffling through the tapes. "Visit? Would that satisfy your craving?" David Sullivan, The Smiths, The Cocteau Twins. Olivia's collection held nothing Margaret liked. Finally Billy Bragg.

"Well. Long story. Broken heart," Olivia said. "The man involved is staying in my apartment. Crazy, I know. Have I told you about Rufus? I was hooked on him, a manic-depressive, bipolar sculptor." Olivia laughed, grabbing the steering wheel with both hands. "He was totally into me, and we were out of control. You know, manics are sexual *animals*. It was fantastic." She looked at Margaret and smiled, laced her fingers tighter around the wheel. "And then he crashed. Blew my money on blow. Then my best friend blew him, and he blew her brother. I think all three of them did something together and what happened after that I don't want to know." She laughed again. "Oh God, that isn't funny, is it? It's a mess, and Rufus won't leave. I filed a lawsuit. It's going to get worse. I'm hoping he just gets bored and extracts himself from the situation. Until then my dad's monitoring it. I unfortunately loaned him a lot of money and also signed some kind of sublet agreement during the big sex part," Olivia said. "Like I said, a mess."

"Wow, I guess so," Margaret said. "Pretty dramatic."

"It was intense. But right now? This is perfect. You're perfect. *That* is insanity." Olivia pointed over her shoulder as if the past streamed behind them on the highway. "I'm over that. Over him," she said. She leaned toward Margaret and said, "Not really. I think about him every single day." She edged back up, Olivia in the present at the wheel. "Fucking post-pop sculptor asshole," she said, checking her lipstick in the review mirror, dabbing the corner of her mouth. "Don't listen to me complain. I'm never satisfied," she said. "It's the whole New York–centric thing. I quote the *Times*, and then talk about how much better it was five years ago. Sometimes I wonder when that got started, you know? Did the Dutch sit around saying 'it was so much more "real" when the Indians were here'?" She pushed her hand through her bundled hair. "You have to watch out for New Yorkers, Margaret. We say one thing, mean another. We don't eat dinner until it's dark out. Shady characters. Not to be trusted."

Not sure what to say, Margaret said, "I'd like to go to New York some time. Maybe once stuff dies down you could take me there and show me the city?"

"You've never been? That would be fun. I'd love to do that," Olivia said. "Let's plan on it, maybe at the end of the fall? I'll have to take some work into the gallery around November. I'll bring you along, introduce you to everyone. It's a date."

Margaret was flattered. Wesley promised to take her to the city sometime, too. She imagined they'd make a habit of it in the future, traveling in for weekend getaways. She'd visit Olivia once she returned to her apartment, make New York friends.

A classic steel-car diner with sleek, stainless-steel fixtures, the Agawam's chrome clock curved above the line cook's grill, its thin second hand sweeping by the hours, days, and years. Cowboys and Indians etched into the glass windows above each red vinyl booth played out their endless and exuberant clichéd roles. A feisty old woman polished her nails behind the register under a sign that read: "Everything from Scratch." The grill sizzled, dishes clanked. Grilled cheese and mashed potatoes with butter for Margaret. For Olivia, the open-faced roast beef sandwich with gravy and fries.

"How do you stay so *small* eating like that?" Margaret said.

"I know. I should be a fat lard," Olivia said. "Wesley mentioned you were a vegetarian. How long have you been doing that?"

"Since I left my parents' house. At first it was just economical. Then working at the bakery it was just easy. Then meat just became gross. I don't care what other people do, though," Margaret said. "Wesley's a major carnivore, and I think it's cute when he orders a hamburger."

"You *are* falling for him, aren't you? If you think ordering meat is cute, it's serious." Olivia winked.

"Oh, I like him. It's true," Margaret said. "I haven't felt this way about anybody for a long time. We work together. I mean, I can't stop thinking about him."

"Wow," Olivia said, as gravy dribbled from her plate onto the speckled surface of the Formica table. "This is fantastic. I wish I could offer you a bite." She wiped her mouth with first one then another thin, paper napkin. Took another from the dispenser and placed it on her lap.

"Are you from New Hampshire?" Olivia asked.

"Ohio," Margaret said.

"Ohio?" Olivia said, tilting her head as if she needed more information, a small smile forming.

"One over from Pennsylvania?" Margaret said. "The Buckeye State?"

"I know where Ohio is, Margaret," Olivia said, resting a hand briefly on her arm. Her fingers cold and thin. "It's just so unlikely. You're from the Midwest. I don't know if I've ever met anyone from Ohio, although I must have. People hide where they're from once they move to the East Coast."

"They do?" Margaret said. "I mean, I don't live there anymore. It's why I'm here. New Hampshire is definitely a better fit. But, you know, I can't change the fact I grew up two miles from the mall."

"Right. Yes, of course," Olivia said. "I think it's cool. The Buckeye State. That's very cool. Exotic." She sipped her strawberry milkshake, leaving a shadow of lipstick on the tip of the straw.

The fight from the night before stepped forward. Margaret's stomach sizzled. After a few more bites she slid out of the booth to check her messages at the payphone wedged beside the bright red bathroom door. Nothing. The morning caller hadn't left a message. She propped the receiver back into place, floated, unsettled, back to the table.

Olivia mopped gravy with a flimsy roll, her plate nearly empty. "Why the face?" she asked. "You look so sad. Don't worry, we'll get dessert."

"Oh, it's nothing," Margaret said. "Wesley and I had a fight last night. I did my laundry. Ran into Wesley. Fate, you know?" She smiled, suddenly worried she might cry. "We had this weird disagreement about laundry. He told me I need systems. All this after we'd just had sex in the Laundromat bathroom."

Olivia patted her hair, pulled on her elastic and let her black curls fall all around her shoulders. "That sounds so much like his dad. That systems talk, not the sex in the bathroom part," she said, pushing her hair around with her hands.

Margaret said, "Your hair is really lovely."

"Oh, thanks. It's all about expensive conditioner, I swear. Growing up it was a fuzz ball." Olivia pulled a menu from the booth behind them. "Sex in the Laundromat bathroom? Now that's daring. And you said my life was dramatic. Wes has never been a brave soul, you know. Maybe you scared him. At any rate, don't let him bug you. He's spoiled. Just say, 'What's so great about systems, Mr. Khaki Pants?'"

"That's funny," Margaret said. "I did call him Mr. Pickup Truck."

"Right. There, you see? You know how to handle him just fine," Olivia said. "So, after dessert should we head to Boston?" With a raised finger, Olivia brought the waitress their way.

Margaret thought she should keep Wesley hanging for a while, even though thoughts of him still took up space in her head as she contemplated whether to have blueberry or pecan pie. There he was in the darkness, all flesh and action.

Olivia didn't say anything more about Wesley. Margaret thought maybe she wanted her to forget it so they could move on with their day. Or maybe Olivia didn't like talking about other people's emotional issues. Or maybe her loyalty was with Wesley—a conflict of interest. Olivia didn't push her on the subject. Margaret thought that was nice of her.

Later that evening after Olivia dropped her off and barked three short honks, Margaret ran up her stairs, a plastic bag of books spinning at her side. The answering machine's red light blinked rapidly: Susan wanting to return the black skirt she'd borrowed; Gretchen needing to trade shifts.

Margaret waited until midnight before picking up the phone. Wesley answered on the third ring.

"What's up?" he said, nonchalantly.

"Olivia and I went out on the town today. It was good. I like her a lot," Margaret said a little too quickly.

"You did? Just the two of you? Great. Sounds fun," he said.

Margaret hesitated, and then invited him over. An hour later Wesley walked through her door, holding flowers. He got down on one knee in front of Margaret who sat on the couch, her new books fanned at her side. For a moment, she thought he was about to propose. She froze, frightened for her future. But Wesley didn't propose. Instead he pulled her into his arms, straddled her on the floor.

"You can do your laundry any way you want to," he said. "It's just that sometimes I picture us being together forever, and then I see you do something like that, and I just react without thinking."

Margaret looked at him, a gray-green silhouette in her dark living room. "You agree, right? It's just laundry. No big deal?"

Wesley didn't answer. Instead, he kissed Margaret. First in the living room, then the bedroom. Afterward, lying in bed, he said, "No matter what, Margaret, beyond all the bullshit and everything. I love you. Okay? You're the one." He touched her cheek.

They held hands, staring at the ceiling. "Wesley," Margaret said, "do you think it's strange that I'm from Ohio?"

"No," Wesley murmured. "Why?"

"Just never thought about it before," Margaret said.

"I love Ohio," Wesley said, curling his arms around her. Kissing her he said, "I hear Ohio girls are easy."

She edged toward sleep, wondering what "bullshit" he was talking about.

The next morning she ran naked into her bright living room to grab her bag, and they crouched together under the covers, legs tangled, looking at the photos.

"I can't believe you guys did that," he said. "With a kid and his grandmom outside? That's so like Olivia to drag you into something so crazy. Look at her little nipples. Teacups could fit perfectly over each boob. How weirdly, perfectly round. How inferior to your breasts." He lightly touched each of Margaret's nipples.

In years to come, Margaret would wonder if that's when Wesley changed his mind—Olivia's breasts beside her own and their perfect teacup size. Maybe he knew, right then, Olivia was the one, not her. She wondered if Olivia suggested going topless to size up her competition, to see what Margaret had under her shirt and what she would and would not do.

In years to come Margaret lost the photos in her travels—a shoebox full of snapshots and Polaroids and strips and strips of photo-booth pictures left behind in a moldy basement for some landlord to uncover and set curbside.

17
Vivette, Nebraska

Although the sheep seem high strung, they rarely hurry. One minute they're by the tree, staring at Vivette skeptically. The next they're on the far side of the field. They seem hesitant, but as a group they're decisive and organized.

One in particular looks like Vivette's Aunt Martha, who never leaves the house without practical high heels and a tasteful shade of pink lipstick. This morning their baaing also sounds like advice Aunt Martha would give: "Back," they say. "Go back."

The farm is getting to her. Vivette feels a hollowness forming deep inside, like a dry well that would echo if a stone was tossed in. What she needs is a drive down the lane. "Itching to explore," she writes on the back of a postcard with two prairie dogs raised up on their hind legs, kissing. "Back by five unless I meet a cowboy, then I'll be off with the dogies on the range." Vivette puts on lipstick, kisses the edge of the card, and props it up by the kitchen sink.

Jean jacket. Backpack. Vivette hops into the Buick, slamming the big driver's side door. She settles herself on the springy bucket seat and rolls the windows down, enjoying the moment of potential just before the key turns in the ignition. A sense of purpose drifts in through the windows. The silence that drapes the surrounding countryside mixes with the smell of stale coffee and freshly cut grass.

The postcard Vivette pulls out of the glove box has an old photograph on the front of the Donut Queen—a smiling 1950s lipsticked, bosomy, skinny-waisted woman with a glitzy doughnut crown atop her head and a dozen glazed resting in her lap.

Dear Grandad, I'm leaving the sheep and the farm in search of a different kind of adventure on the Plains. The guy here, Peter, you'd like him. He can hold his liquor. I think I'll use him as my guide to the next boyfriend. Did you know back in New Hampshire I had an affair with a married guy? He's friends with the people I'm staying with. It's all very complicated, but it seemed easy at the time. The Plains are sucking me in. Your favorite grandchild, Vivette

P.S. Don't you think Aunt Martha looks a little like a sheep?

After securing a stamp on its corner and scribbling in Joe-Joe's address, Vivette puts the postcard in her bag with the others. The Buick's engine heaves itself into a smooth rumble. A racy breeze wraps itself around the car and skips through the windows. Vivette digs her sunglasses out of her backpack, eases along the gravel road. The sheep run alongside.

The baaing starts in earnest as soon as she passes the edge of their fence line. In the rearview mirror, the herd clumps together, worried ladies looking earnestly after her, warning her to drive carefully, remember her seatbelt, don't talk to strangers.

Vivette zigzags her way to Lincoln. Her plan is to drive through town, get some coffee and gas, mail her postcards, look at her map, chart a course. Meadowlarks whistle longingly from fence posts. A noble hawk looks down from high up in a cottonwood, stiff and indifferent, its wings folded up like umbrellas. The fields, rich and brown, look expectant and ready. The country has opened up, big and flat like a picture book. Vivette drives right on through.

As she nears Lincoln, the capitol is a pointer finger beckoning in the distance. Peter said the locals call it "the penis of the prairie." A tiny sower on its top.

On O Street, she passes bars and restaurants, thrift stores and antique shops. Margaret suggested the old market for decent coffee. Vivette follows the signs along the wide, sunny streets, past the Holiday Inn, card shops, and a clothing store.

Although she's only been on the farm for a few days, Vivette feels like a wild animal set down in the middle of all this. People everywhere. Traffic lights. Workers on their lunch breaks. Dogs straining on leashes. She needs to park, walk, acclimate.

The Beanbag Coffeeshop brims with clean-cut university types. Big rooms and hardwood floors, the smell of freshly roasted coffee. Shiny beanbag chairs in blue, green, and red are scattered in the corners, with students sunk down in, ankles crossed, studying textbooks and working crossword puzzles. Vivette walks out to the loading dock with her steaming paper cup. Everyone is busy reading, talking softly in groups. She feels entirely out of place. They stare at her, smile, and turn back to their coffee and conversations. Vivette thinks of the Buick, how it can take her anywhere.

Back inside the car, door sealed, she's safe and secure, alone. The map takes over the rest of the big front seat, and Vivette charts a course up Highway 77. Late-morning light warms her face as she sips her coffee.

The route has a line of red dots skirting its back, a "scenic drive" according to Rand McNally, which steered her wrong in Illinois, those little polka dots leading her onto traffic-jammed, stoplight-filled, tourist-infested roads that passed miles of strip malls.

She chooses the polka-dotted road anyway, and now the sleek, black highway curves through farmland as it winds its way north.

Winter wheat and drying fields of soybean plants not yet turned under rise up to the horizon. Peter told her that come summer there will be sorghum and milo, wheat, oats, corn, and wildflowers. The plowed fields suggest endless potential, confirmed by the occasional farmhouse, barn, silo. Brown fields everywhere expecting something big to happen.

She passes a prehistoric behemoth of a grain elevator, then a Purina dog food plant, its own industrial revolution right there on the plains. Then it's back to the earth and field, field, field. Long, insect-like, center-pivot irrigation systems sit poised and gleaming on small rubber wheels. John Deere tractors roll around looking exactly like the toys she played with as a kid.

All the fields are transformed into a giant sandbox, the farmer a plastic figurine with a hard yellow cowboy hat. Vivette imagines the Buick is the Matchbox car she drove through the sand as a girl — the tourist watching the farmer sow the fields. There are little-kid car noises, and then the screeching of tires as she brakes for, what are they? Pheasant? Quail? Their fancy-looking plumes party hats on their bobbing heads.

Vivette eases off the road at a rectangular green sign pointing toward Bancroft, Nebraska, on the edge of the Omaha Indian Reservation. She's ready for lunch, maybe a secondhand store.

Another sign tells her that Bancroft is the home of the John G. Neihardt Center. She follows the road markers there. Hers is the only car in the lot.

Vivette read *Black Elk Speaks* in high school, but she doesn't make the connection until she sees the oversized black-and-white photos looming in the center's hushed lobby. Neihardt with Black Elk on the top of a peak in the Black Hills of South Dakota. Neihardt with his wife and family in Bancroft. Soon she's sucked into reading the text panel on the wall that tells how Neihardt and his wife Mona courted by letter. A sculptor who studied with

Rodin, Mona left Paris to marry Neihardt and live in Bancroft with only a cross-continental correspondence as proof of their love.

With the story of this unlikely romance unfolding before her, Vivette thinks of Robert. She had banished him from her thoughts, but now in the dimly lit museum she misses him. As Vivette stares at a photo of Neihardt, who's a serious little man, it comes to her—she needs to write Robert a letter.

Neihardt is short and rugged, standing one step up from an award presenter to match his height. Mona looks happy in the photographs. A classic beauty with wavy hair and a bright smile. An ideal-looking family, a lovely little prairie home with a work studio, which they shared. Vivette reads how Neihardt wrote in the morning and Mona sculpted in the afternoon, taking turns with the kids.

"Can I help you, miss?" the docent Elnora asks—a wide face, rosy cheeks, practical black skirt and shoes, and a tidy metal name tag clipped to her yellow blazer.

"No," Vivette says, "not really. It's an amazing story."

Elnora smiles broadly. "Neihardt was once known as the American Homer. Did you know that?"

Vivette shakes her head no.

"It's true," Elnora says. "But sadly his focus on epic poetry, an archaic form even in his time, caused him to remain relatively unknown to many, even his fellow Nebraskans."

"I read *Black Elk Speaks* in high school," Vivette says.

"That's excellent," Elnora says. She lightly touches Vivette's forearm for emphasis. "Good for you. Neihardt believed the American West's story was the stuff of life itself." She smiles widely again.

Vivette smiles back, comforted by Elnora's sincerity.

"In the 1960s," Elnora continues, her hands folded peacefully in front of her belly, "Neihardt's 1932 *Black Elk Speaks*—as you well know, the strange and haunting narrative of Black Elk's highly symbolic visions during the last days of the Lakota tribe's independence—came into its own and gave rise to an interest in creating this center." Elnora looks around the room, as if to make sure everything is there, just as she says. "Even though it's a little out of the way, people find us. You'd be surprised."

With that, she quietly walks back to her desk near the entrance.

Vivette can't stop thinking about the romance. Mona traveled all over the world before deciding to be with Neihardt in the middle of nowhere. How did Mona know—by letter!—that Neihardt was the one?

Vivette wonders what Mona thought the first time she rounded the bend into Bancroft. Did she say, "Oh, it's beautiful"? Did she love the river? Did she eventually long for the big open landscape, the peace and quiet so different from a bustling city? Or, did she turn the corner into town and say, "Oh shit"? Did Neihardt lure her out in the middle of nowhere, or did she know what she was getting herself into?

Vivette thinks about how Peter said sometimes it didn't seem fair to Margaret, because they were living his dream by moving out to the farmhouse. Not hers.

Elnora highly recommends the pie at Mau's Place, and soon Vivette is seated at the thin Formica counter on one of ten empty maroon stools. Mau herself serves the ham sandwich, potato chips, and slice of coconut cream. Elnora's right. The pie's custard is homemade, thick and rich with eggs and milk, toasted coconut tucked inside and a perfectly peaked meringue rising from its top, the crust nutty and crisp. Lush and familiar flavors. Vivette feels a pang of homesickness. "That'll be $3.25," Mau says.

"For the whole thing? Did you remember the dessert?" Vivette asks.

"Yep. That's about right. I run a hard bargain here at Mau's."
Mau laughs, and then asks, "Not from around here, are you?"

Vivette laughs, too loud. "No, I'm not," she says. "How'd you
guess?"

"Well, you looked a little lost when you walked in. And then
most people around here don't wear dresses with men's shoes. I
mean, it's nice to see," Mau says. "We're glad to have you. Are
you here for the Neihardt Center?"

"I'm just sort of in Bancroft by accident," Vivette says. "I did
find out about you at the center though. From Elnora. I had no
idea Neihardt lived here."

"Every so often we get someone from the university asking
around, doing research," Mau says. "Thought you might be one
of them."

"It's so romantic. Neihardt and Mona," Vivette says. "The way
they met and everything? Do you think they were in love?"

"Elnora told me that Neihardt was never the same after Mona
died," Mau says, leaning in as if she's relaying town gossip. "She
was in a wreck — the brakes went on their car, I guess. He just
had them worked on, too, and they gave out. Isn't that awful?"
Mau shakes her head. "Neihardt's spirit left him the day Mona
died. Broke his heart. That's what Elnora says."

Vivette leaves a two-dollar tip and eases out onto Main Street.
A bar, a general store, a bunch of nearly empty buildings. Wishful
emptiness announcing the West.

She shuffles down the dusty sidewalk thinking about Mona
careening toward her imminent death, pumping the brake pedal
as the car raced faster and faster and nothing she could do to stop
it. For Vivette the world around her isn't careening. It's silent and
clear. Her own heart is the thing flying downward. She feels it
thumping, even now, in a kind of anticipation — wanting more
than Vivette can give it, taking on speed.

Vivette peeks into the general store's big plate-glass window, trying to gauge if it's still in business. The merchandise looks like it was last inventoried forty years earlier. When she tries the door's brass handle, it opens.

Daylight slants in from the street, making the dust in the air glitter and cascade in long, flat rays to the floor. Empty wooden shelves line the walls leading up to the high ceilings. Vivette imagines they were once crammed with merchandise and that this place had been bustling back in the day — selling tobacco to traders and hunters, jeans and shirts to the farmers, bolts of cotton to their wives. A penny-candy counter and a crowd on Sundays after church. Maybe a pickle barrel. Poker games by a wood-burning stove.

Staring at the empty shelves and then the streams of light, Vivette doesn't notice the woman behind the counter.

"Looking for something?" the woman says.

"Oh, wow. I'm sorry," Vivette says. "I didn't mean to be gawking. I didn't think anyone was in here."

A small, fragile-looking Native-American woman sits hunched inside a down parka — too heavy for the spring weather. The ancient sewing machine beside her anchors a piece of faded material with its needle. She smiles calmly.

"I'm up from Lincoln, to see the Neihardt Center?" Vivette says. "I'm doing research at the university?"

"Researching," the woman says. She doesn't appear to believe Vivette, who can't tell if she has just made a statement or asked a question.

Vivette says, "I'll just look around then?"

The woman makes a barely decipherable assent and goes back to sitting perfectly still.

"Oh my," Vivette whispers as she uncovers a whole box of some ancient incarnation of Chuck Taylor sneakers with the tags still on them. They're yellow with black trim and big wide toes. She tries on every pair that looks like they might fit. None are the right size, so she guesses at Peter and Margaret's. Further down the narrow aisle, she finds fuzzy sweaters from the 1950s, still in their stiff plastic packages. Cardigans with big vertical stripes in blue and black. Mohair sweaters in maroon and mustard yellow. From rack to rack, she tiptoes, trying not to make any noise as she opens packages—tries on sweaters, peeks in the dusty full-length mirror again and again. She walks up to the counter with an armload.

The woman looks longingly at each item. She adds up the figures twice by hand, a pencil scratching on the back of a paper bag. "Enjoy Bancroft," she says.

Outside again, Vivette feels like she's traveled to another time entirely. A stagecoach could round the corner and pull to a stop, and Vivette wouldn't be surprised. She looks back at the general store. The plate glass reflects her jean jacket, her dress with gaudy pink flowers, her black shoes. Vivette squints. She fixes her hair, puts a strand behind her ear to keep it out of her eyes, bends down to tie her laces.

The bar is a little stooped building of faded red brick. Vivette kicks her way across the street after stashing her bag of clothes in the Buick. She pushes on the thick metal door, hesitating for a second before abandoning the open outside world for this tiny one within. A dusty window sends a trail of speckled light onto the faded linoleum floor. A couple of ancient sconces flare from the back bar beside a string of liquor bottles. A bartender with two guys in front. Three empty tables line the wall.

Below Vivette's propped elbows, the wood of the bar top has been worn smooth by all the customers who settled in before her. There's a stuffed jackalope attached to the wooden bar back. A bunny with antlers, the West's great inside joke. The jackalope abounded on the Iowa and Nebraska postcards Vivette sent to friends and Grandpa Joe-Joe from the road. Some said the jackalope sang tenor with the cowboys and only mated during electrical thunderstorms. Others proposed they only came out of hiding after a large quantity of bourbon had been consumed. And now, finally, a jackalope in person.

"Nice jackalope," Vivette says. "And in case you're wondering, I know it's fake."

The bartender laughs. "Damn," he says, "There goes our afternoon's entertainment."

There are lines of postcards taped along the wall, sent from all over the country. Seems like a lot of people took the time to send a card to Bancroft on their yearly vacations. Beautiful Hollywood, Beautiful Colorado, Beautiful Ohio, Beautiful Texas, Beautiful Hawaii.

Vivette pulls a stack of postcards from her bag. She'll send one to grandpa. And another to Robert, filled with hidden innuendo.

"So what brings you to Bancroft? From the university?" the bartender asks.

"No, I'm visiting some friends who have a farm outside Lincoln. They're at work today, and the farm was getting boring, so I thought I'd explore. It's a pretty drive," Vivette says, shrugging.

The bartender dries a glass, offers it to her. Vivette shakes her head no as she takes a sip of beer from the bottle. "You sure get a lot of postcards," she says.

He sets the glass back on the shelf. "Where're you from?" he asks.

"Well, I started off in New Hampshire a couple weeks ago. I'm planning on moving to Des Moines," Vivette says. "Thought I'd visit my friends in Nebraska before I did that."

"I thought I heard eastern in your accent. Got a beau in Des Moines?"

"Oh no. I'm driving solo," Vivette says, liking the way it sounds out here on the Plains, as if she has a hardened life and a rig parked down by the feedlot.

The bartender leans against the beer cooler. "Why leave New England? Why not keep on going out to Colorado or the West Coast? You hiding from someone?"

Vivette takes another swig of beer. Fiddles with the damp napkin as she asks, "Why would you say that?" Lately, it seems there's a marquee floating above her head, broadcasting parts of her life story without her permission. "Isn't that kind of rude? A woman walks into a bar in the middle of the week alone and you assume she must be in some kind of trouble."

The bartender says, "It gets pretty cold out this way come winter."

"That's what everybody keeps saying," Vivette says. "I don't know. I thought I'd check it out. Seemed like a good idea a few weeks ago. Now it seems a little bit stupid, but I like to finish what I start."

"I admire that," the bartender says, smiling, overly friendly.

One of the farmers at the bar says, "Twenty-seven below like last January, and you'll be heading on back to the coast. That is, if your car starts."

The one who has just spoken is around sixty, probably drinking with his son who's Vivette's age or younger. They're both wearing feed caps, green work pants, and flannel shirts in contrasting patterns. Strong arms. Big smiles. Their faces are warm and weathered—pink from working outdoors away from neon lights and office buildings.

"I'm not making any promises," Vivette says, fishing out a pen, flipping through her stack of postcards, rattling her foot back and forth to show she's deep in thought. She picks one sporting a jackalope on the front, pink nose tipped up to scout out the Great Plains, another that reads, "Greetings from Indiana."

"Well, it must feel nice being able to up and leave, being out on your own. You're a brave girl, leaving your home behind," the bartender says, setting a shot glass on the bar, filling it with whiskey, and sliding it her way. He sets another shot in the same starting point. Fills that one for himself.

Vivette sets the stack of cards down, saying, "You know, I've been feeling a little brave lately. Let's hope it keeps up. Pretty lonely out here." She eyes the bartender over the glass, eases the whiskey back. It's reassuring to her, this whiskey easing down her throat, this bar, these men, the jackalope and the small bags of chips hanging like gaudy earrings from white metal clips. The buzz of a bar sign, the creak of a chair. The bar is quiet. No music, no pool table, just the clock above the bathroom door.

Vivette's head hums. Talk, she thinks to herself. Say something. "So, it's pretty cool that John G. Neihardt lived here. I read his book in school—the Black Elk one? I guess it's what I think about when I think about this part of the country. Native American spiritual leaders in long johns. Bows and arrows, guns. Teepees. Horses. Visions. What was that Black Elk said about Neihardt when he first saw him? There's a big quote on the wall over at the center. 'This world is like a garden and over it go his words like rain,'" Vivette says, swiping her hand through the air for emphasis.

The old farmer takes his hat off, rubs his forehead with the edge of his palm, puts the hat back on smiling, looks at the bartender. He nods and another beer is set neat and trim where the old one had been. "Well, I don't know about that, but local rumor has it he was a chicken thief," he says. "That's what the old-timers call him. They say he and his friends went out stealing chickens at night. I wouldn't hold much to that though. I think they probably just thought he was peculiar."

The young farmer nudges his dad's shoulder, talking quietly into it instead of at Vivette. "And the skinny-dipping," he says.

"Oh yeah." The hat comes off. "They were known to skinny-dip," he says, massaging his forehead again.

The bartender adds, "On Sundays."

The farmer laughs, "Pretty easy to become a legend in Bancroft. People don't have much else to do but mind other people's business."

To Vivette each statement feels like a running commentary on her own particular situation. She says, "I can't imagine they fit right in."

"They must've liked it though. At least for a while," the older farmer says, motioning to the bartender again. "It's a quiet place, that's for sure. Not too many distractions out here." A shot glass appears. The bartender pours one for the farmer. Takes another for himself.

Vivette finishes the last of her beer, says to the silence that has once again taken away the conversation's momentum, "Well. I'm going to sit over here and write a few postcards."

The table wobbles as her pen nudges the card. It's colder by the tables. Vivette feels more alone, less part of the greater good of the bar in her wooden chair that has duct tape keeping its red cushion together. A second full shot glass gleams in front of her previously occupied seat. Vivette lights a cigarette.

Dear grandpa. I'm drinking alone with a bunch of cowboys. I wonder what makes me do this? I can't seem to help myself. It's easy to walk into a strange bar, take a seat, and see what happens. It isn't half as dangerous as people make it out to be. At any rate, don't tell mom, that goes without saying. There's a mounted jackalope head here. It makes me think most real live animals are kind of boring. From Vivette

Her card to Robert is easy:

*I want to kiss you on the lips. I want you to buy me another shot of whiskey. I want you to leave your wife and live with me forever.
Vivette*

"I need to figure out my life," Vivette announces to no one in particular. Her voice cuts through the silence like static. She doesn't think they believe she has friends. Maybe they think she's a fugitive? A runaway? Maybe she's imagining this whole scene?

"On me," the bartender says as he clears her empty bottle and shot glass, wiping the bar top, erasing Vivette's visit before she's even gone. His good deed for the day. No one will remember her here. Vivette understands.

The two farmers tip their caps as she makes her way out. Her car is like a still life in front of Mau's, the only one left on Main Street besides a big green pickup truck.

Vivette knows she won't be remembered in this world. As the sun creeps around the corner of first one, then another building, she is sure of it. She won't be remembered by any lingering town gossip. She'll come and go out of people's lives. They'll love her or hate her. They'll take her in, and then wipe her visit clean the moment she walks out the door. It's lucid. Her history is written for her. She'll never settle in a place long enough for old-timers to make up tales about her. She'll leave a small, scalding fingerprint and then get into her car and drive. She will not be Mona. She will not be Neihardt. She will not be Margaret or Peter or Susan or Robert.

Vivette walks to her car, her shoes crunching on the soft pebbles. Maybe Mona was the only person who could make Neihardt crack a smile. Maybe she got through that tough exterior. Maybe she splashed the water, and as it fell it caught the early morning light and her naked body sparkled. Maybe she was happy then, here in this place so far away from where things were expected of her.

Wesley had said, "Tell Margaret I said hello."' Something Vivette can't bring herself to do. It was a simple request, but it was the way he said it. And Margaret's face when Vivette lied about sleeping with him. Best kept folded away, his smug hello. Like a note passed in middle school under the teacher's nose.

Vivette holds the Buick's sturdy steering wheel. Rolls down the window. She lets the postcard to Robert drop to the gravel road. It makes the tiniest click. The end, it says. The end.

She drives away, watching the small, white rectangle recede in her rearview mirror. It doesn't blow or move — anchored to Bancroft, to the dust waiting for the wind to carry it away. For now, Vivette drives south. She puts in Hank Williams, a going-away present from Wesley. She sings along to "I'm So Lonesome." Vivette is starting to understand country music. She's feeling her heart break.

18
Wesley, New Hampshire

The mesh on the screen door was tacked into place with thin strips of wood that flaked blue paint. As Wesley knocked, the frame bounced open with a rattle. He wanted to sit with Olivia a while, talk about art in her little cottage, watch her paint, look out the window at the ocean. More and more he was drawn to this place beside the ocean where time seemed to stop. Work deadlines and worries stayed at the doorstep, never venturing inside. Olivia seemed oblivious to the cottage's charms and only saw herself in exile, punished by her father for the sublet mishap.

"Hey, hello," he called, "want me to make some coffee?"

Off in the corner, set up near the window, Olivia raised her hand in an exaggerated A-OK while she stared at a canvas, head bent to the left, one bare foot stuck out to the side, tapping the floor with her toes, the nails newly painted bright red.

The timer on Olivia's coffeemaker perpetually blinked 12:00 a.m., and the milk steamer had never worked right. Abandoned for days on end, coffee dried in hard shellac rings on the bottom of the pot. The filter sprouted dusty mold. Wesley examined the pot and the brittle, ancient-looking grounds in the filter and grabbed two beers out of the fridge. "I'm not touching that damaged piece of machinery," he said, handing her a beer.

Olivia pinched the beer bottle's neck with two fingers, still staring at her work. "Could you get me a glass, please? One of those little juice ones? That's what I like for beer," she said. "Much thanks."

Wesley walked the length of the living room, delivered the glass, browsed through some books on the shelves, continued pacing and looking over Olivia's shoulder at the mysterious patch of blue-green forming under her tiny brush. He glanced at Olivia expectantly, but she continued to ignore him.

Finally, she turned and said, "Antsy today, aren't we?"

"I guess so," Wesley said, drawing his finger along the edge of a lampshade, "I'll settle down soon." He leafed through some paperbacks, tapped the wooden shelves with his thumbs.

"Oh, I don't think you'll ever settle down," Olivia said.

"Oh, really, Ms. Stability. Ms. I-Have-It-All-together. Ms. My-Ex-boyfriend-Has-Taken-My-Fancy-Apartment-Hostage, looking so calm and relaxed and arty over there. Just wait until you put down that paint brush. I know how you get. You're just like me," Wesley said. He opened a window to let sea air rush over him.

"Close that," Olivia said, "the paint dries too quickly. You know, I bet you can't sit still for thirty minutes — just thirty. Try it. If you can, I'll talk to you about whatever you want, even that stupid writing job your daddy got you. I'll buy you a treat."

Wesley sighed, paced a few more steps. "My father did not get me the writing job, Olivia." He stopped at the bookcase, extracted a tattered copy of *In Our Time*, its pages fat with salt air, and sat down on the window seat, the book in his lap, looking out at the ocean. "Ready, go," he said.

By the time Olivia glanced up from her work again an hour had passed, and Wesley was asleep, stretched out on the window seat, the book a tiny blanket over his chest, his ankles crossed. She drew him just like that. A quick pen and ink, a present she would give him later at Christmastime, a drawing they would hang in their den.

Olivia crouched down at head level and lifted the book, browsed its pages. "You win, sir," she said.

"Will you buy the coffee, too?"

"Sure. I'll buy the coffee, too," Olivia said, "but I need decaf. I've given up caffeine for good. I'm giving up all of my vices."

"Except Rufus," Wesley said as he grabbed his coat, held hers aloft as she inserted each thin arm. "Except alcohol."

"The jury is still out on Mr. Rufus, if you need to know. I guess my father had a perfectly decent conversation with him the other day. In fact, I think Dad is starting to like him more than me. And alcohol is not a vice," Olivia said. "It's a basic requirement."

"Why not find a nice guy for a change? Someone you can re-late to? Why seek out these damaged cases with so many leaks? Why not start with something decent and work from there?" Wesley asked.

"Oh, dear Wesley. You're not talking about me, are you? You're talking about Margaret. When will you learn? Margaret is humor-ing you. It's what women do. I mean, I love Margaret, but I'm sure she just pretends to want the same things you do. I know she does. It's hard to believe it, but she adores you. I'm sure she's insane, too. You just haven't discovered it yet. With Rufus, what you see is what you get," Olivia said, "and I like that. No secrets. Plus, have I mentioned the sex?"

"You've mentioned the sex, Olivia," Wesley said as the screen door slammed behind them.

19   *Margaret, New Hampshire*

Olivia made a pitcher of Manhattans in honor of her officially permanently lost apartment and her latest bookstore score: a 1956 *Esquire* magazine drink guide for the swinging bachelor. She phoned Margaret, asking her over to the cottage for cocktails, just the two of them.

"Here, have another," Olivia said, leaning toward Margaret, delicately pouring from the shaker into her glass, plucking a cherry from the jar next to them and letting it settle down through the bourbon murkiness. "You should sleep over. Don't go," Olivia said. "It's too lovely here with you." One camisole strap hung loosely off her shoulder, her wild, messy curls were alive in the candlelight.

Margaret held the stem of her glass steady, sipped the drink before it could trickle onto the rug. "It is lovely here," Margaret said. With candles scattered all around the living room, they had turned out the lights and read each other's tarot cards. The cottage cool in the filmy evening air, the windows open, the surf lapping the beach, the tiny flames flickering, they had already gone through half a jar of cherries.

"I've got things I want to talk with you about. Stay, stay right here," Olivia said, patting the floor beside her. "I'll get pajamas for you." She ran upstairs, feet thundering above Margaret's head. Dresser drawers opened and banged closed. Margaret stretched her legs across the scratchy rug. She tipped her head back to rest against the window seat cushion. Her brain spun clockwise, then counterclockwise.

"Here. These are perfect for you," Olivia said, running back down the stairs holding out men's cotton pajamas, light green with white piping. "God knows where they came from. Probably my dad's or my brother's. They're yours tonight, though. They're all yours," she said.

"Thanks," Margaret said, hesitantly trying to weigh the positive side of staying over, deciding she just didn't have enough energy to say no. "They're very cool. I love men's pajamas. In fact, I stole Wesley's. They're bright red. I wear them all the time. He likes when I run around in the top."

"Oh, I'm sure he does," Olivia said. "I bet he likes when you run around without the top, too," she laughed. "Well, you can have these if you want. In case Wesley takes his back. You can have a back-up set."

Margaret kicked off her jeans and pulled off her shirt and slid into the pajamas. She reassessed her world, drink in hand, and said, "This is nice. I haven't been to a sleepover since middle school. Although we never had drinks this fancy, of course. More like cans of warm beer stolen from my dad's garage."

"Oh, that's too bad. I had tried many top-shelf drinks by that age," Olivia said. "Finishing up the dredges of cocktails was one of my favorite pastimes. In fact, I could make a mean martini by my freshman year of high school. I took to assisting the bartenders at my parents' parties, more control over selection that way. 'Mr. Smith, would you like that up? With an olive or twist?'" Olivia pitched in a lisp.

Margaret could see her then, frizzy hair and braces, a too-skinny frame barely filling up a fluffy party dress.

"But yes, you're right, middle school," Olivia said. "Let's toast to sleepovers." They clinked their glasses, peered out at the darkness as the tide continued to slip away.

"Do you want to go for a walk on the beach?" Margaret asked.

"Do you ever do that late at night?"

Olivia crinkled up her nose. "I do, I guess. But I don't feel like it tonight. It's so nice and cozy here. Let's just stay in and talk."

"Oh, okay," Margaret said, disappointed. She liked the idea of walking up to the pier in pajamas, the feel of the sand beneath her feet.

"So," Olivia said looking at Margaret knowingly, an eyebrow raised. "What is Mr. Wesley like in bed? Do tell. I already know from your tarot cards you're born for love. What about him?" She looked crazed in the flickering light.

"Well," Margaret said, leaning toward Olivia. "It's definitely the best sex I've ever had. So, right there, you know?"

"Really. The best?" Olivia said. "Scout's honor?"

"For me, I want to have sex all the time. Sometimes he actually says, 'Not tonight, Margaret.' Sometimes," Margaret said, laughing.

"So, why do you think it's so good? Do you think he's just good all the time, or is it the two of you?"

"Good question," Margaret said, talking lower. "I think he's probably exceptional, then I think we're really good together. Without much practice at all, we pretty much had it down. I think we're in love."

Olivia smiled. The soft candlelight made shadows that climbed along the wall of books. Margaret reached forward and tucked a piece of Olivia's hair behind her ear so she looked less crazy. Olivia was still smiling as she turned to look out the window. "I know. Let's blow out all the candles so we can see the ocean."

They sat in the dark, staring out at the night beyond the windows. After awhile they could make out the white edges of the waves. "See," Olivia said. "Now that's sublime. That's what I need to capture in my work. It's scary, but exquisite. Perfect."

They sipped their drinks with less frequency. Olivia said, "I miss my guy in New York. My Rufus. Even though he's done me wrong. I'm afraid I'm going out with wackos the rest of my life, and if that's the case, then I want to go out with him. Oh, man. He really broke my heart into tiny pieces."

"Oh, Olivia. You'll find a guy," Margaret said. "Don't worry. I mean, look at you. You're gorgeous and successful and young. You'll find someone, and you'll have amazing sex, and then you'll forget about Rufus, and I'll never see you again."

"What do you mean? Look at you. You've found Wesley, and I still see you," Olivia said.

"That's true," Margaret said. "But that's because you're so persistent. Most people kind of disappear once they find somebody. The relationship changes."

"I'd never do that to you. I'd never leave you," Olivia whispered, putting her head on Margaret's shoulder. "You're so cool. I think you're totally cool." Olivia seemed to fall asleep, then she started talking again. "And it won't be that easy for me to find a guy. I'm really messed up. I'm going to be messed up for a long, long time. But hey, does Wesley like to be on top or bottom?"

Margaret put a hand to her forehead to steady her vision. She said, "I think he likes to be on bottom."

"Good, good," Olivia said patting her on the shoulder. "That shows fine character. Good for you."

20

Vivette, Nebraska and New Hampshire

Margaret clutches two handfuls of salad greens, their little dirt-clotted roots still attached as she props open the door with her heel and scoots inside the house. "Robert called for you," she says to Vivette. "There was a message on the machine when I got home. If I knew how to work the thing right I could tell you what time — but I don't, so I can't."

"Robert? Really?" Vivette asks, sitting up straight from her slouch, wedging her book into the crevice between the couch cushions.

"You weren't around, I guess. He called today sometime. Said he had a question he needed to ask you."

"That's strange," Vivette says. "Did it sound urgent?" She thinks of the postcard she threw out the car window in Bancroft. Unstamped, she reassures herself, no address. Could it have skidded and floated east and east and east, up to Robert's doorstep? No. Vivette tells herself. "No," she says out loud.

"What?" Margaret asks.

"I mean, no, it couldn't have been urgent, or he would've called back."

"Right," Margaret says, "it didn't sound urgent. I'm sorry. I accidentally erased it. I just don't understand this new machine — it randomly decides what messages to keep, what to erase. Anyway, he specifically said it wasn't urgent. I do remember that. Maybe he just found something you left behind."

"Yeah, maybe," Vivette says. "I'll give him a call later."

"Yes, sometime later. You should," Margaret says, sitting down too close to Vivette, the greens still poking from her fingers. "Peter was thinking we should have a few people over tomorrow. Have a little party. Is that something you'd be interested in?"

Vivette quickly takes inventory of the reasons Robert might call. He called . . . *with a question.* Could he want to move to Des Moines? That would be urgent, though. A question? Her heart. How ridiculous. Her face, it must be flushed. She smiles at Margaret. She says, "I'm sorry?"

"We thought we'd invite a few people over tomorrow," Margaret says. "Or would you rather we didn't?" A thin crease has formed between Margaret's eyes.

"Oh, that's fine. That's great. I can help make food if you want. I'd love to meet your friends," Vivette says, although she's not sure she wants to meet any of Margaret's friends who will size her up in the same nonjudgmental way Margaret does, with little jabs and prying questions. "Invite some single people though, will you? I just don't know if I could bear being around a bunch of couples as happy and adjusted as you guys." She picks up her book again, says, "It'll be fun. I'm sure."

Vivette's can't let go of Robert's call, his question, unasked. Unanswered.

Vivette had told Robert first, as a courtesy, before she put in her notice at the bakery and let the world in on the big move. The last night they spent together was more like a first date than anything — everything in reverse order.

After she told him, Robert asked in a low voice if she'd like to go to dinner. Just the two of them. Somewhere away. Up north, in Maine maybe. They lay side by side in bed.

"We can go out to dinner and talk anywhere, Robert," Vivette said. "No one knows about us. Unless you want to fuck on the table. Why are you suddenly whispering?"

"I want to do something special," he said. "I wasn't thinking we'd do it on the table, per se."

Vivette was happy then, in that moment, happy he saw their relationship as special. She thought maybe he'd surprise her with a hotel room. Something unexpected and lusty.

The night of, Robert called at the last minute to say he'd be late, that a few things had come up he needed to tend to before he could get over to her place. He sounded frazzled.

Vivette put on a gauzy, low-cut white shirt, and then changed into a pink v-neck. Pulled her hair up, took it down. She guessed Robert was probably doing something for Susan. Walking the dog or grocery shopping or having sex.

Finally she gave up. Pulled a plaid polyester dress on over faded jeans. She laced up old Puma sneakers. *It doesn't matter*, she chanted to herself. She was leaving. She was gone. She put on mascara.

Vivette grabbed her bag and a sweater, went outside to sit and wait. Already her apartment was emptying out — things she put into storage, dragged to the thrift store, gave away to friends. She didn't spend too much time there these days, what with the boxes asking so many questions.

Everything she owned had to fit into the Buick's big trunk or in the passenger seat beside her. That was the rule, so she could sleep on the back seat in a pinch. She wanted to travel light so quick decisions could be made, so she would be leading the way, not her stuff loaded down with memories and warnings.

Robert's red vw Rabbit sputtered into view. He leaned over and opened the passenger door from the inside. It creaked as she walked up the sidewalk.

"Hey, sorry I'm late. Had to run a few errands," Robert said.

Vivette hated that he wasn't specific. Errands were a front.

"That's fine," she said. "I spent most of the time having one fashion crisis after another. No biggie."

"Well, that outfit you ended up with is pretty interesting, sort of track team slash polyester car wreck."

"Thanks, I'm feeling very secure right now seeing as how I'm uprooting my entire life. Let's get out of here," Vivette said, slamming the door.

Robert zoomed through town, missing stoplights and barely tapping the brakes for stop signs. He eased onto I-95 toward Portland and accelerated to 85 mph.

"Hey," Vivette said, clutching the armrest. The car felt like it was about to vibrate into pieces. "I had no idea you were such an awful driver."

Robert slowed down a little. "Oh, sorry," he said. "I know, everybody gets on me about it. I grew up in Boston. It's in my veins. I can't obey traffic signs of any kind. Haven't you driven with me before? Hiking or something with Melinda?"

"I guess I never noticed," Vivette said. "Maybe I've never been in the front seat."

"It would help if I wore my glasses, I guess," Robert said. "Could you grab them? They're in the glove compartment."

Among crusty oil-change receipts Vivette found an ancient-looking case with wire-rimmed glasses folded inside. She handed them to Robert. He wrapped their fragile temples over his ears. They didn't sit straight on his nose and seemed to press up against his eyelashes. Vivette laughed.

"I guess you see why I never wear them," Robert said. "They're from high school."

"Well, they're too small for your face," Vivette said. "Maybe you could get an updated style? They're as bad as my outfit, so we're even. Keep them on."

"That's fair," Robert said. "So hey, I was thinking we could try this Afghani restaurant I've heard about in Portland."

"It's good. I've been there. There's only one thing," Vivette said. "You have to promise you'll share. It's much better when you share. Last time I went there with five other people and no one let me try their dish," Vivette said. "Can you promise that?"

"Sure, I'll do that, whatever you want. This is your party," Robert said.

He got fidgety and silent, pushed in a tape, and turned up the volume making further conversation impossible. The Talking Heads' *Stop Making Sense* led them into Portland.

The Afghani restaurant took up two tiny storefronts with tapestries on the walls and colorful candles on each table, dim and romantic. "They have this rosewater drink here. You should try it," Vivette said. "It's like drinking rose petals."

"Okay," Robert said, closing his menu. "Why don't you take charge of ordering since you're the worldly one? I'll just sit back and eat."

The waitress had long, shiny, black hair hanging straight down her back, a single stud earring in her nose. It shimmered as she moved her head from side to side, walking from table to table in the crowded dining room. Little bells jangled on her ankle bracelet. She smelled of jasmine.

Vivette picked out two entrees. The waitress nodded, and then turned to Robert as if Vivette's choices remained optional. "I'm wondering. Did you see the specials?" she asked. "There's a lamb dish that's fantastic." She leaned one hand on the table, made eye contact with him, smiled briefly at Vivette.

Robert stared at her, folded his hands on top of the table and said, "Sure, that sounds great. I've never been here before."

"Get whatever you want, Robert," Vivette said. "I don't like lamb, but that shouldn't matter."

The waitress said, "Good. Good choice. I think you'll like this." She tapped twice near Robert's plate. Smiled at him and walked away.

Robert patted Vivette's hand, smiled, looked around the place. He rubbed the top of her thumb with his own. "This is good, isn't it? I'm glad we came here. It's a sweet place."

After their meals arrived, the waitress leaned toward Robert. "Isn't that better?" she asked. Robert smiled with his mouth full, and she walked away, a shimmering jangle.

"So, you're leaving," Robert said. He wiped his mouth twice with his napkin.

Vivette sat back in her chair, looked at Robert, took a deep breath. "Yes, I am."

"And it's Des Moines? Is that what you said?"

"I think so. It's this idea I have in my head," Vivette said, nodding. "I'm thinking Des Moines." Vivette picked at her Kabob Palaw, setting the raisins aside in a neat pile before she ate the chicken.

"That's crazy, you know. I mean, nobody leaves New England and moves to Des Moines unless they have to. Unless they have a job, a reason, family there, something."

"Except me, of course," Vivette said. "I want to go there because I like the name. It intrigues me."

"Right. You mentioned that," Robert said. "The name. Well, you know, you should visit Margaret while you're out there. She's in Nebraska now. She and her husband Peter have a farmhouse out in the middle of nowhere they fixed up. It's supposed to be lovely, according to Susan, according to Margaret. Susan keeps wanting to visit, but Nebraska isn't exactly on the way to anything. It's definitely a special trip. You should give her a call, though. I know she'd love to have a guest."

"You talked to Susan about my move?" Vivette set her fork down, put her hands in her lap, had trouble swallowing.

"Well, yeah. I mean, why not?" Robert asked, setting down his fork in response to Vivette.

"I thought you kept the two separate, remember?"

"But we're over, so it doesn't matter anymore. That world in my bedroom is gone. Poof. Done. Doesn't exist," Robert said, picking up his fork waving it back and forth like a magic wand. He cut his lamb into careful slices, forked in rice between bites.

"That's it?" Vivette said.

"You said it was over. You're the one who said that," Robert said. "You said that in bed the other day, and you said it on the phone the other night. So, okay. It's over. I told Susan you told me you were moving to Des Moines and after her initial confusion over your choice, she suggested Margaret. Visiting her," Robert said.

"I guess I didn't expect such an on-and-off switch for our affair," Vivette said. She needed space. Immediately. She stood, walked quickly past the other tables with their snippets of enjoyable conversation, and toward the bathroom, down a narrow hallway. The wooden door clicked assuredly behind her. Vivette stared at her reflection, decided she had too many freckles. She looked sixteen years old in this plaid dress, with these green plastic earrings. She fiddled with them, put her hair into a long, loose braid. The waitress probably thought she was Robert's daughter. She whispered, "Robert, Robert, Robert," and leaned against the sink, her back to the mirror. "Going," she said.

Vivette returned to the table, doing her best to look refreshed, trying to begin again. "Hello," she said.

Robert said, "Oh, I don't think that's the right word. What you said before, 'affair.' That seems so scandalous."

"What would you call it?" Vivette asked, struggling to retain composure. If nothing else, she wanted to claim the word *mistress* from this period in her life.

"Oh, I don't know." Robert cleared his throat. "A little fling, maybe?" He turned his fork over, somersaulting it slowly along his plate. "Something between two close friends? I'll miss you. But I'm married, Vivette. Happily married," Robert said. "You've known that all along. No surprises there."

Vivette took a sip of her rosewater, swallowed liquid, velvety petals down her throat. "I'll call her," she said. "I'll try and hook up with Margaret. Nebraska is just one state over from Iowa—very close." She fiddled with her linen napkin, flopping it one way and then another. She thought about Robert in bed, how that time was so unlike this dinner date, how those weekends were placed out of the real world entirely—extracted. Looking at Robert in his clean shirt and jeans, she couldn't imagine having sex with him. She couldn't even imagine him naked.

Robert raised his hand for the waitress. "Could we get some coffee? And do you have some kind of dessert? Something with that rosewater in it? She loves the rosewater." He nodded to Vivette. "That'd be great."

He leaned toward Vivette, whispered, "I know you like the rosewater. I'm sure they'll have something nice."

Nothing was random. Everything up for grabs.

After leaving the restaurant, they stopped for a drink at a pub near the harbor. Vivette picked a tiny table at the window facing the street. It wobbled when she put her elbows along its edge.

In the next few weeks, as her remaining evenings in New Hampshire dwindled, Vivette met up in bigger and bigger groups. Everyone, it seemed, loved a going-away party. She tried not to think about Robert, who often left early with Susan. Melinda said they looked more in love than ever. "If that's possible," she said.

For Vivette it was just the end. She didn't know what she was looking for, but it was over, and Susan would never know. Vivette didn't have a lover or a job, and soon she wouldn't have friends or a home. Soon she'd wander the country alone in her car, searching to fill the kind of loss she already felt.

This was her comfort.

21 Margaret, New Hampshire

Margaret's TV offered only gray fuzz. For days she thought maybe Wesley needed some time to himself, some space. But with her patience dwindling, she called to see if he wanted to come over for dinner. Wesley was slow to decline, then when prodded reluctantly said he'd stop by, probably around ten o'clock.

The late-evening air trickled through her open windows. Margaret wore the button-down shirt Wesley had left hanging on the bedroom doorknob the week before. The silence of her apartment closed in on her. This act of being alone, of waiting, made her tense. The shirt's smooth cotton reassured her. Margaret rolled up the sleeves, checked herself in the hallway mirror, unfastened another button to show the top edge of her new lace bra. Wesley was two hours late.

In the kitchen the percolator hummed on warm by the stove. When she lifted it to pour a cup, the thick black handle snapped off, sending the chrome base to the floor like a giant slow-motion bullet, pulling the plug out of the socket on its way down. Soggy coffee grounds erupted out of the percolator's middle. Steaming brown liquid settled at the lowest point of her uneven kitchen floor.

Margaret pulled the mop out of the closet. Stale coffee mixed with Mr. Clean. The smell would linger for months.

Finally a knock at the door. When she opened it, Wesley looked confused. "What's wrong?" he asked.

"Why didn't you just use your key? I broke my grandmother's coffee pot," Margaret said. "It was important to me."

Wesley hugged her stiffly, formally, saying, "Let's sit down."

Margaret curled herself onto one end of the couch. Wesley sat awkwardly at the other. She stared at the far wall, tracing a fine crack in the plaster above and below a photo of herself and Susan on the beach. "Do you want a drink?"

Wesley hesitated and then said, "Sure. Yes, I'll have a drink, thanks."

In the kitchen, the open window fluttered some papers caught underneath the battered percolator on her kitchen table. She took two juice glasses from the kitchen cupboard, cracked ice cubes, poured whiskey halfway up, added a dash of water. Wesley stayed on the couch, looking around the room as if he'd never been there before.

He set his glass on the coffee table without taking a sip. "I want to break up," Wesley said.

Margaret laughed. "You want to break up? Come on Wesley, what are we, in high school? I'm sorry I was frustrated about the percolator when you came in."

Wesley stared at her and simply repeated himself.

Margaret focused on his hair, his eyes, his strong arms, trying to figure out what had changed between last week and now. She wanted to nestle up to him, but she suspected if she did those arms would stay at his sides. "Because I don't know how to do laundry?"

Wesley sighed, laughed. "No, Margaret," he said. He picked his glass up from the coffee table, jiggled it so the ice moved in a circle. Took a sip, set the glass down again, further away. "There's somebody else," he said. "This isn't how I wanted to tell you, but you were really persistent on the phone today."

Margaret smiled, forgetting herself for a moment. "I can be determined," she said.

"I've been meaning to come over," he said.

Margaret clutched the glass, moved her thumb in stiff circles over the purple flower painted on its side. She feared the glass would crush in her hand, and so she let up, saying, "We're breaking up? I wish I had a class ring to give back to you. No one, absolutely no one, says, 'I want to break up,' Wesley. They say, 'I want to see other people' or 'It's not working out' or 'I don't want to do this' or 'It's over.'"

"It's over, Margaret," Wesley said. He reached out and touched her knee, looked at her the way he always had, like he cared, like he wanted her to be happy, like he wanted her. Then, just as suddenly, he took his hand away, his face retreated, and Margaret couldn't find him again. "Olivia feels awful about this," Wesley said. "She wanted me to tell you that she just feels awful."

"Olivia," Margaret said, carefully setting her glass on the floor. "O.K. Kingsley." She didn't look at him and instead stared at her arms on her knees, the juice glass going out of focus at her feet. Everything far away now. "Of course," Margaret said. Then she couldn't stop herself. Words came freely before she could rein them in. "You'll regret this, you know. You aren't thinking it through, Wesley. It's a bad decision. You'll look back on your life and know this was when everything went wrong. Olivia is in love with Rufus. Everybody knows that," Margaret said. "What do you think you're going to do, save her? Is that it?" Her eyes watered, and Margaret could only study the ribbed pattern of the rug now. She grabbed a Kleenex, made herself stop crying. "What in the fuck are you doing? Don't you understand? You're the one. I love you, Wesley." The words sounded foreign in her mouth.

"Olivia and I have been trying to be friends for so long now, and it isn't working," Wesley said. "There's more to it though. I just don't see a future in you and me." He raised his hands to demonstrate the futility. Then Wesley leaned back and looked out the window.

Margaret realized he was already gone, already outside, away at high-society events with Olivia using the correct fork and laughing smugly at a dinner table buzzing with snippets of French.

"Why? Why won't it work out?" Margaret said.

"Margaret," Wesley said, "don't do this,"

"Will you still be my friend? Will both of you still be my friends? You were supposed to take me to New York."

Wesley looked at her, looked down at his hands. Looked at her again. "I've got to get going, Margaret. Olivia is waiting for me. I was just at her place, talking all this over. She's expecting me back."

Margaret leaned across the couch and buried her face into his chest. She could smell his familiar earthy scent. She whispered, "Hold me." And he did. She closed her eyes. They held each other for what seemed like a long time before she said, "I'm going to miss you."

"I'm going to miss you too," Wesley said. And then he left.

The next day Margaret regretted it all. Regretted the hug, that she listened to his footsteps on the stairs, that she waited to hear her front door squeak open and click closed, and then waited to hear his truck drive away. She regretted sitting on the couch, listening even after that. The motor on the refrigerator. The breeze carrying her neighbors' muffled laughter. Jangly pop music bubbling in from a passing car.

She'd refilled her whiskey glass and continued on that way through to the first light of day — its muggy start at her windows, its slow creep across her rug. She called in sick, and then wouldn't answer the phone when it rang. She didn't change her clothes or eat. She knew the second she moved from the couch her entire world would pop and zip across the universe like a deflated balloon.

Her coffeepot was broken. Wesley was gone. She wore his coffee-stained shirt. Olivia's painting hung in her bedroom. The morning light turned against Margaret, made her apartment ugly and dirty, her reflection in the TV sad and gray. Wesley was gone, and she regretted everything.

22 *Wesley, New Hampshire*

After leaving Margaret's apartment, getting away as quickly as he could, Wesley put the key into the ignition, looked up at her windows. He remembered the first night he pulled into her gravel driveway. Finally he'd met the pretty woman at the bakery with the blue eyes. He'd nearly thrown his back out lugging a dresser up her skinny staircase.

He started the truck, hesitated, drove away.

On the outskirts of town, nearing the ocean, he pulled over. Big rocks heaved up silhouettes at the edges of the dune. Wesley scrambled up their rough sides through the darkness.

The sharp salt air stung his eyes as the dark waves crashed and settled beneath him. Wesley marveled at how much of his life came down to chance. Running into Margaret, visiting Olivia. He could have met two totally different women, lived an entirely different life. With a tight orbit, he knew the possibilities weren't endless, though. He liked his routines. People knew his name. No big-city address needed. He made this clear to Olivia. There was no going back to New York for him, and no discussion about it.

"Done," he said softly. He stared out at the waves without another thought.

Back at the cottage he struggled with the front door, jiggling the key. He could never lift the latch the right way. Olivia, anxious on a stool in the kitchen, her back rigid, legs crossed, wore a tank top and shorts, her hair pulled up, which meant she'd just been exercising. An unlit cigarette wobbled between two stiffly extended fingers. "There you are," she said, relieved, as the door gave way. "I thought you'd never come back. How was it? How's Margaret?"

Wesley told her the story, starting with Margaret and her broken percolator, leading to her giving him a whiskey, and finishing with her asking for a hug on the couch. Olivia paced, nodding her head like she was counting off a checklist.

"And did you give her a hug?" Olivia asked, looking up to study his face.

"That wouldn't have been a wise thing to do," Wesley said.

Olivia patted him on the back. "You were good to her, Wesley. You were good, but why were you gone so long?"

"I stopped to sit by myself for a while, Olivia. Get my head together. I stopped to have a few minutes to myself." He walked toward the window seat. "What are you doing with a cigarette? You don't smoke." Olivia shrugged, set the cigarette on the kitchen counter, trailed behind him.

"Did she say anything about me?" Olivia asked, crossing her arms over her chest.

"Well, she basically said, 'I can't believe you two are doing this to me.' And, 'How can we all still be friends?' Does that come as a surprise?" Wesley rubbed his eyes.

"She's upset," Olivia said. "Of course. But it's over. We just need to remain autonomous." Without lipstick on, she looked like a little girl practicing a vocabulary list. Faint dark moons puffed under her eyes. She stole a quick glance at her latest work in progress.

Wesley hugged Olivia, her thin, hard body curving into his. Over her shoulder, the sand, the ocean, the moon smeared the rolling clouds. "It'll be fine," he said. "I told her nothing happened between us. I told her that, okay? Just like you suggested. It went fine. I don't think she was that upset. Give her a few days."

"You're right," Olivia said, putting her feet on his lap, curling her arm around his neck. "I wanted to try and fit in here, find my place. I thought Margaret could be part of it. But now you're a part of it. You're it, Wesley." She kissed his rough cheek.

Wesley returned Olivia's kiss with a peck on her creased forehead. "Let's take a walk on the beach," he said, "a long walk before the sun comes up."

23   *Margaret, New Hampshire*

Gert took one look and said, "What happened?" when Margaret made it into work the next week. A baseball cap pulled low to cover her limp hair, a gray T-shirt and cut-off shorts. Margaret's eyes were liquid, and she had a cold.

Margaret smiled. "Wesley broke up with me."

As soon as she stepped foot in the bakery, Margaret knew in her version of events there would be bad guys and good guys. It wouldn't be a modern love story with mature and complacent players. No. She would set things straight.

Gert turned up the music, whispered, "Who's Wesley fucking?"

"Olivia," Margaret said.

"That super-fit little New Yorker?"

"Yep. That's her. I was starting to like her, too. I mean, she was pursuing me, working hard to be my friend. It was like a courtship. But all along it must've been a way to get in with Wesley." Margaret sniffed, pulled a Kleenex out of her pocket, and blew her nose. "She and Wesley have been friends for years. They went to some stuffy prep school together. Their parents know each other. I don't know," Margaret said. "Wesley's with Olivia, and I can't get it out of my head."

Gert gave her a hug. "Well," she said, "at least you know he has good taste."

"Good taste," Margaret said. "Gert, he dumped me. What am I, runner-up?"

"That wasn't what I meant," Gert said. She started a new pot of coffee. "I mean, at least he's going out with someone you like. I know that sounds lame, but it's something, isn't it?"

Margaret rolled her eyes.

Gretchen strode in through the back door wearing her tan fly-fishing vest adorned with hand-tied flies, fuzzy hooks with names like Wooly Bugger and Yellow Sally Descending. As she grabbed a baguette to take on her fishing trip, she eavesdropped on parts of their conversation. "Wesley was at the Press Room last night drinking wine with some swanky dark-haired type," she said. "When did all this happen? Last I knew you were in love, love, love." Gert and Margaret stared at her. "What? Am I being insensitive again? Sorry. I never liked the guy."

"Gretchen, you don't like anybody," Gert said, making herbal tea for Margaret and pouring it over ice.

Gretchen shrugged, went out the back door. Came back in,

gave Margaret a whisper of a hug, said, "I'm sorry," and walked out again.

"Don't listen to her. She probably doesn't even know who they are," Gert said. "You sit in the back for a while, pull yourself together. It's slow today. I'll take care of this." She waved her hand back and forth at the line of customers.

Margaret lay on the back counter where no one could see her, the icy mug resting on her chest, pressure building in her sinuses. It was no use. She sat up, her head a balloon. After swinging her feet a few times for momentum, she sighed and grabbed an apron, made her way back to Gert.

Margaret tried to focus by making a list on the back of a lunch bag of the cookies she needed to bake. When she looked up, she saw Wesley and Olivia strolling through the parking lot, swinging their clasped hands, walking through town for all the world to see.

"Perfect," Margaret said.

That night she eyed the road beneath her kitchen window, listened to her downstairs neighbors laughing, fighting, making up. She couldn't sleep. Empty plates and silverware had found their way into her bed. Half a newspaper, dirty clothes, photographs, and a pile of half-read books. She burrowed underneath.

The next day Susan barged in, picked out clothes, and pulled Margaret to State Street Saloon. There they took up stools at the dark end of the bar to drink scotch and watch Robert and his friends play pinball.

"So do you think they were doing it all along?" Susan asked, swirling her drink with her straw, sticking it in her mouth like a cigarette, plunging it back into her drink again.

"I don't know," Margaret said. "There was a night when Olivia asked me about my sex life with Wesley." She stared at the tin ceiling above her, then at Susan. "It was good sex. I mean, that can't be one-sided, right? I mean. I don't think they were doing it, because why would she have to ask me anything? I was the scout on this expedition. Olivia let me go in, check out the territory, and then she invaded. Pow."

"He did seem really into it," Susan said. "A little too fussy for your tastes, if you want the word on the street. Everybody thought you'd end up walloping him. But when I saw you two together it seemed like he adored you and all that." Susan shrugged. "Minimum requirement."

"I hate break-up stories, and now it's me," Margaret said. "Never again. Next time you have to give your seal of approval before the first date. An actual A-OK stamp on his forehead. I'll bring him by for an interview."

"Definitely," Susan said, laughing. "I'll put him through the wringer." She took a long look at Margaret, smoothed the napkin under her drink. "Hey, what's wrong? It's a breakup. You'll be fine. I promise I'll stamp the next guy. I'll write up a questionnaire and ask for references. It'll be rigorous. Don't you worry about that."

"Here's the problem," Margaret said, "How many more relationships can I stand? I mean, he implied he wanted to be with someone more cultured. He implied that our relationship was futile. Actually, what he said was he didn't see a future in it. Like a stock. I've been divested." Margaret worked away at her own damp napkin, shredding it around the base of her glass until just a rough, pulpy circle remained.

The pinball machine popped a free game. The guys cheered. Margaret looked down at the swirling center of her drink.

"It's a weird scene," Susan said. "I think Olivia's crazy. It's good you're out of it."

"I'd take him back in a heartbeat," Margaret said. She stopped for a moment to think, and then said, "Yep."

"Oh Jesus, Margaret," Susan said.

"I'll always be a part of them, the glue holding them together," Margaret said. "They're wallowing in me right now." She rested her chin on her cupped palm. "You know it."

They both stared at the Miller beer sign behind the bar. It boasted two men dressed in flannel and corduroy, fishing from a canoe on a peaceful lake. "Live the High Life," it read.

Susan picked up a fresh napkin from the stack at the bar, wiped both of Margaret's cheeks. She smiled at Sally the bartender who crinkled her forehead and frowned. "Margaret," Susan said, "knock it off."

"The problem is going cold turkey. It messes with your head," Margaret said. She grabbed a menu off the counter. "I don't know, I think maybe we should order something. Garlic toast?" She pushed her old drink away, pulled her new one in, drew her straw around in circles.

The pinball machine, idle while the guys waited for quarters from Sally, played the *Addams Family* theme song, the flippers magically making the double snap at the end without anybody pushing them. More quarters and someone pushed the illuminated start button three times. The bar filled and smoke wafted to the ceiling, lazing around and heading in a puff out the door each time it was opened. Margaret and Susan drank. Talk circled back to Wesley and Olivia, making a deep groove through the conversation as the night wore on.

Margaret picked at her garlic toast, peeling the mushy buttered bread away from the crust. She looked toward the blinking pinball machine and said to Susan, "There's room for a fourth. I want to play." She sauntered over and offered up a quarter. Shoulders parted when it was her turn. She knew how to work the machine, how to use her hips to give the flippers a boost, nudge the metal frame to keep the ball bouncing in the right direction. Lights flashed. The score tallied. "Thing," a rubber hand, edged up from the underworld of the machine and took her ball. She was given another and another and soon four balls were spinning toward her at once. She was ready. Bells chimed and then came the reassuring tap-tap: free game. The guys high-fived her before she walked back to Susan and her seat. Margaret said, "Culture, my ass."

"From where I sit?" Susan said. "Wesley doesn't know what he's missing."

24
Vivette, Nebraska

Vivette rinses strawberries at the sink. "So, who's coming tonight?" she asks.

Margaret focuses on making brownies while thinking about the introductions, the clever anecdotes, the overlapping worlds and times of her life, all the expectations of a party at her house. "Well, I don't know exactly," she admits. "We don't have parties very often."

Margaret measures out flour, oats, cocoa, salt, and baking powder. Bittersweet chocolate and butter melt in the double-boiler on the stove.

Vivette reminds herself that she's a guest, and that her job is to make it through the party without offending anyone, and then get into her car and drive away the next day. The strawberries in a big colander, she slices each one into thin sections after cutting off its spiked green cap. "You know," she says, "it seems like I think better out here where it's flat. There aren't any hills or coastlines to hem me in. When I was out walking the other day before the storm, I had all these crazy thoughts ricocheting around in my head. It was kind of peaceful to just let them go. That had never happened to me before."

"Yeah, some days it's like my brain starts to hum," Margaret says. "The plains can definitely stretch things out to make room for some unexpected epiphanies."

"I don't know about that, but it did make me take some deep breaths," Vivette says. "You know, it's easier to let go when you know someone's not going to come up and tap you on the shoulder."

"You'll be spic and span by the time you head out into your new life," Margaret says. "And you're still thinking Des Moines?" She cracks eggs and whisks maple syrup into the velvety chocolate-butter mixture.

"I'll start there, for sure. I mean I'm out here to move to Des Moines. That's the goal," Vivette says. "There's supposed to be this cool, restored hotel there, the Kirkenwood—from the 1930s? I saw a postcard of it. They have a big neon sign out front. I thought I'd stay there for a week, see if they can give me a discount. I mean, they can't be crowded, right? I think they'll be psyched to have a week's commitment."

"Unless it's rodeo season or the blues festival, I think you're golden," Margaret says.

"I think Des Moines might work," Vivette says. "I can make anywhere work for a year. I'll give Des Moines a year."

"That's funny. That's the same thing I said about Nebraska, and look at me."

The timer rings, and Vivette pulls her tart shell out of the oven. It's just starting to crisp and brown along its short scalloped edges. She sets it onto the cooling rack, then pulls the piece of waxed paper off the top of the custard she made that morning. She heats up the currant jam for glazing. Margaret asks her to take the oven down to 350.

"Did you miss the bakery after you left?" Vivette asks. Already she feels pangs of homesickness.

"I missed making food for people who appreciate great food. It was fun being a part of all that. I just needed to leave, you know. I guess if I could've taken the bakery with me, I would have. In some ways I did, right? That place whipped me into shape."

"Yeah, it's great knowing any time of day or night you can stop in and someone will be there baking. I love that part," Vivette says. "Sometimes in the middle of night, I'd think about Francie baking on through. It was like having a town crier saying all's well."

Vivette takes the glaze off the stove, feels the bottom of the tart. Still too warm. "Did you ever think you'd move back?"

"Just once," Margaret says. "just after I left, actually. I headed out into the great unknown in my old beat-up Datsun. It was December, and I was towing one of those little U-Haul trailers? God knows why I felt the need to leave in the dead of winter, carting all my stuff with me, but it seemed important at the time. Anyway, I was halfway across Nebraska when this ice storm hit. Cars and trucks were flying off the road. Pretty scary.

"I edged my way off into a truck stop and just sat there shaking. It was snowing ice, everything seizing up. Right then I thought, 'I'm going home.' And I realized that's what happens when people come back a month later. You know, you see them waiting tables but at a different restaurant? Something comes up, it seems insurmountable, and they buckle under the pressure, turn around, and head back home to what they know, tail between their legs.

"I just couldn't face everyone after I'd wrapped everything up. I felt like I had something to prove. So I got out my atlas and figured if I drove back east, back through Nebraska on Interstate 80, I could get to a major highway that went south. Then I could take the southern route to the West Coast, change my plans. So I did that. I went into the restaurant and drank tea and wrote furiously in my journal until the waitress told me she heard the roads were getting better. I got back onto the highway and started driving. Of course, I had to retreat a little, which was discouraging. That's when I realized how big Nebraska is. No way around it.

"It was pretty driving through New Mexico and Arizona at night. The stars were unbelievable. Roadrunners and armadillos. It worked, and I kept going until I hit California. It was my first test, and I passed."

Margaret finishes spooning the brownie batter into the baking pan. It's glossy and thick with chunks of chocolate and roasted walnuts. She rests the wooden spoon in the bowl and runs her hands along her apron, spreading a thin line of chocolate down her front. After she puts the dish in the oven, the gas kicks on with a hiss.

Vivette checks the inside of the tart shell again, spoons the custard in, and smoothes it flat. She lines up the strawberries on the creamy bed, like she's dealing a hand of cards. Vivette says, "I wonder what my test will be?" The strawberries glisten as she brushes them with the glaze.

Margaret takes off her apron, leaves the brownie bowl soaking in the sink. "I need to get ready," she says. "Do you mind checking the brownies when the timer goes off?" Margaret shuts the bathroom door and has the water running almost immediately. Vivette stares out the kitchen window.

The sheep are moving in big circles. It looks like gym class, running, running, their little hooves dead set on getting nowhere. Vivette looks at her hands covered with strawberry goo, rinses them clean.

The party is bustling. A small group of people near the fireplace, a few more at the dining room table. The smokers are out on the porch creating a cloudy exhaust that rises up tidily through the yellow cast of the porch light.

The tart is gone. The brownies, just crumbs. The chips and salsa are still in good supply. Peter, thinking ahead, rummages through cupboards looking for the popcorn. He pulls out a bright red box, puts a packet in, shuts the microwave's door, and presses start. The machine rotates the flat bag as it shakes to life.

Vivette keeps Peter company.

"So, did you meet everybody?" Peter asks, holding the steaming bag by its edges. He puts a second one in.

"I think so. I was talking with Elaine? The woman you work with? About quilts? She says you can find amazing handmade quilts at the thrift stores around here."

"Elaine would know. You should see her kids. They're totally hip in outfits that cost about two dollars each."

The second bag done, Peter dumps it into another bowl.

Vivette pulls herself up onto the counter. Peter hands her a beer from the fridge.

"So, you didn't grow up in Nebraska, did you?" Vivette asks.

"Me? No, no. I grew up in Chicago. My whole family is still there. I left behind a whole big thing. I was married before, you know. Did suburbia full on. Don't look so surprised. It happens to the best of us."

"I remember you mentioned being married before," Vivette says, "but suburbia? I guess I didn't put that together with a whole different life. What was your first wife like?"

"Oh, I don't talk about it much. She was fine. She was nice. Ann," he says. "Two people in the wrong place at the wrong time, wanting totally different things but not knowing it. I was afraid if I didn't leave when I did neither of us would ever be happy." Peter dumps a third bag of popcorn into a basket he has lined with a pink napkin.

"Did you guys get along? I mean, did you have stuff in common or were you a totally different person then?"

Peter grabs a bottle of vodka from the freezer and two small glasses from the cupboard, raises them in Vivette's direction. After Vivette accepts the invitation to a shot, Peter says, "I always end up in the kitchen at parties, how about you?"

Vivette holds her glass up, Peter splashes vodka in, then hits his alongside.

"To the kitchen," he says.

"I'm sorry I'm asking so many questions," Vivette says. "I'm trying to revise my life."

"I'm sorry to say it," Peter says hoisting himself up onto the counter beside her, "but it's a complete accident that Margaret and I found each other. I don't think it had anything to do with revision on my part."

"Oh," Vivette says, "that's not the right answer. I need to have hope that being happy has something to do with making something happen. I have to believe that. It's amazing to me that you're so well-adjusted after the divorce, that you don't have any lingering animosity toward Ann."

"Ann? No. That was a long time ago," Peter says. "If anything I harbor a lot of guilt, because I knew it wasn't going to work way before she did, and I stayed in the thing because I was a chicken."

"Wow. Blow my mind," Vivette says. She grabs two of the popcorn bowls, puts her beer into the pocket of her overalls. Peter grabs the third and follows behind her.

Vivette finds Margaret, stands near her the rest of the evening when she isn't out with the smokers. Margaret has come alive with small talk and makes a point of introducing Vivette to everyone as her good friend from back east. Vivette walks into the kitchen every so often to sip from her vodka glass, kept waiting for her by the sink. If she meets Peter, they toast to the kitchen, to popcorn, to the diligent smokers on the porch.

At the end of the night she holds up her glass to tap his and has an overwhelming urge to tell him about her postcard to Robert. *Wesley was right,* she thinks. *Once you tell a secret, it just keeps leaking out. No wonder Joe-Joe insisted on a tire gauge. It's symbolic. Keep to yourself. Stop the leaks.*

Beyond her control, her confession forms into sentences that she whispers to Peter. Words she can't keep straight combine with facts in combinations she won't remember in the morning.

Later in bed, after all the dishes have been stacked in the sink, all the empty beer bottles shoved into boxes, Peter rubs Margaret's shoulders.

"I told Vivette about Ann tonight," Peter says. "She seemed shocked that I was married before—like she had to revise her ongoing 'How to Get a Man' guide. I don't know. I think Vivette needs to relax a little."

Peter rotates Margaret's shoulder blades in little circles.

"That feels amazing," Margaret says. "Can you hear all the crackly things in there moving around? I know *I* need to relax a little. You, however, seem very, very relaxed. Exactly how much of whatever bottle you started did you finish?"

"Finished. But I had help," Peter says, not feeling half as drunk as he is.

"I always think no one is going to show at parties," Margaret says. "Then when they do, I'm worried about running out of food." She's buzzing from all the words, from all the effort of sustaining the conversations like spinning plates to move the evening forward.

There's a patch of silence. Peter stops rubbing. Margaret stares at the smooth skin on her own forearm, thinks that the glow from the bedside lamp makes it look beautiful, like someone else's perfect skin, not her own.

"You know," Peter says. "I think there might have been something between Vivette and Robert."

"Robert Gooding? Nah. I mean, he called for her the other day. Was that yesterday? Yes, he called then, left a message," Margaret says.

Peter says, "He did? Well, that's interesting. I can't really say why, but Vivette mentioned some weird stuff about a postcard and heartbreak and impulses. That's the word she used. Impulses. Then she went a little stream of consciousness, and I couldn't follow her. She kept leaving out verbs and pronouns. She was pretty drunk, and she was whispering. But I did hear Joe-Joe and something about a tire gauge and then Robert. I think they were having an affair."

"Hmmm." Margaret is nodding off. She wants to hear this story, but she also doesn't think it's true so she remains suspended near dozing.

"I don't know," Peter says, sitting on the edge of the bed. "There was something about John G. Neihardt and one true love and letters and Robert? Or no, postcards to Robert? Postcards to Joe-Joe? Throwing them out the car window?"

"No way," Margaret says, "Robert and Susan are the couple I can count on—everyone counts on them. And your argument shifts the entire axis of the earth. Thus, it isn't true, even if it is, because I'm too tired to think about it tonight. In fact, I think this may all be a dream."

Peter kisses her neck. "Let's make up," he whispers into her hair.

"Are we fighting?" Margaret asks.

"No, but it's good to do it anyway, just in case."

They try not to make the bed creak in the silent house. The comfort of Margaret's arms around his neck, playing down his back, pulling him toward her. After kissing, after smoothing Margaret's hair against her pillow, pulling the sheet up close around her neck, after she's asleep, Peter stands by the window looking out over the fields he knows are there but can't see with the new moon hiding it all.

25

Margaret, Lincoln, Nebraska

Handmade shelves lined the walls of Peter's apartment floor-to-ceiling. Little glass bottles and stones were scattered in front of the books. Freshly vacuumed carpet. In the kitchen, three white plates stood single file in the drying rack.

"Anticipate we might end up at your apartment?" Margaret asked as she peeled off her coat, threw it over a chair in the living room.

"I've had to keep this place spotless through four dates," Peter said. "Don't know how much longer I could've kept the kitchen clean."

"Are these yours?" Margaret asked walking over to the photographs on the opposite wall.

Peter rooted around in the kitchen cupboards. "I know I have filters somewhere," he said. "I just bought some."

"Who's that woman? She's beautiful," Margaret said, as her shoes squeaked across the kitchen floor. "You mopped?"

"Well, it needed it anyway," Peter said, opening a kitchen drawer, shutting it. Opening another. "That's Angela. Someone I used to know. No, no they aren't mine. They were a gift."

"They're very good," Margaret said. "Is she a model?"

Peter pulled a bag of coffee out of the freezer and promptly spilled beans on the counter. "I swear. I do this every day all by myself," he said. "Yes, she's a model I used to date. Those were taken by some famous Brazilian photographer. She thought my walls were too bare." Peter suddenly stopped his search and stood perfectly still. He turned to Margaret and was about to say, "Those will be down by tomorrow," but instead he took both of her hands and asked, "Do you have any idea what I could use for a filter? I can't find the pack I bought at the Hinky Dinky yesterday, and I've promised coffee to this lovely woman I've lured to my apartment."

After improvising with a paper towel in the coffeemaker, Peter handed Margaret a mug. In the living room, he turned off the overhead light, switched on a lamp, and put in the Cowboy Junkies.

Margaret said, "I hate to ask if you have any sugar."

"I do. One minute," he said. Three cupboards opened and banged shut, one drawer, the refrigerator. Finally, Peter held out a pink and white bag of sugar for Margaret, a spoon extended from its top. "Found the filters in the refrigerator with the sugar," he said, flopping the plastic packet back and forth.

Peter sat close to Margaret on the couch, his arm around her, tapping his fingers on the backrest to the beat of the music. Slowly he rubbed the thin cotton of her shirt between his fingers, lifting it from her shoulder, pressing it down again, smoothing it. He ran his fingers through the ends of her hair and smiled at her when she turned to face him.

Margaret wondered about diving in. There was the brief moment on land when she was still dry and safe, the hesitation, and then the sudden sinking as she became weightless.

She rested a hand on Peter's thigh, leaned her head on his shoulder, pushed off and swam far from shore.

Side by side, they listened to the music, knowing that the rest of their lives was beginning. Knowing there was time to patiently usher it in. Cautiously they met their future. No games or false starts. They refilled their mugs.

They kissed.

26 *Robert, New Hampshire*

The phone is a black bug, ready to bite. Robert checks the bedroom door, makes sure it's closed. He fingers through Susan's little blue address book.

He waits. When Peter and Margaret's machine starts in, he hangs up.

Deep breath. Again. Redial.

He smoothes the fringe of the blanket into straight lines, messes it up. Smoothes it.

Peter's voice, then a long double beep.

Robert leaves his message, puts the phone on its base, opens the bedroom door, walks down the stairs, and out onto the front porch where Susan rocks in the porch swing. Reading, one toe of her foot on the floorboards, the rusty chains making a nostalgic creak. The puppy scampers back and forth, its leash tied to the rail. Susan looks up when she hears the screen door slam.

"Hey, baby. Where have you been?"

Robert smiles. "I love you," he says, as he sits beside her. She smiles, pats his knee, goes back to reading, puts her feet up into his lap. Robert rocks them both, his feet planted firmly on the floor.

As he rocks, a final Saturday morning with Vivette comes to mind, making coffee in the kitchen. The Italian stove-top espresso maker. NPR on the radio, twisting the bent antenna to get better reception. A package of shortbread cookies in the old chrome bread bin on the counter. Robert picked two teacups that had pink flowers circling their rims. Milk into another small cup. The sugar bowl. Everything on a tray he carried to the bedroom.

In the doorway he listened, head turned to the side. Vivette was asleep. He walked back downstairs, set the tray in the living room, turned up the radio, and opened the newspaper. He knew if he made enough noise, she'd wake up on her own, head home, start her day away from him so he could begin his trek back to Susan.

27   *Margaret, New Hampshire*

Streetlights popped on in rounds down the chilly street. Margaret hurried through the swarming dusk of her apartment to get out the door. Splashing water on her face didn't clear the fog. She preferred the rooms with no lights, covered in deep shadows, fading sun melting into dark night, the color of dreams.

Margaret floated through these days. Sleep was a relief. No problems there, just dreams and clear, black infinity. Off work, she hurried home, but with nothing to do. She took any baking shift offered. This made her sleeping schedule chaotic and unbearable, but she gathered some savings. Days collapsed in on themselves. Dreams bled into waking thoughts. Six in the morning and six in the evening were twins.

On the street she was better, the fog clearing. The fall air made her long for something she couldn't place, which gave her comfort. Her wool sweater, the brown and green and mustard-yellow scratchy yarn, helped keep her calm with its sweet musty smell.

Hands in pockets, head down, she willed herself forward. Susan was waiting for her. But still it was a burden, all this movement, all this undoing of what had so recently dominated every thought.

She wasn't good at it, after all. She couldn't get on with her life. Or wouldn't.

Susan sat at the table closest to the bakery door, tapping her foot, reading a crumpled *New Yorker* three weeks old. Tracy Chapman bubbled over the stereo system. Susan, her bobbed brown hair caught behind an ear, looked calm, happy, and content as Margaret scraped the chair across from her back from the table.

"Hello, Missy," Susan said, looking up. "What's shakin'?"

Margaret smiled, touched Susan's cheek, "Oh, you know, sleeping too much, working too much. Wondering what I'm doing with my life. The usual." Margaret swiped a loose strand of hair behind her ear.

"Get some coffee," Susan said. "I'll split a dessert with you. You pick. Whatever your heart desires."

Margaret nudged her chair back, grabbed two forks from the bin, and snuck behind the counter to get a slice of linzer torte. At the table, she absently held the forks suspended in one hand, staring out the bank of windows at herself in the reflection and the streetlights beyond, the parking lot, the glass bubble of the bank drive-through lane.

Just then, a woman rushed across the lot, loaded down with shopping bags and a bouquet of bright red and yellow roses wrapped in green tissue paper. A puff of pungent perfume followed her through the front door to the table beside Susan's, where another woman cupped a mug of Earl Grey and skimmed *Redbook* with bright red fingernails.

The woman tipped the bouquet this way and that as she peeled off her long, leather coat. "Hello, Joy," she said breathlessly. "I hope you haven't been waiting too long. I just had to stop and pick up some flowers. It's something I do for myself every week these days, because I deserve it," she said. The woman smoothed her short jean skirt, her bright red top on her skinny, wilted frame.

Her friend said something, a soft murmur. "Yes, I know, divorce does have its advantages. I never would've bought flowers for myself when I was with Steve, and we both know he certainly never did." Her bracelets jangled as she made her way to the counter, her boots a dull click, her anxiety palpable. The bouquet lay sideways across an empty table.

Margaret pulled the magazine down from Susan's face, whispered, "If I'm ever like that, do whatever it takes, okay?"

"Like what?" Susan knew not to look.

"That woman there," Margaret twitched her head, "with the *flowers*. If I'm ever just running around spending all my time chasing nothing," she whispered quickly, "tagging after men who don't give a shit about me, if people start pitying me, if I start fucking buying flowers for myself once a week and parading them around like a prom queen, just kill me, okay?"

"Oh, Margaret, you're going to be just fine," Susan said slowly, distracted now by the woman at the counter. She shoved the magazine into her bag. "What's up?" she said.

"You know, the usual, contemplating a life of celibacy," Margaret said. "I don't feel like I'm good at judging anything lately."

"Honey," Susan said, taking a bite of torte and rolling her eyes. "You're going to have sex again. Probably tonight, knowing you. I just don't see that being a major problem heading into your golden years. You need some time. You need to kick some ass, here, okay? Don't let them win."

The woman returned from the counter with two cookies balanced on top of her mug. Her smile expanded as she glanced around the room. "This place is cute, isn't it? I love exploring. Here's a treat for us."

Susan nudged Margaret. "You need a strategy. Maybe a haircut? A new apartment? A one-night stand?"

"I'll try anything," Margaret said. "Maybe I can start with a really short haircut? Move on to a really long one-night stand?" She made designs in the raspberry jam with her fork. "How are you and Robert so happy? What's the secret? You guys make me sick. What if all the Roberts in the world are taken?"

"Margaret, it isn't that easy," Susan said. "It's hard sometimes. You also lose some freedom in a long-term relationship, you know? I envy how you can make decisions all on your own. I know you're lonely right now, and I know I'm lucky I found somebody, but you have to remember there's frustration on both sides of it." Susan's face clouded. "There's a lot of compromising," she said. She took a deep breath. "Sometimes I think you're too up, too full-on, all the crazy-fun guys rush to you, zoom right in. You need to decide what you want." Susan gazed into her coffee cup, tipped it back and forth.

"I need some more coffee," Margaret said. She carried her mug to the counter, leaned across to grab the coffee pot so Gert wouldn't have to stop midway through cake decorating, poured her own, carried the pot to Susan, and then refilled a few mugs at a friend's table near the bathroom. "But I like to have fun," Margaret said after she returned to their table. "I need spontaneity."

"I know," Susan said, "that's the flip side. I feel lazy some days. I miss the electricity."

Her chin in her hands, elbows on the table, Margaret said, "Do you think we're ever really happy? Any of us? Or are we all just looking for what we don't have?"

"Robert says women think too much. Maybe he's right," Susan said. She looked at her watch, looked at Margaret, shrugged, and grabbed her magazine again. "Better than thinking too little, is what I always say."

The bakery world rotated on its tiny axis. Margaret watched, her head somewhere else entirely.

A young woman strode through the bakery door with purple suede sneakers, a pair of polka-dotted men's boxers hitting her thighs, and a T-shirt with a big, glittery red heart riding high on her chest. There was a spark, a desperado spunk to her step, as she studied the cookies in the case, gravitated toward the pies and the "counter help wanted, needed" sign, up once again.

Susan said, "I swear. This place, there's some magnetic pull. A home for wayward women, and they get younger every year."

The young woman leaned over the counter, rocking onto the very tiptoes of her rubber soles. She watched Gert, patiently hunched over a cake with a tube of pink frosting. "Hi, I'm Vivette," she said, putting a hand up to mess with the clip in her hair. "That's a really gorgeous cake." Gert and Vivette talked as Margaret and Susan eavesdropped. Vivette was new in town, in to go to the university at Durham, but after a semester she had lost interest and was taking some time off from being an undeclared liberal arts major to find a job. Vivette asked for a piece of pecan pie, walked past Margaret and Susan to a table at the far end of the room, a brown paper bag tucked under her plate.

Susan watched Margaret over the top of the magazine.

"What?" Margaret asked.

"I have something to tell you," she said.

"What?"

"I'm afraid to tell you because you'll lose your shit. But I have to tell you because you're my best friend."

Margaret sighed. "You're engaged," she said.

Susan flipped the magazine to the floor. "How did you know?"

"It just came into my head," Margaret said.

"That's incredible," Susan said. "My mom didn't even guess, and she's practically psychic."

"I'm so happy for you," Margaret said. "Really, I am. And I won't lose my shit, I promise."

But she already missed Susan. Right there on the spot. She could feel her shifting away, floating into another category of woman. Like switching lines at the grocery store, regular to express.

28
Margaret, New Hampshire

On a Saturday morning, as winter weather hit full-on, Margaret walked into town in a green wool jacket that hit at her waist, a blue-and-white polka-dotted scarf wrapped tightly around her neck, a short black skirt with black leggings, and dingo boots. At the last minute, she put on sunglasses to complete the outfit. Susan, Robert, Scott, and a bunch of friends had planned late-afternoon mimosas at Scott's house and then a movie. The air was crisp, her cheeks red. Puffs of fog came in quick bursts from her lips as she hurried along, happy to be walking to see her friends, the people who loved her unconditionally, loved her even though she was a pain in the ass. A bottle of cheap champagne tucked under her arm, the newspaper in her bag, purple mittens, and a new haircut. She felt too good to be true.

If she'd thought about it, she would've guessed it. As she rounded the corner of Market onto Library Street, she stumbled into Wesley, but it felt nothing like fate.

Margaret feigned indifference as she looked at him over the top of her glasses. She looked good, and she knew it. Wesley, on the other hand, looked tired. She'd never seen the coat he wore and didn't like it. It was puffy and had a metallic sheen. He stepped back, away from her, as if to confirm his view.

"Hello, Wesley," Margaret said, then she walked away.

That evening Margaret picked up the phone. She still knew the number by heart. Phoning Wesley was forbidden. Susan told her not to call under any circumstances, and she was right. Margaret would just be feeding into Olivia and Wesley's weird shit, making their relationship about three people instead of two. She made Margaret promise never to call. And yet, seeing Wesley on the street nudged her back into an old pattern.

But now it was done. The call placed. The message left. Margaret's rocking chair squeaked with each backward movement. She already regretted telling Wesley she'd be home on a Saturday night. She wondered if they screened her call, huddled there over his slick, black machine, if they discussed in detail whether or not he should return it, or if he'd already pressed delete. When she answered on the third ring, she tried to sound cheerful.

Wesley's voice seemed far away and disengaged. "Margaret, good seeing you today. You called?"

Margaret rocked faster. "Wesley," she said. "Here's what I'd like. I know you have this thing about the bakery, coming every day, but I'd like for you to stop." She pointed out that it was her territory and that surely he could find another place to go at exactly 11:00 a.m. "The Croissant, for instance," she said, "is just around the corner. That's what I'd like, and it's what other people who work at the bakery would prefer, too." Margaret pushed toward the end of the conversation. "Actually, it's the least you could do."

"I'll think about it," Wesley said after a long pause. "I could try doing something else, but I'm not interested in changing long-term. For a little while I could try." He cleared his throat.

Margaret ran a hand through her short hair. She liked its new spiky feel. Susan had also hennaed it to a deep burgundy, pouring merlot into the soupy, clay mixture. A toast, they said, to a new and improved Margaret.

"I've been meaning to call you," Wesley said. "There's something I need to ask you, too."

It was like flying, this rocking, the phone cord expanding and contracting as she went. Margaret felt a tinge of generosity forming in her chest. Wesley wanted a favor of her. An even exchange.

"It's about the pajamas I left at your place," he said. "The red ones?"

Margaret screeched her ride to a halt. She hung up the phone in one quick motion. Irrationally, she disconnected the cord where it met the little plastic box on the wall. She picked up the phone itself, an old light blue rotary that she loved, and carried it to the hall closet, setting it on a shelf between a bag of half-finished knitting and her straw cowboy hat. She walked away, into the kitchen, half expecting it to ring again anyway, like in a low-budget horror movie.

She would destroy the pajamas before she let Wesley wear them again. Into the trash. That's where they were going. In with yesterday's coffee grounds and the pair of yellow socks with holes in the toes.

Margaret's face burned. In that moment, she hated them all over again. Even though sometimes it felt like her heart was literally breaking in two and there was nothing she could do about it. The least Wesley could do was forfeit the fucking pajamas.

The San Francisco snow globe kept vigil on her windowsill.

29

It was the dead of winter and nearing 10:00 p.m. when Margaret finished loading the U-Haul. A band of friends wrapped in colorful wool and fleece stood by as she clasped the padlock and said, "There we go."

It had taken two weeks for her to pack. She offered her apartment—furniture included—to a grateful friend of a friend. Gave notice at the bakery to a line-up of stunned faces. A call to U-Haul, an oil change for her car, a new pair of boots, a withdrawal from savings, and Margaret was ready. Her Datsun tugged the little trailer over roads packed with snow. Her headlights searched the town's empty streets. She rounded the traffic circle and edged onto the highway. She'd drive through the night until the hazy start of day edged up from the ground.

Margaret had never been so sure of herself.

The final decision came one night at the bowling alley with Susan and Robert and the rhythm of step-step-step-pause-throw.

As Susan cleaned up on a spare, Margaret thought, *I don't have to live here.* It was a revelation. Next up, Robert got a strike. He high-fived Susan, and Margaret thought, *Change only requires determination.* She marveled at this new thinking, so like a motivational speech but so true. The blue-speckled ball heavy in her hand, she approached the shimmering wooden lane, lifted her arm, released. To her left and right the hollow echo of other people's pins crashing. Her ball rumbled down the lane, knocked out four. When the pins reset one remained in front of the gate, careening like a top. *I am in charge*, Margaret thought, waiting for her ball to burp back up from the oily chute. *I am in charge.*

Margaret pushed the lighted button that told someone some-where to fix her problem. A lanky boy appeared from behind the counter, ran down the lane, threw the wayward pin into the black guts of the machine, and a gleaming triangle of ten perfect pins realigned themselves.

Margaret was astonished at the size of the world. All the deci-sions she could make. She knew that this idea set her apart from Susan and Robert. They were here to stay, committed to each other and this place. It was their life she was living, not her own. She thought, *It's time.*

Wesley's pajama's, Olivia's lost friendship, the tight circle of friends, the bakery, this town. She didn't have to belong to it forever.

"Pretty quiet tonight, Margaret," Robert said. "Fuming over your inevitable bowling loss?"

Robert scratched and doodled in the margins of the big paper score sheet. He'd given all of them bowling names. Margaret was Gus. Robert, Slim. Susan, Big Bob. "I'm moving," Margaret said.

"What do you mean you're moving?" Robert asked.

Just then Big Bob finished up a second spare.

"I'm moving away," Margaret said.

"Since when?" Robert said.

"About five minutes ago."

"Okay," he said. "Let me know if this train continues. I can't imagine this place without you. Susan will be devastated."

"At what?" Susan said rubbing her hands together. "Why isn't anyone cheering for my spare?"

"I'm moving."

"What do you mean you're moving?" Margaret didn't answer. Susan asked, "When?"

"Two weeks," Margaret said.

And that was that.

30

It's barely morning. A hazy veil of gray covers the fields outside the farmhouse. Squirrels and birds scurry about halfheartedly, slick with dew. It seems the party has just ended, but Vivette stumbles to the kitchen groggy and hungover.

Sneaking out to the front porch, wrapped in a blanket on the Adirondack chair, she waits for the day to begin. Her bags packed, she's ready to get on with it — away from Nebraska and the routines she has already fallen into here on the farm. She's no longer afraid of the possibilities awaiting her in Des Moines.

Dear Joe-Joe,

You have to be careful what you say to people. I keep learning this same lesson over and over again. Maybe Wesley was right. I can't keep a secret. If that's true, then I'm a dangerous person. I know you can keep secrets. You are one big mystery. And you always will be, won't you? V

Vivette hears someone in the kitchen, wanders back inside. "I'll be as good as new by the time I reach Omaha," she says as she takes the glass of water, tips her head back, and swallows the ibuprofen Peter has handed her.

"We made a serious dent in the vodka last night," Peter whispers, leaning against the stove, his arms folded, one hand holding a wooden spoon he has grabbed without a fully formed idea of breakfast. The coffeemaker gurgles and puffs.

Peter pulls up a stool, discards the spoon. Vivette fills her coffee cup, nudging the pot aside to let the steaming liquid pour directly into her mug from under the filter basket. They sit in silence.

Soon they have their heads hunched over an atlas, charting a course. It feels like they're planning a top-secret mission, with the overhead light shining on them and the rest of the room dark except for Vivette's yellow Spider-Man T-shirt. She has her hair pulled up into a ponytail and wears ankle-length sweatpants: driving clothes.

Her finger lolls somewhere near Omaha. Peter has his planted at Des Moines. He talks Vivette through the complicated route he thinks she should take.

Peter says, "Well, yes, it'll take you twice as long. I'm not saying it won't. But Interstate 80 is a killer. It's so boring and just above it are all of these pretty little roads that go through towns and fields." Vivette tilts her head to get a better look.

Peter cradles his mug. Choosing his words carefully, he says, "If I recall correctly, last night you were telling a story about a postcard that you sent by throwing it out the window?"

Vivette frowns. Her memory is thick, gray sludge. She pokes this way and that to see if she actually named names, right or wrong. "Yes. Abstract. I have no idea what I was saying, Peter. I'm sure it was only half true, whatever it was. Postcards. They're everywhere in my life right now. I dream about postcards and write postcards about my dreams. You know, reeling in the stories for Joe-Joe."

"That's what I figured," he says. Peter stares at Vivette, and then busies himself with more sugar for his coffee.

Vivette silently begs for the conversation to veer away from her.

The refrigerator kicks on. The wind picks up outside with a tiny, low-pitched howl through the closed windows. Rain is near—big overcast clouds will soon stomp a deliberate march across the sky. The sheep are nowhere to be seen, probably huddling behind the barn.

Vivette thinks then she might be alone forever.

31

Susan nestles into the couch in a patch of late-morning light, a mug of tea in her hands. The sun ripples across her arms as the wind shakes the tree branches outside. Sunlight plays through the small beveled-glass ovals at the top of the big living-room window, scattering tiny rainbows on the wooden floor.

Susan is, without preamble, a new woman. She knows it will remain untrue until she tells someone. Soon her body will change and expand and fill up with a tiny, whole person inside, and she has no idea what that means. She's in the midst of mystery, unsure of which emotion to latch onto. Shivers down her spine, and this same indescribable epiphany for twenty-four hours now.

Everything morphed between the time before she talked with Dr. Hatcher and the time after. A tiny bit disappointed that bells and whistles hadn't gone off, and instead this quiet morning, this first official day of being pregnant. She takes a sip of tea. Raisin, the puppy, is splayed at her feet — asleep for once, not chewing up something. His paws stretch out in front of him so the tips of his little claws touch Susan's calf, his two hind legs akimbo in the air. She knows if she moves, he'll wake up. So she stays.

She'll work at the historical society throughout her pregnancy, and then once the baby is born Robert can shift his painting and teaching schedule around to cover the hours she works. They'll need to start looking for a house, maybe one with a little yard. They'll have to search outside of town, nothing for them here with prices climbing through the roof. She'll miss the porch swing. She'll miss this apartment where they've lived all these years, although recently Robert has wanted a change — a new place to start over again. He says he wants to "declutter."

Susan just wishes Robert could calm down, learn to relax a little. She wishes he could sit on the couch with her and drink tea. But she has always wished this and knows it's never going to happen. He's consistent, she thinks. This morning Robert's off somewhere, doing something or other, "getting stuff done," he calls it. And here she is, not moving so the puppy can sleep, so she has an excuse to stay put, to drink her tea. To think: *mom*.

She calls the bakery to see if anyone there has seen Robert. Gretchen answers, hands the phone over.

Susan can hear the clatter of the bakers and voices rising and falling in the background. "Let me pull the cord around the corner so I can hear you," Robert says. "I'm at Penhallow with a hundred million people. Oh, guess you know that. Can't hear a thing." Susan waits what seems like a surreal amount of time while Robert stretches the cord around the cookie case.

"Susan," he says. "You're up. Want to go for a hike today? People are talking about driving up into the Green Mountains. It's lovely out. Have you been outside?"

"No. Not yet. I'm just here with Raisin," Susan says. "It is pretty out though. But hey, I have something to tell you. Something I found out yesterday that I need to talk to you about."

"Oh, okay. It isn't bad, is it?" Robert says. "You aren't mad, right?"

"No, I'm not mad," Susan says. "Why would I be mad?"

"Is there something wrong with your mom?" Robert asks.

"No, no. She's fine," Susan says. With the bakery noises and her friends in the background, she's reluctant to let her news out into the world. It seems easier just keeping it in her head.

"So shoot, I really shouldn't stay on this line long," Robert says.

"I'm kind of getting the evil eye from Gretchen. Is everything okay? I mean, is everything okay with us?"

"I think everything's fine. Really fine. Super fine, Robert," Susan says. "I don't want to tell you this over the phone, though."

"What's going on? Tell me," Robert says. "I mean, you called. I hate when you do this, Susan."

"I'm pregnant," Susan says. It's the first time she's said the word, except to herself, and she blushes even though she's alone. Her palms are sweating. She moves her legs, which makes Raisin shift, crawl on top of her, and fall back asleep with a short grunt.

"What? Wait. You're sure, right?"

"Yes, I'm very sure."

Before Susan has time to stop him, to make clear she wants to ease into this new stage privately, Robert yells, "Susan is pregnant!" Then he yells it again, as she tries to get his attention.

She says, "Robert, wait."

"I'll be right there," he says, and hangs up.

Susan continues to hold the receiver, realizing these are her last few moments alone. She looks out the window, uncertainty setting in as she thinks about the future, how summer is coming and then fall and by the end of winter there will be a baby. By spring, everything will be new and different.

After a while she hears Robert running, first in the driveway, his feet crunching on the gravel, and then slamming the front door. He's breathing hard as he rounds the corner. He looks at Susan, who is already softly crying. Robert starts crying too, waking up Raisin making him howl and run in circles. Before Robert can kneel in front of Susan he has to discipline the dog, bat it on the nose a couple times, drag him over to his kennel and shut the door. In his anxiousness Robert pushes a little roughly, and Raisin yelps. Robert then feels like he has to get a toy for the puppy, grabs a rubber ball and throws it in. Then, to the background of its methodical squeaks, Robert kneels in front of the couch, and puts his ear on Susan's flat belly. He rubs the skin with his thumb — over and over.

"Forgive me," he says softly.

32
Margaret, Nebraska

Voices in the kitchen, low murmurs. The sky is dim and subdued, not quite morning. Margaret smells coffee. The clock says 5:00. Vivette's quick laugh. But Margaret can't get out of bed. She curls her knees toward her chest, slowly, deliberately reviewing every word she remembers saying at the party the night before.

Margaret scrutinizes herself, already regretting almost everything. She thinks through making the brownies, talking with Vivette, taking a bath, getting dressed, picking one outfit, then another. She replays setting a pile of plates on the table, pouring herself another glass of wine. A neat stack of pink napkins. Talking with Elaine and Joe and Allen.

Margaret would like to take every word back; none were what she meant to say. Then she thinks about Bailey Johnson, forgotten for days, but then the kiss, the slam of the car door, the Zoo Bar, cigarettes, Nick the bartender, the origami swan, standing in front of hotel room number 345, the cast of the fluorescent lights in the bleak hallway.

She thinks about Peter, how she's about to let him say goodbye to Vivette by himself. She thinks about his body, his strong arms, his voice in the kitchen breaking now into the rhythm of a long story. She thinks about him working in the garden. But still Margaret can't get out of bed. She's ashamed to know this about herself.

The pink napkins, the smell of popcorn. Vivette in her over-alls—her long hair cascading down her back. Laughing with Vivette. At ease. Pouring herself another glass of wine. This methodical recapping lulls Margaret into an uncertain state of half-sleep. In the kitchen, the voices are far away, and the bed is her safety net. A cocoon.

In this half-sleep Margaret gets into a car, her old Datsun. It runs like a clock. There's a waxy cup of ginger ale in her plastic cup holder, a full tank of gas. She has a map but doesn't need it. Getting into the car, dozing and waking, starting over again. Margaret turns the key, a twist of her wrist. She leaves. She leaves her life on the farm, drives away, and there is a release—a joy so unaccountable—involuntarily she replays it again and again. She drives. The breeze is warm as it trickles through the windows. The sky is big and blue. The road is endless as it points to the horizon. It goes on forever. She starts the car. The tank is full.

There's Wesley on the side of the road beside his pick-up truck. Margaret laughs as she pulls up, and Wesley gets in. Margaret drives away.

It's five fifteen. Vivette's voice in the living room now. Margaret's eating lunch at the bakery, waving to a customer, pulling orange pound cakes from the oven. The pinball machine pops a free game. Images flip by on metal plates. A little motor. A brass viewing piece, Ocean Beach. Sand dollars. Seal Rock. The promised road trip she never took with Wesley.

She picks up Wesley. They drive and talk. They're laughing, but now Margaret can't hear the words. She forgives him, though, forgives him for everything. Just like that. She starts the car. The tank is full.

The road, a distant horizon. Wesley. She pulls over. He opens the door, gets in. She's walking on the farm with Vivette, pulling up salad greens from the garden, driving to work, into the

Zoo Bar, Bailey Johnson. She's knitting in front of the fireplace, hugging Peter in front of the fireplace, another glass of wine, setting out the pretty pink napkins. She's walking to the bakery, pulling pies from the oven, walking to meet her friends, sitting in Olivia's cottage, talking to Wesley, to Susan, to Robert, to Scott, to herself. She gets into her car. She drives away. She meets Kevin. She meets Fred. She takes the N Judah to Ocean Beach. She grabs her horoscope at Museé Mechanique before it floats to the floor. She drives away. She takes a bath. The doorbell rings. The smell of popcorn. Voices from the kitchen. In the middle of everything now. Wesley leans against the truck, waiting for her. She stops, he gets in.

The tiny tap of the door slamming shut. She forgives him. He's standing on the side of the road. She drives away. The tank is full.

33 *Vivette, Nebraska*

Every so often Peter looks toward the bedroom door. He doubts Margaret will get up. He knows she'll make him say good-bye to Vivette alone. The party was probably a bad idea.

"I had a great time hanging out with Margaret last night," Vivette says. She, too, looks cautiously down the hallway.

"You'll have to forgive her," Peter says. "Wiped out. She gets like this after parties." Peter feels like all the wrong angles are coming at him, sharp and jagged. He'll cover for her. Later, he'll tell Margaret it's okay, that Vivette didn't mind, that he didn't mind.

Vivette turns from the kitchen window. "I'm feeling good," she says, although Peter hasn't asked. "I'm feeling ready to go. I'm anxious, actually, to get started."

Peter asks, "Do you have everything you need? Did you check the pressure in the tires like Joe-Joe warned you?"

"I swear I'll check them as soon as I stop for gas," Vivette says, closing the atlas. She slaps her hand on its battered front cover. "I really appreciated this time to get my head together," she says.

Peter remembers the basket Margaret has put together for Vivette's departure. He clomps down into the basement to retrieve it.

Vivette looks down the hallway. The closed door to the bedroom, a mouth shut tight. It's 6:00 a.m.

"Margaret made this for you. I won't tell you what's inside," Peter says, handing the picnic basket to Vivette. "Just wait until you stop. It'll be a surprise."

"Okay, then. Let me just grab my suitcase and I'm off," Vivette says.

"I'll get that," Peter says. He rolls Vivette's suitcase out the door. Cool air rushes into the kitchen.

Peter puts her bag onto the back seat. He hugs her. "Now, part of what's in that basket is for use *after* you reach Des Moines. My contribution."

Vivette thanks Peter again, and then hesitates before getting into the car. "I didn't sleep with Wesley," she says. "I told Margaret I did, and I'm not sure why. I never slept with him. Can you tell her that? Tell her Wesley said to say hi, okay?" With that she pecks Peter on the cheek and gets in.

Vivette drives down the rutted lane, waving good-bye to Peter, so long to the sheep who have magically reappeared, crowded into a bon voyage committee near the fence. Peter stands on the porch, getting smaller and smaller in her rearview mirror. Vivette turns right at the end of the lane.

As she drives, the clouds roll away, and the sky begins to blush pink. With the rain pushed aside, it feels like a whole new morning at hand.

Vivette nears her first rural route, the road Peter had insisted she take, and a flock of wild turkeys coasts down, casting bulky shadows over the hood of her car. The fat bundles of feathers make her swerve and miss the turn. The giant, unlikely birds pecking there in the grassy strip beside the road are a sign. *Of what?* Vivette thinks. Instead of quaint lanes with pretty flowers, Vivette decides to follow the stoic blue markers to Interstate 80. She merges onto the big road with the trucks and the minivans and the traffic, sets her eyes on the horizon, and goes.

34 *Margaret, Nebraska*

Peter laces up the new sneakers Vivette bought him in Bancroft, props his feet on the rail of the front porch. Tractors hum in the distance. The storm clouds have passed them by. Summer lurks behind the breeze.

"You know, I think we should get a porch swing. Wouldn't that be nice?" he says to Margaret.

"Susan and Robert have this porch swing on the first floor of their apartment. It was the after-hours meeting place," Margaret says. "The bars would close and people would wind their way over there. Robert was always up for entertaining. Susan would usually slink away after a while — go up to the apartment to read or listen to music. Sometimes I'd go up there with her. It was nice. We'd be upstairs, quietly talking, drinking wine, but we could hear all our friends downstairs on the porch laughing and making jokes. It was comforting. A family, really."

"Do you think Robert sleeps around a lot?" Peter asks. "It seems like he's always on the go. I mean, I don't know the guy, but from all the stories you tell, Robert and Susan seem to be different people. I wonder if they have lives they keep from each other."

"It's true. They definitely go at different paces," Margaret says, "but they offset each other, you know? Robert makes Susan more social. Susan helps Robert settle down. They've made it work. You just don't understand how much everyone loves them in Portsmouth. You also still have no idea what you're talking about as far as Robert sleeping around goes."

She thinks about all those murky nights, people whispering in different corners at parties, Robert with his arm around a mutual friend. They were all so close then. It was hard to tell who was flirting, who was with somebody for sex, for friendship. She says, "I mean, everybody there is close. My theory was always that the idea of sex was out there more than the sex itself. If Vivette and Robert were doing it, which I don't think they were, it must have been foolproof, whatever they were doing—because I just don't think he'd risk losing Susan. It's Wesley she slept with, anyway. Wesley of all people."

Peter sits back in his chair, his arms resting on his knees. "Let me get you some more coffee," he says. "I'll make a fresh pot."

Alone, Margaret sits back to take in the view, her bare feet propped on the edge of her chair. The endless horizon. A few birds on the fence posts. The sheep lazing about. She's amazed at her need to reconsider happiness even now. Never settled. Never safe. What is it, anyway? A special moment? A kiss? Years and years of working out two lives, putting them together, taking them apart, making sure everything is up and running like a reliable old car? She doesn't know. Happiness is elusive and fragile. She's sure that finding it means making other people unhappy along the way. It means being okay here in the desolate fields of her mind, deep in the trenches of her heart.

The phone rings. The machine picks up by the time she gets

to it. Margaret stands and watches the little black box as Peter's voice announces they aren't home, as Susan's voice comes onto the machine. Margaret can't bring herself to pick up the phone. She walks away. She'll call Susan later when she's feeling like a normal person again.

Peter walks back out onto the porch with his garden-supply catalogs and a big plate of toast. Margaret reaches over for a piece as Peter says, "You know, it was kind of fun sitting back and watching Vivette try on anything that came her way while she was here. It's too bad you weren't awake when she left. I think she really wanted to say thanks. She wanted to see you."

"Sorry," Margaret says. "I slept right through it all."

"It's okay," he says. "Everything's fine. Let's get Sparky and go for a long walk."

35
Vivette, Des Moines

Two hands on the wheel, Vivette sings Bruce Springsteen's "Born to Run" at the top of her lungs. Interstate 80 is a bustling blur of noise, speed, and exhaust. Trucks zoom past and then slow down once in front of her. She passes them, and they rip by again. Smaller cars zip in and out of traffic like gnats, and every so often there's a pickup truck with bales of hay piled in the back, holding steady at 45 mph in the fast lane.

Easing by a truck filled with cows, she can see their scruffy black fur, the hint of a large eye, a glossy nose. She wonders if they know their first road trip will be their last, if that fear is passed on from generation to generation. Stay put, their mothers warn them. Whatever you do: DO NOT GET ONTO THE TRUCK. A cowbell hangs from the truck's hitch and waves languidly back and forth, just skirting the asphalt.

Vivette hasn't been driving long, but already she feels a break coming on. She wants to look in her basket. A rest area overlooks a rolling field with cows grazing in the distance — black spots against a field of green.

Her sights set on the farthest picnic table, she passes an older couple who've also stopped for a break. They pour coffee from a faded plaid thermos, a small box of donut holes between them.

When she reaches her table, Vivette opens the basket. Inside are homemade brownies, a small baguette, muffins, a hunk of cheddar cheese, a bottle of juice, a container of soy milk, an apple, a plum, a salad in a plastic container, mustard, dressing, a packet of cream cheese, a little paring knife, a juice glass, and a flowered tablecloth. Tucked neatly alongside, still in its paper bag, is a small bottle of Jim Beam.

Vivette eats the muffins — fresh apple with walnuts and honey — and drinks the juice.

There are so many things Vivette wishes she had told Margaret, but the words were never in the right place. Vivette understands that she's doomed to figure out the world on her own. She believes she can put it all together before the desperate years are gone when anything is possible.

She pulls a postcard from her dwindling stack. IOWA in big block letters, with flowers and grains filling in each one.

Dear Joe-Joe, I'm finally on my way to Des Moines. My friend Margaret whispered all of her secrets into my ear each night as I slept. I feel so well informed, but I have no clue what to do. I think part of it has to with learning that there's no way I can stop this momentum. There's no way I'm just going to forget Robert like a Saturday morning dental appointment. V

Vivette feels omniscient as she sits in the rest area with Styrofoam cups rolling in slow, loopy circles near the imposing green garbage can. A blue plastic bag puffs and floats off toward the highway like an unlikely deep-sea creature searching for water.

We did it in the bedroom? Vivette thinks. What was Robert thinking? What if Susan had come back early from her mom's? What if they'd been caught? And then they are caught, there in the rest area, there in the bedroom. Vivette imagines Susan opening the door, a bright, tired smile on her face right before she notices Vivette—naked. Vivette stands up and paces the length of the picnic table. Her heart races. The old couple stares at her.

"It's over. It's over. It's over," she mumbles to herself as she gathers her food into the basket. She feels an urge to call Margaret and tell her it's over. She wants to confess to Susan. Someone out there needs to know her story. Instead, Vivette stands stock-still and looks at the field, at the birds flitting from tree to tree. She listens to the drone of traffic, the voices of milling travelers at the vending machines behind her.

Holding the plum in one hand, resting her other hand on the basket, Vivette runs her thumb over its silky firm skin. She'll never know what Robert thought about it, how he really felt about her. She'll make that part up.

Over, she says to herself. *Over*. She lets the plum roll into the basket.

Vivette looks at her watch, and she's overcome with a sense of urgency to get to her destination.

By ten, she's almost there. At ten fifteen she takes her exit, looking for Walnut Street and the Kirkenwood Hotel. Ten thirty she parks.

It's quiet, with just a few people walking the wide city streets. The Corner Cafe is full and bustling, though. Through the big plate-glass windows, Vivette sees the waitresses behind the counter in their pink-and-white uniforms. They're chatting up customers, topping off coffee, writing down orders, delivering plates piled with food. The comforting smell of fried eggs and hash browns hovers over the sidewalk.

The hotel's big red neon sign buzzes the length of the building and draws Vivette in. In the lobby, art deco light fixtures and a mural that reads KIRKENWOOD HOTEL, the block letters filled with scenes of 1930s Des Moines. A fancy chandelier, some couches. A placard propped on an easel advertises a jazz trio that evening in the lounge. The hotel registry's big wooden desk has cubbyholes for each room from a time when people anxiously awaited and received telegrams, letters, and postcards. Vivette feels a little unstuck in time and place.

Two men stand behind the counter—one thin and the other fat. One wears a jersey T-shirt and dress pants, the other a western belt buckle. Vivette imagines them as uniform-wearing bellhops with little hats. They watch her marvel at the deco lobby, standing side by side.

"Hi," Vivette says.

The men smile in unison.

"Um, I'd like a room? Can I get a room for a week? Maybe get some kind of discount if I pay in advance? I'd like to stay for a week. I'm planning on moving here, and I need to look for a job, find an apartment. Would that work for you guys?"

The two men stare and smile. Vivette smiles back, trying to figure out what she said wrong, what more she needs to say. Just then the skinny man moves slightly forward and looks at something, a piece of paper, maybe a wanted poster, on the other side of the booth. He smiles again. Softly and slowly he says, "Are you thinking single or double?"

"One bed would be great," Vivette says. "Whatever's most convenient, whatever's cheapest."

He checks at the hidden piece of paper again, looks at Vivette.

Then he pulls another sheet from a drawer, points a finger at fine print as he squints.

Vivette smiles, absentmindedly fixing her ponytail.

"Where you from?" the other man asks.

"Oh, I'm from New England, but I just drove here today from Nebraska? I was visiting friends there before I came here?"

The man nods.

With both hands at his sides again, the skinny man says, "We can give you a room for forty dollars a night if you stay a week. Plus tax. Pay in advance."

"Thanks," Vivette says. "If that's your best rate, I'll take it. That'll work just fine." She begins filling out the registry card, saying, "I might have some questions for you later, is that okay? Oh, I'll need a key. Yes, thanks. Room 718. This is great. Super."

"Just stop on back when you're settled," the fat man says.

Vivette runs to the car, still feeling a sense of urgency to say, *I'm here, that was then, and this is now.* Des Moines. She grabs her bag and the picnic basket. Her suitcase wheels rumbling along the marble floor are the only noise as she wanders back through the empty lobby. The two men, still standing side by side, motionless, smile at her. She smiles again. Waves at them. They both wave back.

There's a brass mail chute that runs the height of the building. She envisions her postcards to Joe-Joe fluttering down seven floors through that contraption, and then out and off to Wilkes Barre. She pushes the button for the elevator. It's slow but steady as it lifts her upward, the doors opening with a ding to another mural in the seventh-floor hallway, recently painted, of downtown Des Moines. It looks like it's from the 1930s, but in the corner it says 1992. In the mural, Des Moines is portrayed as a major city, like New York or San Francisco, with tall buildings and lights aglitter. It's an evening scene, and there's the Kirkenwood. There's the neon YMCA sign she'll see from her hotel-room window. The Des Moines River and the two graceful stone walkways that slope over it.

Later she'll talk to the bellhops and venture over the bridges to find the Thai restaurant they assure her is good. She'll see the Salvation Army thrift store where in a few days she'll find a quilt, hand-stitched in white, blue, and yellow overlapping rings, an orange sale tag dangling from its corner. Later, when she moves into her apartment on Woodland Avenue, she'll put it on her bed where it will glow in the morning light.

Before she finds her apartment, she'll find Joe's coffee shop with its tall ceiling and comfortable mishmash of tables and chairs. Homemade muffins and cookies. A bulletin board with flyers for upcoming bands, plays, calls for artists, and apartment vacancies. Vivette will rip a tab off a handmade flyer announcing a room for rent. Complete strangers will say hi to her as she sits at a little table and writes her postcard to Joe-Joe.

Dear Joe-Joe,

Moving eventually becomes standing still. This is the part I have trouble with. The stopping. The deciding. But here I am, eating a muffin, drinking coffee like I belong here, and maybe I do, maybe Des Moines is the place for me. Say it while you fall asleep tonight. Whisper it into your pillow: Des Moines. It is lust, it is hope, it is my home. For now. Love, Vivette

After the Thai restaurant, she'll walk back to the Kirkenwood and take a long bath. Later she'll ride the elevator downstairs to the Mint Lounge. In a corner booth, smoking cigarettes, she'll feel mysterious. She'll pretend she's an old-time movie star listening to jazz. Only the two check-in guys sitting at the bar will know she's arrived.

The cute bartender will make her a martini. She'll ask him where he got his western shirt, and he'll direct her to the Salvation Army, which she already knows about but pretends she doesn't. On the way back from the thrift store, the quilt under her arm, she'll buy a newspaper. In the help-wanted section there'll be a position in the admissions department at Drake University.

She'll apply and get the job and work with three older women, who will introduce her to the Saturday farmer's market and help her plant a garden in the yard outside her Woodland Avenue apartment.

When she runs into the bartender again, she'll say hi and tell him about the quilt. He'll invite her to a park outside of town for a walk. They'll walk in comfortable silence after they get the small talk out of the way. After a few more dates, he'll hold her hand as they make their way across the big stone bridges with the water lapping beneath them, summer descending on the city. Vivette will feel her heart shift just a tiny bit. In a few years, she'll move away from Des Moines, move to a bigger city, lead a different life. But she'll always remember this time.

But all of that is later and tomorrow and her future tumbling forward. For now, Vivette stands staring into the mural, trying to get her bearings. She needs a nap. She's over-caffeinated and was talking way too fast for the two clerks downstairs. She needs to slow things down, get off East Coast hyper-speed and join the pace of Iowa. She wants to be well-rested before her premiere. For some reason, she craves Thai food, and she sees that as a bad sign.

She turns and walks down the hallway to the second wooden door on the left. 718. The room is clean, but vintage Kirkenwood. The bathroom has a delicate glass sconce over an etched mirror. The floor is an intricately laid tile mosaic. A short but deep claw-foot tub gives her hope. The room has a narrow closet with a bar that pivots out for hanging clothes. The walls are uneventful, as are the single bed, small desk and chair, dresser, and a stand with a TV. She opens the curtains and there before her is the city. The red YMCA sign, the brick buildings, the streets. In the distance, a gigantic neon umbrella that says TRAVELERS.

Civilization, she thinks to herself. *Civilization at last.*

She lies down on the bed, the basket sitting at her side. She is instantly asleep, home.

36
Wesley, New Hampshire

The clock says 2:00 a.m. Wesley closes his eyes again. When he opens them, it's 2:01. Nicole cries in the nursery. Wesley feels the empty flannel sheet on Olivia's side of the bed.

He rolls back over, curls into a ball. His eyes are raw. He knows he won't catch up on his sleep until Nicole turns eighteen, and then he'll be an old man, unable to sleep anyway.

Nicole breaks into a high-pitched shriek. Wesley knows it well. He sits up, grabs his robe from the chair, and stumbles down the hallway to the nursery. He cautiously puts his head through the doorway.

Olivia looks up at him. With her hair cascading from a loose bun on top of her head, her nightgown half off her shoulder, she looks like a Mary Cassatt painting, except Nicole is a writhing, crying mess in her new Winnie-the-Pooh onesie. "I don't know what to do," Olivia says. "I've fed her. I've changed her. Nothing is working, and I can't carry her across this room one more time."

"I'll take over," Wesley says flexing his arms, like a reluctant Mighty Mouse.

He still finds it hard to believe that someone that small can generate so much noise. The shift from one parent to the other makes Nicole stop for a moment and reassess her world. The nursery is silent. The dim elephant light on the dresser. The rocking chair with the sheepskin draped over the back. Wesley says, "See?" Then Nicole howls again, and the room is a nightmare circus scene.

"Okay. Good luck," Olivia says. "Don't come get me if this keeps up. She pats Wesley on the shoulder. "Good boy," she says.

Wesley looks at Olivia, watches her turn the corner — gone, a ghost.

Nicole opens her tiny eyes, a huge teardrop suspended on one cheek. "Oh, come on now, those tears are way too big for someone so little," Wesley says. She closes her eyes and screams, kicking her legs.

Wesley grabs his running pants hanging over the nursery door, finds a T-shirt, a flannel shirt, a sweater, his coat, wool socks, and boots. Sometimes a ride in the car puts her right to sleep. Wesley changes his mind when he looks out the window. A light snowfall that started a half hour before dusts the streets and sidewalks. "Okay, little girl," he says. "We're going on an adventure."

Wesley puts Nicole into her yellow fuzzy zip-up with the big duck on the front, into her big fluffy "happy capsule," as Olivia calls it — a bright-purple, down, snap-up body suit. He pulls a hat over her head and puts her into the baby backpack. At each step of the way, Nicole stops to see what comes next and then starts in again, like she means it.

He quickly turns her around and puts the frame against his back, adjusts the straps, and shuffles down the stairs. Each wail edges further under his skull like a mini crowbar. Lots of people have kids and remain sane, functioning individuals, he thinks. He just never anticipated taking his baby for a walk at 3:00 a.m., changing so many diapers, having to think so much about what he should do next. Wesley opens the door. Tiny flakes spiral all around.

Nicole stops crying. Then, a few muffled sobs. Wesley says, "Isn't it amazing, Nicole?" Then she screams again.

"Okay, I hear you. Let's get a move on."

Wesley walks up one street and down the other. Like hiking inside a snow globe, he thinks. Past houses all closed up and silent, he keeps up a steady pace and soon Nicole quiets.

He realizes what Margaret meant years ago when she talked about the early hours just before morning—the strange quiet that descends. She said she always felt like a voyeur in her own town, walking to her baking shift.

There's a blue TV glow from a few windows, insomniacs waiting for dawn. Strange muffled bird noises, and a garbage truck rumbles down a side street. Then it's silent. Wesley walks on.

Nicole still quiet, Wesley makes his way to the park and looks out at the Piscataqua River. Streetlights play off the swirling current.

He nears Pennhallow Street, his legs numb from the cold, his cheeks plastic. The lights are on, and he hears music through a window slightly ajar. In the back a lone figure rolls bread. At first, through the frosted glass, the woman there looks like Margaret. And for that moment he lets himself believe his entire walk was a dream.

He tries the door. It's locked. Rubbing some frost away, Wesley looks inside, cupping his mittened hands around his face. He thumps on the glass.

Francie is in the back. When she hears the noise she stops like a deer in headlights. She can't see a thing with all the lights on. Reluctantly, she walks over to the stereo, turns down the music, listening.

Wesley pulls his keys out of his coat pocket. Makes three tiny rapping noises, not wanting to wake Nicole.

Francie comes forward, squinting and frowning. She sees a man with a pack on his back. He's smiling, and he looks crazy. She unlocks the front door from the inside, pokes her head out.

"Closed," she says.

Wesley has never seen this woman before. He thought he knew everyone who worked at the bakery. He smiles, says, "Hi, I'm Wesley. I come here a lot during normal hours. I'm a regular? I was out walking my daughter to sleep and now I'm freezing. I'm wondering if I could get something to go?"

Francie says, "We open at five."

"What time is it now?"

"Four." She shuts the door, locks it, and walks away, stopping to turn the music up again. Wesley looks at the closed door for a moment and then stands in front of the bakery, his back to the door, looking out at the big town clock, which just then strikes four, just to rub it in. He sighs. He'll walk home, hoping Nicole doesn't wake up once he climbs the stairs and puts her into the crib. He'll make himself a stiff drink. Coffee and whiskey maybe. That could be a morning drink under certain circumstances. But the lock turns in the door again.

Francie looks at him. "You got a kid in there?"

Wesley laughs. "Back there? Yeah, she's all bundled up. That's Nicole. I'm sure she looks like a perfect cherub right now, but we call her The Screamer."

"Okay. Come in," Francie says walking away, the door shutting behind her.

Wesley isn't sure what to do. He tries the door again and it's open, so he steps inside. Warm bread, cinnamon rolls, coffee. It smells so comforting. The snow melting off his boots makes two small puddles in front of the cookie case.

"Just finishing up the hot chocolate," Francie says. "Here," she pours some into a to-go cup. She has turned off the music and now the only noise is the hiss of the ovens, the motor on the big Hobart mixer.

"Perfect," Wesley says. "I don't know how to thank you."

"No problem. You look like you need it." Francie dusts off her T-shirt, stretches her arms above her head like a welterweight champion warming up for the big lift, and walks back to the wood-block table. She checks on some rye loaves, grabs the peel, and slides five pans out from the oven and onto the table in one swift motion. Francie lifts each crusty loaf flecked with caraway seeds out of its pan and sets it on the bread rack.

"Aren't those hot?" Wesley asks.

"You get used to it," she says.

Wesley nods.

Francie walks over to the Hobart to check on the mixing bread dough, adds a scoop of flour. The juice case gives off a dim glow—the bottles lined up in neat rows like a marching band. Plates of cookies and cakes are wrapped in plastic beside colorful signs clipped here and there with the prices of today's selections. Francie pulls a sheet tray lined with rising cheese danish onto the table, egg-washes them with a thick brush.

"What do I owe you?" Wesley asks.

Francie seems surprised he's still there. "Nothing. We aren't open. No way to pay," she says. "It's on the house."

Wesley smiles. "You just made my night, or my day, whichever it is right now."

Francie looks up at him, her mouth a straight even line, then she smiles, just slightly, and gets back to work.

If he remains very quiet and Nicole doesn't wake up, Wesley decides he can stay for a little while. He props Nicole in her backpack in a chair and sits in the chair facing her. He stares at his daughter's pink cheeks and the black tuft of hair peeking out from her hat. So clean and clear of worries. All her mistakes are ahead of her, he thinks. It's a face that trusts him, a little person that hasn't been messed up by anything yet, not by him or Olivia or anyone. She's pure, and Wesley is envious. He marvels at her deep slumber after the screaming back at the house.

Wesley sips his hot chocolate, rich and creamy. It seems important to make it last as long as possible. Francie pulls a tray of fat cinnamon rolls out of the oven, plucks a few muffins from their tins on the cooling racks, tumbles them into baskets. The oven door creaks with each opening and closing. She stacks a mound of whole-wheat baguettes on the middle row of the bread rack.

When Wesley looks out the window again a small group of old men is lined up. They wear parkas and stand immobile by the front door, flakes of snow collecting on their hoods and hats. At 4:55 Jeanine shows up, rushing in. The men follow. They all turn to watch sleeping Nicole as Wesley puts a finger up to his lips. The men order coffee, gather their newspapers, and scatter across the bakery with Wesley and Nicole at the center of their lopsided constellation.

Once everyone is settled into place, Wesley stares out the bank of windows again. First he studies his own tired reflection holding his near-empty paper cup. He crosses one leg over the other, thinks about Olivia at home, dead to the world.

He's lost in thought, but then Nicole's blurry image catches his eye in the frosty glass panes. Her sleeping face is round and peaceful. The men are reflected to Nicole's left and right. They hunch over their papers and randomly sip coffee from identical steaming mugs — their arms raising and lowering, the pages of their newspapers fluttering softly. Jeanine moves back and forth behind the counter.

Wesley looks out the windows, beyond himself and the interior of the bakery, at the snow falling on the streets, filling in the footprints.